Barbara Richardson
about 91,000 words
341 W. Michigan Ave.
Au Gres, MI 48703
(989)903-5000
barbrichar@gmail.com

STOLEN HOME STOLEN INNOCENCE

By

Barb Richardson

**Part One House of Lies**

According to Miriam Webster online:

**Home:**
-a family living together in one building, house, etc.
-a place where something normally or naturally lives or is located

**Innocence:**
-lack of experience with the world and with the bad things that happen in life
-lack of knowledge about something

**Steal:**
-to take (something that does not belong to you) in a way that is wrong or illegal
-to take (something that you are not supposed to have) without asking for permission

## CHAPTER ONE

### Learning to Tiptoe

She stood back and stared resolutely at the building across the street. Mixed emotions seared through her burning, memory clouded mind. She hadn't thought about this place in years and yet it seemed directly imbedded in her daily life. This was probably the reason that she was standing there pondering its very existence.

The physical appearance of the building itself had changed immensely from that of her faded and scattered recollections or perhaps the vague memories were just distorted with time. She had a strong feeling that this was the beginning of a long journey for her but whether she could follow the trail of pain was yet undetermined. Her stomach felt like a vat of molten steel as she released the tortured grip on her thoughts and allowed her emotions to disembark on whatever path they were going to follow. Squinting in the fresh June sunshine she let her legs fold beneath her as she lowered herself to the sun warmed sidewalk.

Now completely absorbed in the past she concentrated on the memories now flickering like old film strips dancing on the movie screen of her mind. Some of the pictures were vague and snowy while others danced before her with the crystal clarity of bright, three dimensional technicolor. Finally what came to focus was a drab gray day, with dirty melting banks of snow scattered about. Inside a tiny girl with chocolate eyes and tendrils of ringlets escaping from her ponytail was inside peeking curiously through the doorway of what had once been her father's meat store. Now the room was different. It was filled with tables covered with white cloths, pretty pink flowers and many other gala decorations. Many people were gathered in the room but the little girl's gaze fell on the woman standing next to her daddy. She thought that the lady looked really pretty all dressed up and smiling. Somewhere behind that smile she sensed some sort of anger but the commotion and merriment of celebration distracted the child so she couldn't quite figure out why she thought the lady was mad. Lots of people were gathered around the woman and her daddy. They seemed to be smiling, talking and laughing all at once. The men were taking turns shaking her daddy's hand and kissing the dark eyed woman on the cheek that she turned toward them.

Spying the familiar brown head of her brother she began to venture from the relative security of the doorway. Robby would tell her all about this party and who all these people were. He always explained things to her if he wasn't too busy and his friends weren't around. She inched her way toward him but when she saw the other boy standing next to him she froze as still as a stature. Thinking quickly, she ducked under the closest table so as not to be spotted.

She didn't want to bother Robby when he was talking to that boy. She remembered the pretty lady talking to her a few days before. Her daddy had sat down next to the lady on the couch upstairs then pulled her onto his knee so she was cuddled tightly between them. Her daddy really hadn't said much. He had just kept smiling and nodding agreement as the lady spoke. "I once had a little boy." She paused looking like she was going to cry. "He was just a little older than you." The lady's voice shook and the little girl saw her throat move as she looked across the child to her daddy. Daddy had reached across her lap and took the lady's hand in his. With that the lady continued to speak. "His name was Donald. He died and went to Heaven to live with God just like your momma did. Now God wants me to live with you and be your momma." She paused again then gestured across the room where the chubby black haired boy sat with Robby. "Wade is going to be your brother and we'll all have lots of fun together. Your daddy and I are going to get married and we'll all be a family."

Both she and Daddy were smiling as Daddy leaned forward and finally spoke. "I think it's time that you two start calling Ellen mom. Wade already calls me Dad." The little girl saw her father's eyes shining with pride as he looked toward the lady's son. Through big eyes the little girl watched as the focus of her father's adoration crossed the room to stand near her daddy who quickly put his arm around the boy's shoulders. The boy stared back at her with olive pit eyes that looked as if they contained all the secrets of the world and his chest thrust forward in a self-important stance. It was just like the dominoes that Robby lined up in paths to make chain reactions. As Daddy hugged the olive eyed boy Robby had quickly jumped to his feet and made a running dash toward the hallway leading to his bedroom.

"Rob, go after him!" the lady stood as she spoke and Daddy rose with her, his arm still draped around Wade. Daddy shook his head with what seemed to be disgust. "He'll just have to get used to it." Daddy had grumbled. "The other two have probably filled him with their lies just like you said."

Looking out from the harbor of her hiding place under the table, she once again studied the lady whose white gloved hand was entwined with daddy's large dark one. She didn't think that the lady looked at all like the pictures of her Mommy that had used to be upstairs, but she couldn't be sure because the pictures were gone. She had watched the lady take them and put them in a box one day when Daddy was at work and Robby was sitting on the porch in front of the store door. Now when she closed her eyes she couldn't see the smiling face she knew was her mama so maybe she should just call this lady mama. After all, she had bought her the pretty new dress that she was wearing.

    Suddenly as she was peering out from her hiding place she heard the adults laughing and looked toward the source of their laughter. Spying what had captured their attention made her gasp with delight. There on the floor, under the table with the lacy tablecloth that went clear to the floor and the cake with the pretty flowers on the top, was a little boy no taller than her. As she inched closer along the length of the table she was under she could see that the boy was grinning from ear to ear as his Cheshire blue eyes sparkled with impish delight. One of the ladies stepped toward him from out of the crowd. She had dark hair and eyes just like the lady with daddy but she was quite a bit taller. "Bradley Michael!" she shouted, "You get out of there right now!"

    Quickly the little boy retreated back under the tablecloth but not without sticking his tongue out at the fast approaching woman first. The devilish little boy scurried quickly away as the little girl ran hunched over down the length of the table trying to catch another glimpse of his retreating form. About midway down the length of the table she was under, the little girl ran head on with the metal support bar of the table. Both of her little hands went directly to clutch desperately the top of her scalp as the quick hot tears of pain filled her eyes.

Without any warning two white gloved hands reached under the table quickly pulling her out from the safe haven of her hiding place. The pretty new mama lady was clutching her firmly by the shoulders and that angry look was very apparent in the glare she bestowed upon the child. "Now you straighten up right now!" were the harsh words that woman hissed toward the girl as she pulled her hands away from the throbbing spot on the top of her head.

As she clenched the little girl's hand in hers tugging her forward the mama lady spoke out loud. "Well Delores here's Bethie. This is Rob's youngest and look, she's bawling again. I don't know if she can smile. She just bawls all the time!" The lady's whispering tone was very scornful and the child was far too shy in front of so many strangers to speak out about the painful injury she had incurred. She wished fervently that she could pull away and run upstairs where Kaylin or Sharon would hold her and make all the hurt go away. Instead, she was propelled forward where she was posed in front of what seemed to be an endless line of strange faces. Trying hard to blink back her tears she faced the curious looks of children and smiling adults. Finally, Bethie managed to quell the flow of tears and shyly mumble the various responses that were expected of her, via the coaching of her new mother.

The memory faded and once again she found herself blinking in the brightness of the summer day. The heat from the sun was reflecting off the sidewalk and radiating around her but she hardly seemed to notice as she drifted from one retrospection to the next. This time she was alone upstairs in a hallway. There was a large storage cupboard along one side of the hallway. It had deep roomy shelves and large wooden doors with shiny metal handles.

The little girl wandered down the hall apparently deeply involved with the doll she was carrying. She chattered to her doll as she clutched it to her. "Let's go shopping and I'll buy you a new dress." Just as the child came parallel with the end door to that cupboard it suddenly burst open toward her and a snarling growl filled the air around her. The child jolted from her world of make believe by an electrifying fear that coursed through her entire body. There directly in front of her jumping out of the closet was the scariest monster that she had ever seen. She screamed pushing all of the air her small lungs would hold out as fast as it would go. When she could scream no longer she became aware of two things. The first being that the sound that was now coming at her from in front of the cupboard was the sound of malicious laughter and the second was the fact that the horrifying face was just a monstrous Halloween mask with the round face of Wade hiding behind it. Slowly the girl realized that the source of her self-consuming fear had been the boy who had come to live with them because his daddy and little brother had gone to heaven to live with her mama. Footsteps fast approached from behind her and when she turned and recognized the familiar figure of her sister Kaylin she flung her sobbing little body into the awaiting comfort of open arms.

There on the sidewalk, though still in bright sunshine, memories assaulted her as if she were centered in the eye of the hurricane. Some of the recollections now blurred quickly through her mind with a strong feeling of unrest and impending doom. There were brief glimpses of faces filled with rage matching voices raised in tones of anger and accusation. It seemed that the little girl was always tiptoeing lightly so as not to contribute to the unease of the dark cloud that had pervaded her home. When her mother went away to the hospital a sad feeling had crept into her house but now the feeling that dominated the house was darker, and angrier than sad. No matter how hard the child tried it seemed that there was always some sort of disturbance or confrontation going on around her.

Everything was different. Despite the frequent angry and often tearful words between the people around her this new life wasn't all bad. The new mama seemed nice but she sure had a lot of new rules. Bethie now had to play in her room with her toys. She was to eat only when and what the lady said and it had to be at the kitchen table. She was not allowed to cut paper in the living room and Kaylin didn't watch the Horse Court with her anymore. The mama lady had said it wasn't a horse show. She said the show was called *Divorce Court* and that young ladies shouldn't watch such nonsense.

The adult standing on the sidewalk now remembered that the child had felt that her whole world had changed. Kaylin and Sharon weren't around very much anymore. Now everyone seemed different Kaylin cried a lot. When Bethie asked what was wrong she always dried her eyes and hugged the little girl close. It seemed that Robby was gone a lot and Daddy kept him busy with the new brother when he wasn't in school. The little girl didn't know what to think of the new brother. Sometimes he ignored her totally. Then at other times she would be playing and would look up to find him standing nearby staring at her with a look on his face that scared her almost as much as the Halloween mask had. If he didn't leave when she noticed him she would quickly quit what she was doing and scurry off to a different part of the house.

Once he was nice to her and gave her a piece of gum. Then one night he came to her room. She was dressed in her nightgown playing quietly with her Betsy doll on the bed when he came in. "Mom says I should tuck you in cause it's your bedtime but if you are good I'll read you a story first." With his words her heart soared with delight. No one read to her anymore. Kaylin and her husband Tim used to read to her often before they moved away. Her brother Robby was much too busy with the new brother or he spent his time alone in his room. She had asked the new mama to read to her but she said that she didn't like to read stories.

Wade sat down on the edge of her bed and opened the little golden book that he had helped her retrieve from one of the shelves in her closet. The story was her very favorite. The princess book. He looked it over for a moment then turned to Bethie. "Wouldn't it be easier for you to see the pictures if you sit on my lap when I read?" She thought for a moment then slowly and with great shyness she inched closer to him.

Something about his eager expression puzzled her. When Robby read to her it was usually not quite so enthusiastically. When she was next to him he reached out and lifted her onto his lap. As he settled her there he held her tightly against him so as he lowered her to his lap her nightgown bunched up around her midsection. When she fidgeted trying to straighten it he tightened his grasp around her waist. "You're all right," he explained. "Every princess has to sit on a throne." With that he began to read the book. Even when he stopped to show her the brightly colored pictures he still kept his arm tightly around her middle. She noticed that sometimes he even sounded like he had been running because he got so out of breath from reading to her.

As he was reading to her, Daddy stepped into the room. "This is nice," he commented. "Thanks Wade," and with a quick "Goodnight," toward Bethie he retreated from the room.

When Wade finished the book once he turned it over and started reading it over again. This time as he read he began lifting himself off the bed. "Look, you're riding a horse just like the princess in the story." He held her tightly against him as he pushed himself harder and faster off of the bed and against her bottom. When the story was over she had to push hard against his belly before he let her go. When he finally set her free she looked at his face. His eyes were cloudy and his complexion was a blotchy red color.

He rose quickly off the bed pulling the covers back in one rather jerky motion. In a rather low voice he croaked breathlessly, "Just get in bed now or Mom will be mad and you don't want that to happen." He was fidgeting with the waistband of his pants as he turned toward the door. She climbed onto the bed and as she did she felt an odd wetness on the back of her panties. She pulled her covers up as he shut the light off and closed her bedroom door.

As she lay alone in the dark room a tear leaked from her eye and traced a torrid path across her cheek to the pillow below her head as she wondered when she must have had the embarrassing accident and hoped it would dry before the new mama found out. She knew from experience that the new mama didn't let accidents like that go unnoticed. The last time it had happened she had rubbed the wet sheets in the little girl's face growling with her actions. "You must like the smell of piss and how it feels to sleep in it! Maybe if you get a good whiff you won't be too lazy to get out of bed and go to the bathroom next time!" Bethie couldn't bring herself to explain that she had gotten out of bed and headed into the hall toward the bathroom, but when she had reached the cupboard from which Wade had jumped and scared her, she was sure that she had seen the door move. This filled her with so much fear that she ran terrified back to her room. Once back under the covers she had lain as still as she could trying to hold it for as long as she could. Then it came to the point where in order to keep from wetting the bed she had to squirm from side to side. Then when she could stand it no longer she gathered all of her courage together and sat up intending to dash right past that scary cupboard to the bathroom where she could find relief. Her hopes sank quickly. The motion of sitting up was just too much for her extended bladder as she scooted toward the edge of the bed it emptied and there was absolutely nothing she could do to stop it. Now she hoped desperately that her new mama wouldn't notice this latest accident!

The unsettled waves of emotion that filled the household eventually began to calm with time. There were occasional upheavals but they were getting fewer and farther between. The little girl was too young to correlate the emotional calming with the fact that the family dynamics had changed to accommodate the bidding of the new mama and her son. However, the adult woman standing on the sidewalk zoned directly in on the cause and effect relationship.

Occasionally Kaylin and Tim would come to visit or to take Bethie out for the day. It was always a pleasant, secure time for the child but when it was time for the visit to end she was devastated. Tears rained making the new mama very angry. Bethie often heard her Mama complain to Daddy that Kaylin was making the child unmanageable. She didn't understand this at all. Her big sister didn't do anything to make her be bad. Bethie told herself that she was going to have to try even harder not to be sad and cry when Kaylin and Tim brought her home after their outings. The little girl knew that she just couldn't stand it if her Daddy decided not to let her see them anymore.

As it was now it seemed to Bethie as if everyone was always disappearing from her life. First her mommy had gone away to the hospital and then they said she was dead and never coming home again. Then, when the new Mommy and Wade came to live with them both of her sisters, Kaylin and Sharon, seemed to stay away. The little girl had hardly seen Sharon since and Kaylin's visits were only occasional even though Bethie suspected that wasn't her sister's choice. Robby was always with Wade now because Daddy told him that he had to help him find new friends. When Robby was home and he did talk to her it was different. It seemed to her that he always looked sad. The new mama and Robby fought a lot. She said he was always making messes and getting into trouble. She had even told Bethie that he was just a "bad boy" and not to act like him.

Easter came with a hint of spring in the air. It was Good Friday. Bethie remembered because Robby told her it meant that if she was really good all day Friday and Saturday the Easter Bunny would come on Easter Sunday. This thought scared her a little because, after all, she didn't know if she could be good for that long. Again last night when Wade read to her she had wet her panties without knowing it. This time her panties were really wet and sticky. So bad that she figured that she had to have wet Wade's lap when he was reading to her. But as hard as she tried she couldn't actually remember doing the deed. Maybe it was when he was bouncing her as he played horsy and held her tightly against his lap. At least he had been nice and didn't mention it. Kaylin had always been like that too. She would just wash the soiled laundry and pretend it didn't happen. Not the new mama though.

The new Mama got really mad and had recently spanked her bare bottom when she discovered Bethie's soiled sheets. It had happened once again and she had tried to wait but Wade was in the bathroom and wouldn't get out. He had told her just to go pee with him in there. When he told her this he had been wearing his scary look and there was no way she would use the toilet while he was in the bathroom. That's why this time she had carefully taken off the soiled panties and stuffed them behind the corner of her bed that was closest to the wall. No one would find them there she hoped.

Easter finally came and she must have done okay because there was a fully loaded basket just for her. Robby and Wade each had one too. The new mama had spent a whole week cleaning and getting the house ready for company. The new furniture that had recently been purchased was polished and neatly arranged. Bethie was proudly wearing a pretty new dress complete with a flower adorned bonnet. She posed proudly for a family picture with her brothers in front of the fancy new spinning wheel lamp that her daddy had bought as an Easter surprise for her new mama. The pause for picture taking was brief. The household bustle continued as Mom explained that there was lots of company coming for Easter dinner and we should all be on our very best behavior. Shortly after her father slipped a large roasting pan into the oven and the woman, who she now thought of as her new mother, put finishing touches on a beautiful pink cake the company began arriving. She kept watching for Kaylin and Tim or her sister Sharon to arrive but they didn't appear. Some of the faces of the people who did come were becoming familiar to her. There were the new aunts and uncles she had gotten when her Daddy married her new mama. Bethie was very excited to see that her new cousins were among the guests. One cousin in particular captured her interest. He was the impish little boy who had hid under the table at the wedding.

Even though she hadn't been introduced to him she still remembered his name. It was Bradley and he was staring at her with as much open curiosity as she had for him. His mother who was standing behind him gave him a gentle shove. "Run along and play with your cousin Bethie."

"Take him to your room and show him your toys," her mother added. Shyly she led the way through the suddenly crowded house. As soon as they were out of sight of the adults Bradley reached out and flipped the new Easter bonnet down over her eyes. As she reached up to push the bonnet out of her face the devilish little boy leaned forward in front of her squishing his expression into a silly face with crossed eyes and lolling tongue. As soon as Bethie raised the bonnet and caught a glimpse of that silly face she giggled with delight. All of the shyness quickly disappeared and the twosome was soon deeply involved with an assortment of toys. Occasionally they were joined by other cousins but most of them were older and quickly retreated to join Robby and Wade. The only younger cousin was Bradley's baby sister, Jamie. The two soon becoming fast friends decided that Jamie was much too young to play with the big four year olds and the holiday ended much too soon to suit the children.

Time passed in a childhood blur. Bethie tried really hard to be good and not cause problems, but it seemed that sometimes no matter how hard she tried, it happened anyway. After one visit with Kaylin and Tim she returned clutching a large stuffed goose. The toy was a gift from her sister and brother in law and the little girl treasured it dearly. She took it everywhere with her especially to bed where she cuddled it close when she went to sleep. With the goose nearby it was like having her beloved sister by her side. Then one fatal night the goose slipped from her grasp and tumbled under the bed.

Late at night Bethie awoke and noticed the empty space next to her pillow. Frantically she groped through the dark covers searching by feel for her missing treasure. Panic rose in her when she failed to find it. Unfortunately, the child gave voice to her loss in a melancholy howl. From the hallway Bethie heard the sound of hurried footsteps. Soon her bedroom light snapped on and as the little girl blinked in the painful brightness she recognized her mother illuminated in the doorway wearing a sleepy look of confused concern. "What's the matter?"

Bethie turned with tears flowing freely down her cheeks. "I can't find my goosie! Kaylin gave it to me and now it's gone!" she bawled.

The mother's expression quickly changed from concern to a mask of fury. She moved from the doorway in a huff of anger. She quickly closed the gap from the doorway to the bed where she angrily snatched the goose from where it lay just slightly under the edge of the bed.

Bethie's smile of relieved gratitude quickly vanished as her mother clutched the toy roughly and stormed back toward the hallway. "If this thing is going to cause that much trouble I'd just better keep it so we can get some sleep around here." Even before Bethie's tears could start anew her light was once again turned off and the bedroom door slammed shut tightly. That was the last time the little girl ever saw the prized stuffed goose. Dejectedly she lay in the darkness with silent tears leaking down her cheeks and soaking into her pillow. Once again she had gotten into trouble.

Wade, on the other hand, never seemed to get into trouble. He was always doing well in school and helping Daddy with chores around the house. His report cards were always a case for admiration and compared glowingly to Robby's average to struggling grades. Many times Bethie had heard her Daddy telling someone how smart and well behaved Wade was. Then he would shake his head with disdain and say he just didn't know what they were going to do about Robby.

It seemed that the two boys were frequently an object of comparison. They were outside in the garage one day, Bethie didn't know the cause, but a fight broke out between the two. She watched wide eyed from the yard where she sat with her parents as the two boys stormed into the yard with both fists and voices raised. Her mother jumped to her feet as if to put a stop to the fight but Daddy stopped her with an arm to her shoulder. "Just let them go Ellen. They need to figure out who is boss."

Bethie gazed in wonder as the two red faced boys circled each other. They were angrily spitting words that she couldn't hear. She watched as Robby punched toward Wade. Wade took the punch with his shoulder and brought his leg around behind Robby's. She winced as she witnessed the action tripping Robby to the ground where Wade, driving his knees first, quickly dropped onto his stepbrother's back. Bethie flinched as she heard the ooaaf of air escape her brother. Once again her mother made as if to intervene and as before her father put a halt to the action. "It's almost over." He explained. "Let this happen this time and it won't happen again."

Her father was right. The child had looked on as Wade grabbed her brother's arm twisting it upward behind his back until Robby yelled his words of surrender. Wade got to his feet and strutted proudly toward his parents. Robby was a bit slower but he too headed angrily toward them until he heard his father's chuckled remark. "It looks like you showed him who was boss."

Robby changed his course and headed quickly toward the house. Bethie wasn't sure but she thought that there was tears in his eyes as she watched him climb the stairs to their living quarters two at a time. Bethie had tried to follow him but she couldn't' keep up. When she got to his room the door was shut tightly and he wouldn't acknowledge her knock.

It was only a few days after when Betsy, her favorite doll, went missing. Bethie looked under her bed, under her dresser, in the closet and in her toy chest. She looked in all of the places that mama had said to look and she still didn't find her. That night Bethie didn't want to go to bed without Betsy. When her mother found her crying she threatened the child with a spanking. Bethie clearly remembered what had happened to her goose so she did her best to hide her lonely tears in her pillow. Oh how she missed Betsy. She had been sleeping with Betsy a lot lately. Betsy had been given to her by her first mama and even though Bethie couldn't remember what that mama looked like she could still hold Betsy close and think about her.

Eventually she fell asleep but even in the morning she still felt sad. She tried to tell mama about it when she sat at the table for breakfast but as soon as the troubled child mentioned her first mama the new one got really angry. "I told you that she's not coming back and I'm your mama now!" she growled at Bethie through clenched teeth. "That doll was all old and ragged anyway."

It was later in that same week when mama was vacuuming the living room that she wandered out into the sun room to get away from the noise. She was just climbing onto one of the chairs when she realized that she wasn't alone in the room. Robby was in school but Wade had stayed home to go to the dentist that morning and now he was perched on a small sofa at the other end of the room.

"What ya got?" his deep voice asked.

For some reason Bethie's heart began to pound harder as she held out her coloring book and crayons for him to see.

"Bring it here. Let me see your pictures." He commanded.

Suddenly she felt really shy even though he had been living with them for nearly three months. Her feet could only take the tiniest of baby steps as she crossed the room toward him. Once she was there he scooped her up and sat her on his knee making the hem of her sundress push upward around her waist. She tried to pull it down but he held her tighter making her endeavors useless.

"Do you like it when I read you stories?" he asked seriously.

She didn't want to hurt his feelings so she nodded ever so slightly. Daddy had told both her and Robby that they should both do their very best to make Wade and Mommy feel happy that they were now a part of the family and living with them.

Wade took the coloring book and crayons from her and quickly leafed through the book. "These pictures are really good." He told her. "You are a very good artist." His words made Bethie smile broadly. She had heard other people say her sisters were good artists too. She didn't mind being just like her sisters. Wade set her things aside as he asked, "What happened to that pretty baby doll I usually see you hauling around here with you?"

"She got lost." Bethie's voice was timid and her expression quickly changed to one of sadness.

"That's too bad." He looked genuinely sympathetic as he thought for a moment before he continued. "I know how you could get a real live baby instead of some dumb old doll."

"How?" she asked. Her brown eyes rounding with curiosity.

"I could give you one." He paused and then continued. "That is if you are a really big girl that can keep a secret."

"Oh, I am, I am." The tiny child nodded. She adored secrets and she was enjoying the fact that someone as old as Wade, a whole twelve years old, would trust her with a secret.

He looked at her very sternly. "You have to understand that this is a very, very important secret and that if you ever tell something very very bad could happen."

Her already wide eyes grew even wider. She didn't like it when bad things happened. It was a bad thing that happened when her mama went away to the hospital. She never came back and that was a really bad thing. "I don't like bad things." She whispered.

"But you do want a real baby don't you?" he prompted as he ran his hand up and down her back.

"Yes." She answered so quietly that he had to lean forward to hear her.

"Then just don't tell the secret. Okay?"

Bethie nodded.

Wade went on to explain. "All you have to do to get a real baby is touch me and I'll touch you. That doesn't sound too hard does it?"

Again she nodded her response. Her little heart was pounding so hard that she could feel it in her throat. Imagine a real live baby all her own. She could hold it and feed it when it was hungry. The thought made her so excited that if Wade hadn't been holding her so tightly on his lap she would have danced with glee.

"This is going to be only our secret." Wade was saying as his hand moved from her back to the inside of her leg. "You can't tell anyone. Not Mom, or Dad, or Robby, or Kaylin, or anyone else. Do you understand?"

"Yes." She wished that Wade would just hurry up and give her the baby now. She knew how to keep a secret. After all she hadn't told him or Robby about their birthday presents that Mama had bought when they went shopping last week.

"If you ever tell something very bad will happen. If you told our secret Mom and Dad would be so mad at you that they would get divorced and you'd never see Mom again." Wade paused for a minute as he stared seriously at her. "You don't want that to happen do you?"

Bethie shook her head firmly back and forth. She didn't know what divorced was but it sounded a lot like what happened when her first Mama died. She never saw her again and the little girl was sure that she didn't want that to happen to her new mama.

"Then you just do exactly what I tell you to and nothing bad will happen." Wade instructed. He was breathing so hard when he talked that the little girl figured that he was even more excited than she was about giving her a baby.

The hand that was stroking her leg had moved farther between her legs and up higher. It was now up under her dress with his fingers tugging frantically at the crotch of her panties. As they pulled it aside the little girl squirmed and tried to push the probing fingers away with her hand. "Hold still!" he spoke sharply between clenched teeth. "You have to let me do this if you want to get a baby."

She really wanted a baby so she did her best to hold still. He was rubbing the area right between her legs and making her feel very uncomfortable as he did. No one had ever touched her there before. Wade paused in his endeavors for a moment as if listening. Bethie listened too. She hoped that he was listening for the baby to cry but all that she could hear was the vacuum hard at work at the other end of the house.

It wasn't long before he turned his attention back to the little girl on his lap. With his left hand exploring the area inside her flowered panties, where her legs came together, he used his right hand to undo the fly of his blue jeans. When this was done he reached inside for a moment then took one of the child's small hands and guided it inside the white cotton of his underwear.

"To get a baby you need to touch me here." He explained as he took her small hand and wrapped it around something that felt like a hot rubbery finger. "Now move your hand back and forth like this." A soft whooshing moan escaped from his parted lips as he demonstrated the motion with his hand wrapped tightly around hers.

Bethie was very quickly becoming frightened. "I don't want to." The child whimpered trying to pull her hand away from his iron grasp.

"Then you don't want me to give you a real baby." Was his quick impatient sounding retort.

"Yes I do but I don't want to do this!" Tears were filling her eyes threatening to spill over her thick dark lashes. Wade's hand was still wrapped around hers guiding it in a rapid stroking motion along the hot finger.

"Just relax I won't hurt you." The fingers on the hand between her legs were still massaging the area. As the motion of his other hand picked up the tempo becoming even more frenzied. "You are doing really good. I'll be able to get you that baby real soon." He spoke through clenched teeth.

Bethie squeezed her eyes shut tightly as if that could hide what was happening. She wanted a real baby all of her own but she didn't know how much more she could endure. He took the hand that was guiding hers away and instructed her not to quit the motion. When she slowed he admonished her with a growl as he used his newly freed hand to spread her legs farther apart. The fingers between her legs began probing even harder.

"When you have a real baby this is where it comes from." He demonstrated by pushing his finger inside of her. Bethie yelled in pain and he quickly covered her mouth. He sat very still and listened again as she realized that he was listening to make sure that the vacuum was still running. It had stopped but Mama must not have heard her scream because it started immediately as they listened.

"Calm down!" was Wade's disgusted command. The tears were now running down her cheeks and spilling freely over the hand that he still held firmly clamped across her mouth, "Stop crying you are acting like a baby!"

She wiped at the tears on her cheeks as he pulled one hand from her over mouth and the other from between her legs. She could tell that Wade was very angry with her but what he had done to her had hurt badly.

He was staring hard at her as he asked the next question. "You still want a real baby don't you?"

Suddenly it just didn't seem so important to her, but not wanting to make him any angrier than he already was, she managed to drop her head in what to him must have resembled nod of affirmation.

"I'm sorry. I didn't know that would hurt you. I thought that you were a big girl." His tone was scornful as he spoke to her. "Big girls like it when boys put things in there. I think we are just going to have to wait until you get bigger before I can give you a real baby. Until then you'll just have to play with this dumb old thing." He reached behind the couch and pulled out Betsy. Shoving the doll roughly into her arms he pushed the little girl from his lap. "Don't forget," he warned, "If you ever tell anyone about our secret very bad things will happen. If Mom sees you crying just tell her that you miss your real Mom." He rose off of the couch closing the front of his jeans as he spoke.

With that Bethie fled from the sun room quickly seeking the shelter of her own bedroom. When she got there the scalding tears that were hanging on thick lashes spilled over so she firmly closed the door. She dropped Betsy to the floor asking herself what she had done wrong. He told her that if she did what he wanted that she would get a real live baby. Now all she had was Betsy! Looking at the doll seemed only to remind her how bad the spot between her legs was aching. She picked up Betsy from the floor and threw her in the very back of her closet. Next she went to the dresser and retrieved her old blankie from her bottom drawer where Kaylin had helped her put it when she convinced her that she was too old to haul it around all the time.

With Betsy locked away in the closet she clutched the blankie close to her cheek and climbed up on the bed where she could lay with her legs pressed tightly together trying to quell the ache. The tears finally subsided and she lay there hoping that she would not somehow tell the secret. She certainly didn't want anything bad to happen. She also hoped that Wade never decided to tell her any more secrets.

Unfortunately, her hopes were soon crushed. It was only a few days later when Wade had another opportunity to explore his secret relationship with his new sister. It was a Saturday. Daddy had taken the car to get new tires. Bethie knew this because she had heard Daddy ask Wade if he wanted to go with him and in turn heard Wade decline. Robby had gone somewhere with a friend and one of the aunts needed mama to help her hang some wall paper. Mama told Wade to look after Bethie for a little while because she would just get in the way while the two women were working.

Mama could only have been gone minutes when Wade strutted into Bethie's room where she was playing at a small table in the corner of her room. With an echoing snap he closed the door tightly behind him and continued across the room where he perched proudly on the edge of her bed. By his flushed cheeks and sparkling eyes, the little girl sensed that he was once again up to something. "Come here." He commanded patting the bed next to him.

Bethie's gaze fell to the floor as she remained firmly rooted to the spot where she was. Suddenly her stomach was tied in a giant painful knot and it was hard for her to take in a breath.

"Come here." He repeated a little more firmly.

"No." she croaked in a tiny hoarse voice.

Wade got off of the bed and stepped toward her. Instinctively she flinched away. He reached out and took her by the shoulders. "What's the matter? Don't you like me anymore?" the little girl stared intently at the floor refusing to meet her step brother's gaze as he went on. "You don't have to be afraid of me. I won't hurt you." His tone was pleading as he pulled her from the miniature chair. "You're my sister and I love you. I didn't mean to hurt you the other day and I won't do it again."

At this she felt a small surge of relief and allowed her gaze to rise as she began to watch him intently. Still her expression was that of a trapped animal. She could only hope desperately that the words he spoke were sincere. "Now come over here and sit down." He put an arm around her shoulders. She tried to resist but his strength was just too much for her. Wade pulled her to the edge of the bed and sat down next to her. "Now isn't this better?" he said as he lifted her into a sitting position next to him.

His voice deepened and his voice became serious. "It sure is a good thing that you didn't tell our secret. Did you hear Mom and Dad fighting again last night?" His stare was intently focused on her.

She nodded the affirmative. She had heard them having a terrible argument last night. They had still been yelling furiously at each other when the child had finally fallen asleep from exhaustion. She wasn't exactly sure what the fight had been about but she knew that it had been something to do with Robby saying that their new Mama was not his Mother. With lots of drama and tears the new Mama had cried out if that is how he felt she would just take Wade and leave. Bethie started to hope that she would do just that but that was when Daddy had gotten really mad and started yelling too.

Robby's face had reddened when he saw Daddy's anger pointed at him and as he trudged from the room Bethie was sure there were tears in his eyes. Turning and running past Wade, Bethie had tried to follow Robby. As she passed her step brother Bethie heard Wade mutter something that sounded like "pussy," but more focused on following Robby she didn't take time to wonder why Wade was talking about a cat. At Robby's door she found it closed tightly. There was no answer to her knock and the door knob wouldn't turn in her hand so resignedly Bethie just continued along the hallway to her own room. At least here she didn't have to see the anger of her parents first hand, but even hiding her head in the pillow she couldn't drown out the thundering angry words. It made her feel even worse when no one had even remembered to coma and tuck her in.

"Mom was this close to leaving." Wade held up his hand with finger and thumb nearly touching as an indicator. "If you told our secret she would be gone in an instant!" He snapped his fingers to demonstrate. "Nothing Dad could say or do would stop her from leaving if you told." He shook his head sadly back and forth to stress his point. "You had better never tell or you won't have any Mama! Who knows what Dad would do then?" His vocal tone was so grave and stern that it brought tears to her eyes. He let the point that he was making sink in for a moment before he continued.

"I am still going to give you a real live baby. It will just take a little longer than I thought. We'll have to be very careful and go real slow so it doesn't hurt this time."

He was wearing what had become to her a too familiar look. She didn't like that look and after the other day she didn't even want a real live baby. Without her even being aware that she was doing it she was shaking her head in firm denial.

"Come on," he coaxed. "I won't hurt you this time. I promise." He held up his hand as if he was taking a solemn oath. "We've got lots of time alone together and I am going to be very careful not to hurt you." He began tugging on the hem of her shirt preparing to pull it off over her head.

"No!" she told him tugging at the material. "Stop it!"

"I have to be able to look at you or it won't work." He jerked the shirt roughly over her head and she immediately crossed her arms over her bare chest.

"You go away!" she demanded forcefully stomping her foot. "Just leave me alone! I don't like you! I don't want to do this!"

"Oh, yes you do. You are just being a scared little bawl baby." She used all of her strength to resist but Wade still pushed her down on the bed and began tugging at her shorts and underpants. His voice had turned to a wicked snarl. "You just do exactly what I want or I'll tell everybody just what you've been doing with me and you won't have a Mom anymore! If she found out how bad you are she would leave and never come back again!"

His horrid words shocked the little girl into complete stillness. She by any means was not cooperating as he pulled off the remainder of her clothes but she wasn't struggling either. Her young mind was grappling instead to understand what he had just threatened. If she did not do what he wanted, he would make her new Mama go away. He would tell Mama how bad she was and she would never come back. If her new

Mama went away and it was Bethie's fault, her daddy was sure to send Bethie away too. Just like Kaylin, Tim and Sharon. Just like she had overheard her parents talking about sending Robby away if he didn't straighten up. Tears welled hotly in her eyes as she silently promised herself that she would never let that happen.

Wade had her lying flat on her back on the bed with her clothes in a small heap on the floor next to his feet as he stood over her. He reached out and pulled her hands away from her chest and laid them at her sides. "Stay just like I put you." His words came out in short stuttering gasps that scared her even more. He pushed her knees up in the air spreading her legs as he did. Tears escaped from her tightly clenched eyes and traced scalding paths down her cheeks as she once again felt his touch between her legs. She wished wholeheartedly that someone would come home and stop him.

Suddenly he began talking in a quiet sort of flat voice as he touched her. "Don't cry Bethie. I'm not hurting you am I?" when she didn't respond he repeated his question in a louder more demanding tone. "Am I?"

She managed to pacify him with a minute shift of her head. Actually what he was doing to her did hurt but the emotions she was feeling were far more painful. Letting him explore her body in this way was the last thing she wanted to do. Kaylin had told her a long time ago that girls shouldn't get undressed in front of boys and now here was her step brother staring at and poking and prodding her bare body in all of her most personal places.

"Pretty soon you are going to like doing this with me." His voice was low and gloating as he continued. "You'll want me to do this to you and even more!" One of his hands was still massaging the area where her legs came together and the other was softly pinching and pulling the small rise of nipples on her otherwise flat chest.

"Please don't." she begged, "Please stop. I don't like it!" She tried to roll away from him but he just pulled her toward where he stood at the edge of the bed. Wade then proceeded to educate her on the various names for the places he touched and prodded on her. He next went on to describe in detail all of the different things that he hoped to explore with her on both her young body and his.

After what seemed an eternity Wade finally took a break from touching her. Through a tiny slit in her squinted eyes she watched him as he reached inside his unzipped jeans and pulled out the part of him that he had told her was his cock. His hand was gripping it and she shut her eyes tightly so she couldn't see as she felt him press its rubbery length between her legs. He pulled her legs tightly together and gripped them painfully as he pushed this part of himself quicker and quicker back and forth between her thighs. As he did this he explained in detail how some day he was going to put his cock into the spot made for it between her legs. But until she was a big girl and not a baby they would have to do it like this. Bethie tried hard not to listen to his words and let her mind wander elsewhere but it was hard when her little body was being pushed and pulled back and forth. Finally, Wade groaned and she felt a hot sticky wetness on the skin between her legs. He then moved away from her on the bed and as he closed the opening of his jeans he proceeded to instruct her "Get dressed now." He growled. "If you ever tell our secret Bethie you know what will happen!" He then turned and strode out the door closing it quickly behind him.

Quietly and with the automated motions of a small robot the tiny girl climbed off of the bed and pulled her tangled clothes back on. With her every move she desperately wished that Wade wasn't her new brother and that he didn't live with them. Later that afternoon, after her mother returned, she caught Wade staring at her evilly. Her mother commented that she must have put her shirt on inside out when she had dressed herself that morning. As Bethie looked up to reply she saw Wade's expression and quickly shut her mouth.

Suddenly the memories faded and the adult woman, Beth, was once again on the sidewalk in the warm June sunshine valiantly struggling to separate from the memories of her younger self. The summery weather did nothing to dispel the cold within her. She shivered in spite of the heat as she turned away from the building that had captured her attention and catapulted her down a path of blazing tortured memory.

## CHAPTER TWO

### Wilting Flowers

She drove along the busy thoroughfare hardly noticing the midday traffic. She intently scanned the buildings of the business district. She spotted the building she wanted on the right. It was the local State Police Post and she now clearly remembered that at the next cross road she should make a right turn. She signaled the turn and noted that the small store on the corner had changed but she still clearly remembered what it used to be.

Many memories seemed to flood back to her in a gushing flow. A smile lit her face as she quickly signaled again and then eased into the parking lot. She hadn't even been five years old yet when her brother, Robby, had given her money from the family monopoly game and sent her inside that store to buy him some candy. She had known that the money wasn't real but with some clever fast talk he had convinced her that it was a special kind of money that you could use at this store only. Sort of like the coupons that Mama used at the grocery store.

The adult Beth could hardly contain her laughter as she remembered the wondrous look on Robby's face when she came out of the store happily licking the generous ice cream cone that the man behind the counter had given her. The man had first made her explain about the special money that her big brother had given her to spend for him. It was just too bad for her brother though, the man told her because that special money could only be used once by four-year-old girls whose older brothers were babysitting.

She put the car back in gear and pulled out of the lot still chuckling to herself. She had ended up sharing that ice cream with Robby anyway—just because he always shared with her. It wasn't far to the next corner where she made another quick right turn and slowed her car to a crawl. The landscape in front of the house had changed but the house itself was pretty much as she remembered it. It was a rather large ranch style house with shutters at the windows and a large two car garage at one end.

They had lived at this location for such a short time her memories of the actual house and neighborhood seemed pretty vague. She remembered a blond little girl named Kathy who lived across the street. As she drove farther down the road and turned around another smile of recollection spread across her lips. She pulled to the shoulder in front of a vacant lot where she could study the house without drawing attention to herself. She still wasn't quite sure what was driving her down this often painful road of remembrances but some inner sense told her it had to be followed.

Her smile fading, she forgot the present and ventured down yet another memory she found trailing from her past. It was a hot sticky summer day. Bethie stood with Kathy on the sidewalk leading to the front door of the blonde child's house. Kathy's bright blue eyes sparkled with impish delight and a cherub's grin lit her face. "Let's do it." She coaxed as her whole body danced with excitement.

"Okay." Bethie consented. The two little girls joined hands and sprinted toward a neighboring garage which was surrounded by a variety of brightly colored flowers. When the twosome reached the flower beds they quickly released each other's hand and gathered armloads of the beautiful fragrant blooms.

"You take yours to your mom and I'll give these to mine." Kathy instructed as they parted. Bethie looked both directions then scampered across the road and up the driveway to her own house. She skipped happily and thought about how much Mama was going to like these real flowers. Yesterday her Mama said that the yellow dandelions Bethie brought her were just weeds--not real flowers that go in a vase. This puzzled Bethie because Kathy's mom had really seemed to like them and as the two little girls had watched she had filled a glass of water, added the flowers then placed them in a place of honor at the center of the kitchen table. Now Bethie smiled broadly, her mom would have to like these she thought. These were real flowers. She reached the door and had to stand on tiptoe to open it because her arms were so heavily laden with the present she carried.

"Mama." She called running through the house. "Mama, I brought you a surprise!" Right through the kitchen, dining room and on to the living room. Not finding her there she turned toward the hallway. Her pulse surged with excited anticipation as the door to the basement opened.

Expecting her mother, she was shocked to find Wade standing at the top of the stairs. "Mom and Dad went to the store." He pointed to the flowers she was clutching so proudly. "Where did you get those?"

"I picked them for Mom." Even facing her step brother didn't take away all of her excitement but his next words were quick to throw ice water on that fire.

Wade shook his head sadly. "Boy are you going to be in big trouble!"

"Oh no I won't!" Her voice rose in anger. "Why will I be in trouble? These flowers are a present for Mom! I'm not gonna be in any trouble!"

"Oh yes you are!" His tone was insistently sober. It did a lot to quickly shake her childish convictions. "you picked the neighbor's flowers. That is stealing. When they find out and tell Mom and Dad you are gonna be in terrible trouble. They will be really mad!"

Tears began to form in her eyes. "I don't want to be in trouble." She moaned. "I just picked them for Mom! I wanted to surprise her."

Wade's stern gaze seemed to soften. "Maybe I can help keep you from getting in trouble. Give me those flowers."

She surrendered them immediately. She did not want to be in trouble with her parents or the neighbors. Wade took the flowers and as she watched him he went to the garage, opened the door and dumped her gift into one of the large garbage cans that sat just around the corner. "There," he smiled slyly as he turned back toward her. "Mom probably won't find them there but if she does I'll tell her that you didn't know any better. If I explain it she won't get mad."

Bethie's brown eyes were round with wonder. Maybe Wade wasn't so bad after all. Especially if he was going to keep her from getting in trouble. The thought however instantly froze in her mind as she noticed the look in his shining narrowed eyes. He had moved back to the basement door and was standing with the door open, his hand resting on the handle as he turned back toward her.

"Now that I did you a favor," his tone was gloating, "You have to repay me."

Bethie couldn't find any words to speak. Her mind was filled with regrets and her insides felt as if someone had socked her in the stomach knocking the breath right out of her. The feeling reminded her of the time she had fallen from the monkey bars at the park and landed hard on her back. It only took her moments to forget that memory and figure out what he was expecting as his repayment.

This new house was set up so her bedroom was at the end of the hall directly across from the room Wade and Robby shared. Daddy and Mom's room was at the other end of the house. Late at night Wade had been coming into her room and doing things to her that she didn't like. He always made her promise not to tell and explained in detail the horrors that would happen if she did.

One night when he came to her room he had hurt her badly. He had been trying on a regular basis to fit his thing between her legs and tonight he told her once he got it in it wouldn't hurt. She just had to be tough for a minute as he slid it inside then she would like it there. He had brought the jar of vaseline from the bathroom and rubbed it on himself and her. He was crushing her as he laid on top of her. Bethie could barely breathe but all at once he had raised up allowing her to gulp in a breath of air as she filled her lungs he pushed himself from his middle hard against her. The pain between her legs was so sharp and intense that she cried out very loudly. Wade had been balancing on both of his arms so he hadn't been covering her mouth like he usually did and the sound of her scream seemed to echo through the night still house.

It had only been moments later when they heard a door open at the other end of the house. Wade had quickly sprang up from the bed, righted her covers and rearranged his own pajama bottoms so that by the time Daddy opened her bedroom door he was soothingly stroking her brow and telling her to go back to sleep that all was well and she'd just had a bad dream. Daddy repeated the reassurances and waited at the door for Wade to follow him out of her room. Bethie heard her Daddy Thanking Wade for taking care of her and saw him put his arm over Wade's shoulder as he pulled the door shut behind them. Hot tears filled her eyes as they left but she made sure not to make a sound. There was no way she wanted Wade to have an excuse to return to her room.

Now he was standing before her issuing yet another of his commands. "Come down stairs with me."

She quickly shook her head no and turned away from him. "I'm going to play with Kathy."

Wade's voice dropped an octave lower. "Well if that's how you are going to act I guess I had just better take back my favor and let you get in all that trouble for stealing Mrs. Johnson's flowers."

Bethie glanced at the outside door and then back to the one leading downstairs. Perhaps she could just run outside and play with Kelly. She could just take her punishment when her parents got back home. It couldn't be as bad as what Wade would make her do in the basement with him. Her mind was weighing her options and as if he could read her thoughts Wade interrupted. "If you don't come with me I will make sure that Mom and Dad find out about those flowers. I'll even tell them how you deliberately made Kathy help you pick them after I specifically told you not to. Then Mom will know that you are bad. Just like Robby. You heard what she told Dad about him this morning! She said that she would leave rather than put up with any more of his misbehavior."

The little girl clearly remembered the harsh words. It seemed like her new mother was always threatening to leave and then Daddy would get really mad. With his whole face turning an angry shade of red her Daddy would yell at whoever had hurt her new

Mama's feelings or even worse he would drop his voice to a low angry growl. Bethie hated it when her Daddy talked like that. She had heard him use that voice with Kaylin and Sharon before they had moved away and then lately he had frequently aimed it at Robby. She didn't ever want him to talk to her like that and she hoped that it didn't mean her brother was going to leave too. Slowly she turned toward the stairway and using her tiniest baby steps she inched her way downward descending toward her pasty faced, beady eyed brother who was panting hard as he waited at the bottom of the stairs.

The woman who sat behind the wheel of her parked car shook herself sharply. Coming back to the present she found her hands white knuckled on the steering wheel. As she concentrated to force herself to relax her grip she gave herself the usual pep talk but the same feelings of humiliation and self-recrimination still threatened to intrude.

"You were the victim." She reminded herself as she checked her mirror and pulled away from the curb. "None of it was your fault! He is just some sort of sick pervert who even at that young age knew how to play on the weaknesses of a child!" She choked back another bitter memory of Wade telling her parents how bad she'd stolen the neighbor's flowers and their consequential punishment.

As she drove she again let her thoughts wander back to her life in the house that she had just left behind. Her memory skipped from incident to incident pausing sometimes and then moving on. Her parents had owned a cabin in a small town up north and she remembered many pleasant times there. As an adult she drove on toward that location while her memories also made the journey to that same location in a different time. On Fridays her mother had spent the whole day packing and by the time

Daddy got home from work all that was left was to load the car and they would be on the road to their "up north" retreat.

On one particular Friday, when things had been especially hectic, she and Robby had spent the better part of the afternoon bickering back and forth over numerous little things. Her mother's patience had been stretched especially far and she explained the situation to their father as they finished loading the car. Finally, ready to leave, they called everyone to the car. Wade was the first one there and quickly scrambled into the back seat directly next to the window on the driver's side.

Bethie didn't want to sit in the middle again. She hated sitting next to Wade. It seemed like every time she went to sit down he always stuck his hand on the seat and then did something nasty to her. Just this once she wished that she could sit by the window and not by Wade. She knew that Robby, being older and bigger, would get the window seat and there was nothing that she could do about it. Suddenly, she had an idea. What if Robby got to the car first? Certainly then he would have to slide over and give her the window seat.

She watched as Robby headed for the car. Hoping to time herself perfectly behind him she hesitated a moment. To her dismay when her brother reached the car Bethie heard her father send him back to close the garage door. She was struggling to form another plan as he reached the garage where she was standing. "Go get in the car." Robby told her.

"Not yet." Bethie replied belligerently.

"Just go get in the car, Bethie. I've got to close this door." Robby was reaching up to pull down the overhead garage door as he spoke.

All at once the little girl had an idea. She looked toward her brother and spoke quickly. I'll just go out this way." She took a step toward the walk through door as her brother began pulling down the heavy overhead door. Robby turned his back with the motion and was totally unaware when Bethie changed her direction and made a quick dash to run under the door he was closing.

She had hesitated just a bit too long for when she reached the large opening the descending door caught her squarely on the shoulder sending her tumbling to the ground with a more frightened than wounded scream. In response to the commotion Bethie's father jumped from the car and headed toward the garage.

"Where the hell is your head?" her father demanded loudly as he approached his son. "You could have hurt her badly!"

Robby's summer tanned complexion had turned ashen as he turned toward his father ready to explain that he hadn't seen the little girl. He faced the full wrath of his Father's anger. In horror Bethie watched as her father struck her bewildered brother with his fist sending him toppling to the ground next to her. Her insides clenched in a tight knot as she heard him roar. "Maybe this will teach you to watch what you are doing next time!"

Still crying more from the shame of getting her brother in such trouble rather than pain Bethie got to her feet and climbed into the center of the back seat where as usual her backside once again came in contact with her stepbrother's groping hand. She elbowed him roughly and was quickly and firmly reprimanded by her mother as Robby climbed in next to her. The little girl was bathed in misery. Once again all that she had tried to avoid had only succeeded in getting her and Robby into even more trouble. She wanted to speak up and tell Daddy that it wasn't Robby's fault. She wanted Daddy to see that it was Wade's fault and if he was going to hit someone it should be Wade. Looking to her left from under her lashes she saw Wade perched next to her wearing a satisfied smirk and quickly swallowed the words before they tumbled out of her mouth. Instead she let them trickle down her cheeks in the form of shameful tears.

It seemed, for the little girl, that their angry departure had set the mood for the rest of the weekend. On the way up north they had stopped at a restaurant and despite her mother's objections her daddy had let her order her favorite shrimp dinner off of the adult menu. As the food arrived she heard her parents planning a night out that evening. Robby had earlier been given permission to spend the night at a friend's house and as her heaping plate was set in front of her she learned that Wade would be left in charge of babysitting that evening. Bethie found she wasn't hungry. Between the guilt she felt over getting Robby in trouble, the knowledge that somehow her dinner selection had made her parents argue and the news that she would be left at Wade's mercy she found that she could barely nibble at her favorite crispy coated shrimp and fries. When she offered an explanation of," I've got a stomach ache," she only seemed to infuriate her mother even more. Once back on the road her mother barraged her father with her latest version of "I told you so!"

Once they arrived at the cabin Bethie was sent immediately to bed while her brothers proceeded to go swimming. It just wasn't fair she thought as she laid glowering at the bright daylight that still streamed through the bedroom window. She wasn't sure but she was starting to think that she just didn't know how to be good. She was just going to have to try harder she resolved while more tears trickled down her cheeks.

Later as she heard her parent's car pull out of the driveway and the bedroom door started to open her resolve melted away to more misery.

The next morning dawned bright and clear. The sun was shining warmly as Bethie played along the shoreline. Her father and brothers were busy raking the beach and spreading a clean load of sand that had been delivered. Her grandma was there visiting and all seemed wonderful. It always amused the little girl to think that this white haired short woman was her father's mother. Bethie called to her where she sat talking with her mother. "Grandma watch this!" She hurriedly climbed to the top of the sand hill where she proceeded to bound down the other side. About halfway down in mid stride she saw the rake. It was lying in the sand with the tines pointing straight upward. With downhill momentum carrying her forward it was far too late to stop her small foot from impaling painfully on the yard tool.

The blood curdling scream brought the adults running to her side. There was much debate between them and then finally Daddy held her foot firmly in one hand and pulled the rake from the wound with his other hand. She heard bits and snatches of their conversation as they hovered around her and even through her pain and tears she sensed that her mother was angry when her daddy said that she didn't need to go to the hospital because grandma could take care of the wound.

After he had carried her into the cabin and Grandma had had her put her foot into a steaming bucket of water Bethie again heard her father bellowing at Robby. This time it was for leaving the rake where she stepped on it. The little girl had once again caused him to get in trouble. Poor Robby she thought. He never once meant to hurt her and it seemed she got him in trouble all of the time and Wade, who hurt her on a regular basis, and on purpose, never got into any trouble. Things just seemed so unfair and as she looked into the kind eyes of her grandmother she was tempted to try and explain it to her. But, just as she was about to open her mouth to have a chat with her Grandma she remembered Wade's threats and she decided that it would be unwise to confide in her grandmother.

The adult woman, now freed from memory, drove on trying to grasp the childhood confusions. One memory after another drifted past her. Some were pleasant and she found herself smiling. One specific incident Beth found herself remembering with fondness. Her daddy and mama had taken her with them to one of the aunt's house and on the way home at her Mama's urging they had stopped at a house with a large hand painted sign in front of it. Bethie was too young to read but as soon as they followed the man who had answered their knock into his garage she was sure she knew what it meant. On the garage floor in front of her scampered many assorted black and tan balls of fur. They were all over and the child laughed delightedly when one grabbed ahold of the hem of her coat and began tugging noisily.

Finally, after much consideration Mama chose the blackest one and tucked it inside the front of her coat to keep him warm. Bethie could hardly sit still for the ride home she was so excited but she did manage to contain herself like her Mama told her to and did not spoil the surprise for Robby and Wade when they arrived home.

## CHAPTER THREE

### Trick or Treat

It was only a few days and many nightmares later when the adult Beth, once again, found herself compelled to follow another tortuous path of memory. This time she was walking down a dusty gravel road in much more familiar surroundings. The house she approached on this day was almost completely square and very boxlike. Noting the deserted look and the real estate sign firmly anchored in the yard she walked up the narrow drive, circled the house and then settled herself easily on the cement steps that bordered the side of the house at its midpoint.

This house was much smaller than the colonial that she had previously visited. Looking across the driveway she took in the low setting cottage that snuggled closely to the one that she was visiting. Her mind's eye could almost see the elderly couple who had lived in that cabin. Their last name had been Stiles and Beth remembered them acting very grandparently toward herself and her brothers.

The clarity of these memories were much more vivid than those previous. She could even mentally picture the interior of the Stile's house. The details she pictured were amazingly real. She could even picture the 50$^{th}$ anniversary plaque that had hung over the archway to their living room.

Turning away from the cottage toward the front yard of her family's old house her gaze encountered the sparkling water of the Bay. She remembered that her step-mother hadn't been very happy to move here from the city. As a child she had not known the exact details of the move but she had known that it had something to do with

Daddy not having enough money. She remembered her mom telling her and the boys that she hated the place but that she would live there for Daddy until he got back on his feet again. The barely five-year-old Bethie hadn't quite understood it all. To her, Daddy looked the same as always when he stood up., So she hoped that it would take a while for him to get on his feet again because this place was fun. It was just like being at their cabin. The cabin however was at the other end of this same dirt road. This house had been her grandmother's cabin and she had had many good times here.

The first few years that they had lived there seemed to blur together in her memory with certain days and events retaining more clarity than others. She remembered a dock extending out into the water from which she had learned to swim. Beautiful hot summer days spent splashing in the sunshine with Robby taunting her to jump off the end of the dock until she finally overcame her fear and took the plunge.

She remembered her first day of school. The first step on the big orange school bus had seemed so high that she could hardly make her leg stretch that far. Her mom had walked her to the corner and stood chatting with one of the neighbors until Bethie climbed on the bus and headed for one of the enormous green seats. All at once she had been overcome with fears. As the bus had driven away Bethie pushed her nose against the glass wishing her mom would at least wave to her but instead she had turned her back and followed the neighbor woman into her house.

Despite all of her first day jitters Bethie had found that she liked school and instantly began making new friends. Her life at this new house began to form a pattern. On weekdays her mom would wake the three of them just after daddy left for work in the morning. They would quickly eat breakfast and get ready for school. Some mornings were calmer than others. She smiled remembering some of the arguments that she had had with Robby over which one of them got to look at the back of the cereal box, who used the last of the milk, who spilled the milk, who was staring at who and who had kicked who under the table.

As the memories guided her the adult Beth couldn't help but smile. Being a parent herself made her realize that their constant bickering must have driven their mom half crazy. She now realized the triviality of those arguments but she also remembered that her arguments with Wade had been of a totally different nature.

One morning in particular she remembered very clearly. Mom had stuck her head in the door of Beth's room and called out to awaken her. As soon as her eyes opened the little girl jumped out of bed and ran to the kitchen. She was particularly excited because today in school they were taking a field trip to a circus. She ran immediately to the table where she jumped into her usual chair.

Her brother Robby was still in the bathroom but Wade was already seated in his usual chair next to hers. Just as the prancing child launched her backside toward her usual chair Wade reached out and put his hand palm side up on the seat of her chair. When Bethie's bottom came in contact with Wade's open hand he pushed his fingers and thumb upward and roughly pinched the point where her legs came together. Jumping up the little girl let out a yelp of startled pain and by the time Mama turned from the stove where she was pouring herself a steaming cup of coffee Wade's hand was once again wrapped around his cereal bowl and he was looking at the little girl with what appeared to be twinkling curiosity.

The anger boiled up inside her and Bethie could contain it no longer. She had only one desire and that was to make him lose that taunting innocent look. She struck out as hard as she could with one tightly clenched fist toward his face but with very little effort he deflected the descending blow. The small amount of control the child had managed to hold in check let loose in a tremendous howl. "I hate you Creepy Wade!" she screamed. "I hate your guts! I wish you would just die!"

With one swift motion mama put down her coffee cup and crossed the room. She picked up the child, and sat down in her vacant chair, bending Bethie over her knee and baring her backside in one quick move as she sat. Four quick sharp smacks quickly rained on the child's already stinging backside. "Don't you ever talk like that again!" Mama's face was almost purple with anger as she roughly put Bethie back on her feet. The girl tugged at the panties that were down around her knees. As quickly as she could she pulled them back up underneath her favorite dress. She had put the dress on to proudly wear at the circus. Her mother continued angrily. "Wade is your brother and you should love him!" She shook her finger under the little girl's nose as she spoke. "Now before you go to your room I want you to give him a hug and tell him you're sorry."

Bethie was now crying so hard that her entire body was racked with giant stammering sobs. "Bu…bu…but," she struggled to protest.

Mama raised her hand as if to strike once again. "No buts!" she roared angrily. "You do as you were told right now!"

From previous experience Bethie knew that she had no other choice. Tears flowing, she turned toward her gloating eyed stepbrother. "I'm sorry." She managed to blurt out as she stepped forward and hugged him. She could feel his laughter and it only served to add to her emotions. Her heart filled with revulsion as she quickly ran from the room. Once face down on her bed she let her sobs overcome her. Deep inside she knew she wasn't sorry for anything that she had done or said. She was totally overwhelmed by the unfairness of the situation. She just could not understand why she was being punished when it was Wade who had hurt her.

The next memory that assaulted, the adult version of that broken hearted child, jumped ahead only a brief period in time. Bethie's Mom and Dad had gone next door to play cards with Mr. and Mrs. Stiles for the evening. Robby was spending the night with friends so Wade was left at home to watch over his stepsister. It was a Friday night and Bethie was already clad in her nightgown. She was playing with her Barbie and Ken dolls in front of the television as she waited for one of her favorite shows to come on. Wade was sprawled on his back on the sofa across the room from her.

"Bethie come here." Came the command from across the room.

The child felt the skin on the back of her neck break out in gooseflesh as she pretended to be so engrossed in playing with the dolls that she didn't hear him.

"Bethie." He called again. "Come over here now."

She froze where she was still refusing to answer or look at him.

"If you don't come here right now I'll call Dad and Mom next door and tell them that you are being bad again."

Her stomach did a flip flop with the memory of the spanking that she had received only a few days before. Slowly she turned toward him. "I don't want to."

"Just come here!" he demanded. "I'm not going to hurt you and you don't want me to call next door. Do you?"

Bethie shook her head in reply. After hesitating as long as she could she took a small faltering step toward him forgetting the dolls that she still clutched firmly in each hand. Ever so slowly she crossed the room until she was close enough that Wade reached out and impatiently dragged her the rest of the way to the couch. He then lifted her and forced her to sit straddling his hips where she could feel his hard thing right through the thickness of their clothes.

"Just sit right there." He instructed taking the dolls out of her hands. "I'm just going to play a game with you and we'll use your dolls." He pushed against her with his midsection and when she looked down she was surprised to see that he had already opened the front of his pants and the tip of his naked penis was pinned flat against his pudgy tummy where he pressed it tightly against her crotch.

Tears welled in her eyes. "This is bad. I don't want to." She whined.

"Yes you do." He stated firmly. "I know you do. You are just afraid to admit it. You like to play these games with me. You like it when I touch you. Especially here." He put his hand inside the crotch of her panties and began stroking her with his index finger. She tried to squirm away from him but her efforts only made him push harder.

Please stop. Don't do this. I don't like it Wade and I don't like you."

He took his hand away from her momentarily, licked his finger, then spoke. "Yes.... You ......Do." He punctuated each of his words by driving his finger quickly in and out of her as he spoke.

"Noooooooo!" came her loud howled response.

With his free hand Wade covered the near hysterical little girl's mouth. "Now stop your bawling! I'm not hurting you. If you would relax you would like it. You do what I say or I'm going to call Mom and Dad and tell them just exactly how bad you are being! They really won't like it when they find out that you wanted me to put my dick in here." He again prodded with his finger.

Once again the child could see no way out of the demeaning situation so, as she found herself doing quite frequently, she bit her lip in order to quell her verbal protests but she could not terminate the flow of tears that ran freely down her cheeks.

Very quietly Wade explained his rules to the new game that he was inventing and Bethie could only grimace with her shame and fear as he put the two now naked dolls in front of her. She knew that she had no choice but to do exactly as instructed. She had to imitate all of the actions that Wade made the Barbie doll do with the Ken doll.

It was only an hour later that she stood alone in her room trembling and trying to find a place to hide her soiled panties where her mom would not find them. She sniffled as she stuffed them behind the dresser all the while trying to forget Wade's threats of revenge if she ever told anyone what they had done.

Late that night she awoke with her nightie and covers clinging soggily to her skin for about the tenth time in so many nights. Rather than wake her parents and risk yet another spanking from her mother as she had the night before she stripped off the wet clothing and replaced it with the first thing that she found in her drawer. Once done she took her pillow and curled at the dry end of her bed drearily contemplating the punishment that she knew would come in the morning when her mother came in to see that she had made her bed.

Only a day later Bethie was struggling to pull off the wet sheets from her bed. Her mama was standing in the doorway of her room glowering with anger as she spoke.

"You must really like wearing piss perfume lately." She intoned. "If you would just get out of bed and go to the bathroom you wouldn't have to clean this stinking mess or hide your underpants."

Bethie was thoroughly miserable. She didn't want to keep wetting the bed. As a matter of fact she didn't think that she even knew when she did it and as far as the underpants that her mother was referring to she hadn't even wet them. The only reason that she hid them was because Wade had gotten them wet with the stuff that came out of his thing and he told her to be sure that Mom didn't find them or she would know by the smell exactly how bad Bethie had been.

Now the child didn't know what to do. She knew she was in big trouble for wetting the bed and hiding the underwear. As part of her punishment her mom had knotted three pairs of the soiled panties and hung them around the little girl's neck. "There," she had said. "Now you wear your piss necklace all day so everyone knows what you did." The child's eyes filled with tears which quickly spilled down her cheeks as her heart filled with guilt. If they only knew what she had really been doing she would be in even more trouble. She was shocked that her mother could not tell. Wade had been wrong. Bethie tried to tell herself that she was very lucky that mama thought that the crotches of her panties were stiff with urine and that today was Sunday so she did not have to wear the horrible necklace to school. Mama must have been reading her mind because the next sentence out of her mouth was, "Maybe you should wear that necklace to school tomorrow—what would the other kids think of you?"

Bethie had spent the major portion of that day sitting in the corner of her room hoping that no one came to visit and praying that Wade wouldn't see her wearing the telltale necklace of undergarments. The child knew that her step brother's punishment was bound to be as bad as or worse than her Mama's had been. Just before dinner mama sent him to the door of her room to tell her to take off the stinking necklace and put it in the dirty clothes because their dad had come home from fishing and it was time for dinner.

Bethie's hopes were dashed. She could tell from Wade's evil smirk that she could expect to contend with his punishment at some point in her future. Sometimes she just wished that God would send her to heaven to live with her first Mom. She had mentioned that thought to Robby once and he had explained that people believed that God only took you to Heaven when you had been good enough. He also told her if you died after you were bad you would only go to live with the devil in hell. "So much for that." She had thought. "I guess I'm stuck here with Wade!"

The following few weeks passed quickly for Bethie. She had managed to avoid being left alone with Wade. The one Saturday night that her parents had went out with friends it had been Robbie's turn to babysit her so Wade had gone somewhere with his friends.

Her Mom and Dad were barely out of the driveway when Robby pushed her roughly to the floor and began tickling her until her shrieks of laughter left her breathless. She tried her hardest to tickle him back but he was too big for her endeavors to be successful. When the laughter died away Robby sprang to his feet and strode toward the kitchen. "Come on brat," he called over his shoulder, "Lets raid the fridge."

The little girl quickly followed with delight. Raiding the refrigerator with Robby always proved to be an adventure in treats. This time was no disappointment. Soon the brother and sister were back in front of the television each spooning happily into large bowls of ice cream topped with almost everything sweet that the refrigerator had contained. The evening passed quickly. Robby had played three games of fish with her and even let her stay up way past her bedtime. Eventually, he insisted that their parents would be home soon and they both would get in trouble if she was still up so reluctantly she let her big brother lead her to bed. As Robby was tucking her in the child could hold back no longer. "Robby," her eyes were large and serious as she stared up at him. "Could you babysit me every time instead of Wade?"

"Why would you want me to?" Robby seemed a little surprised at the request.

Bethie thought deeply before she answered. She did not want Wade to think that she had told anyone their secrets. "You just babysit better than he does."

Her brother laughed. "What does that mean? How can I babysit better?"

"He does things." Bethie nearly choked trying to stop the words that seemed to erupt from her. She hoped that she hadn't said too much.

"Oh yeah, like what things?"

Bethie stammered nervously. She wished with her whole heart that she could just tell Robby the truth. Wade's threats won out. He had already told her that he would hurt Robby or anyone else who tried to interfere. She remembered the serious tone of voice and the look on his face as he said, "If you tell anyone I will kill them then do whatever I want to you—and I won't be patient and gentle."

"Never mind." Bethie's tone was so dejected that Robby reached out and tousled her curls.

"Tell ya what," he offered, "If I'm not busy I'll babysit ya the next time Dad and Mom go out. Okay?"

She was all smiles again. "Okay." Bethie agreed. "I hope you're never busy."

"Well I do have friends too ya know." Robby laughed as he pulled her bedroom door closed behind him. "Go to sleep now, before Dad and Mom get home and we both get in deep trouble."

Bethie snuggled down under her covers. Before she drifted off to sleep she smiled secretly to herself. Maybe now she wouldn't have to do all those yucky things with Wade.

True to his word Robby stayed with her the next time their parents went out. Once again life for Bethie settled into a calmer routine. By this time, she had met many of the neighborhood children and the tenuous roots of friendship began to take hold.

The time was passing quickly. The weather had turned brisk as the bright colored fall leaves left the trees. With much excitement and anticipation Halloween was soon upon them. It was Daddy's bowling night so he had left home immediately after dinner. Robby was invited to spend the evening with his friends and being that he had looked after his sister three times in a row it was decided that Wade would take Bethie trick or treating early and then join his friends later. Her mother was staying home to pass out candy.

Bethie was a little nervous about Wade taking her but she managed to quell her doubts with the excitement of the evening. Quickly she donned the clown costume that her mother had made. She pranced all the way out to the porch to admire the pumpkins. There were three of them. One for each of the kids in her family. Robby and Wade had carved them after school that same afternoon. Now they sat glowing eerily on the steps to welcome all of the Trick or Treaters.

Wade met her on the porch. He handed her an old pillowcase for her to collect candy in, called out to their mom that they were leaving and proceeded to lead the way down the driveway to the gravel road beyond.

Bethie's pulse quickened with excitement as she walked up the driveway to the first house they approached. The porch light was on and a smiling faced jack-o-lantern glowed brightly at the base of the steps. She hesitated for a moment but Wade pushed her from behind. "It's alright." He reassured her when he saw the reason for her hesitation. "That monster is just a costume like yours." He pointed toward the group of costume clad children who were just leaving the porch. Feeling a little braver with Wade's hand at her back she approached the house and when the ugly monster along with its ghostly pals trundled past her she breathed a small sigh of relief and picked up her pace. When she reached the porch a small wave of shyness washed over her and her tiny voice was barely a whisper next to Wade's booming "Trick or Treat!"

They continued on down their street in the same fashion until they had been to every house on each side of the road. Wade turned at the corner but suddenly Bethie felt a flutter of fear in the pit of her stomach.

The road was pitch dark with no streetlights. It was bordered on one side by a deep water filled channel and vacant lots on the other. The only house was at the far end of that long stretch of blackness. Bethie knew that just around the corner from the other end of that long dark road there were many more houses to trick or treat at. Deep inside however she was struggling with the effort to find enough courage to traverse all that darkness to get to them.

Wade noticed her dragging her feet. "Aw, come on!" he called impatiently. "I'd like to get this over with so maybe I'll have some time to do something else before I have to be home."

"It's really dark down there." Bethie pointed. "Maybe we could go home and get a flashlight." She suggested hopefully.

"We don't need any flashlight." Wade growled as he turned around and grabbed the little girl by the arm pulling her roughly toward the darker road.

Bethie's heart was pounding so hard that she thought it was going to burst right out of her chest and Wade was pulling her so quickly through the darkness that she practically had to run to keep him from dragging her. By the time they reached the next corner where Wade released her arm and let her slow to a walk her breath was coming in ragged gasps. They rounded the corner and approached the first of the lighted houses.

This street was much busier. There were costumed children scurrying from the house to house clutching bags filled with candy as vehicles carefully piloted by parents pulled to and away from the shoulder of the road. A variety of spooks, princesses, ghosts, vampires and other giggling costumed children climbed in and out of the family cars slamming doors and chatting excitedly. The carnival atmosphere helped to buoy Bethie's spirits.

At the third house on this street Wade met up with some of his friends. As Bethie went to the door to collect another treat he stopped and talked to them. When Bethie returned to his side she heard part of the conversation. "Well if ya didn't have the pip squeak with ya," the big boy gestured toward her as he spoke. "You could come with us right now and get in on the fun. But no way can ya come dragging her along!"

Wade just looked at the boy as if he didn't have a care in the world but Bethie could tell by the familiar glint in his eyes and his half smirk that he was suddenly very angry. She could only glare at the other boy and hope that he hadn't made Wade angry at her.

"Oh well. Maybe next time." Wade replied as he put his hand on his little sister's back and steered her back onto the street. Bethie started to turn toward the next house but Wade pushed her back the way they had come. "We had better head for home. You have lots of candy and we had better not be too late."

Bethie stopped and turned toward him. "But we haven't been gone long." She protested.

"We've been gone longer than you think and I said it's time to go home." Bethie was well educated to the tone of voice he was speaking in so she gave up the argument and turned back in the direction that he prodded her. She had a moment of hope as a few of her friends approached and their mother asked if Bethie could join them. She said that she would drive Bethie home when the children were done Trick or Treating and the child's heart bounced with anticipation as Wade seemed about to accept. Her moment of euphoria quickly dissipated as she heard him politely decline the offer saying he was not in a position to grant the child permission. The mother smiled at him and then hurriedly herded her children along their route.

Once away from the people and back in the seclusion of the deserted road Wade began to speak. What he said made the child's heart stop in her chest and her teeth start to chatter. "So you left those underpants that I told you to hide where Mom would find them. Didn't ya? What were you trying to do? Did you think you were going to get me in trouble?"

Bethie was so scared that she couldn't have spoken if she had wanted to. This was one topic that she had prayed would be forgotten. She had certainly not wanted her Mom to find the soiled garments.

"Thought you were pretty smart. Didn't ya?" his voice was ominous as it came at her through the obscurity of night. "Well you are just gonna have to learn that I mean exactly as I say." Wade had a firm hold on her arm and was pushing her with his other hand on her back into a weed filled vacant lot on the side of the road. When they reached the center of it he knelt down and roughly pulled her down to the weed spiked ground next to him. The weeds folded under her as she crumpled to the ground and the girl couldn't help but notice that the growth left standing around them served as walls that would shelter them from the eyes of anyone who happened to pass along on the road.

Bethie's eyes were completely adjusted to the lack of light and she could see her step brother very clearly. She stole a quick glance at his face and then immediately returned her focus back to the cold picky ground in front of her. The expression that she had read on his face told her that she had absolutely nothing to fear from the darkness surrounding them. It told her that her fears lay totally grounded with Wade. She did not think she had ever saw him so angry.

A pair of headlights cut across the weeds where the twosome sat. The brief illumination gave the little girl a fleeting glimpse of hope which quickly faded as Wade pushed her all the way to the ground and pinned her there with his hand over her mouth. Once the car disappeared he released her enough to allow her to regain her sitting position.

"Well it looks like I just can't trust you anymore." He continued. "If you can't find a good enough hiding place we'll just have to change the way we do things." He was tugging at the fly of his pants as he spoke. Tears were already finding a torrid path down the girl's trembling cheeks.

Bethie was sitting flat on the cold hard ground. Next to her Wade turned toward her. In the darkness she could see clearly what was protruding from the unzipped opening of his jeans. "Now you will do exactly as I tell you or I will see that you have a very bad accident out here in the dark tonight." The growl of his voice turned her insides into a boiling liquid. "Maybe you could fall in the water or trip and hit your head on a rock. You could drown just like my little brother. Do you want that to happen?"

Bethie's teeth were chattering so hard that she could not even verbalize an answer. She managed a wide eyed negative shake of her head.

"Okay then! You are going to put my cock in your mouth and suck on it. Suck it hard and don't even think of biting it. If I so much as feel one of your teeth, you can be sure no one will ever see you again! Do you understand me?"

Filled with complete revulsion the crying child gasped out a reply in between choking sobs. "I don't want to do that!"

"I really don't care what you want or don't want. You do what I want! Maybe if you do this once the next time I get cum on your panties you'll be able to find a better hiding place for them." Wade rose taller on his knees and turned to face her. She was still tightly clutching the pillowcase containing her Halloween candy, and as Wade filled both of his hands with the hair growing on each side of her head, she clutched the cool smooth fabric even tighter.

Wade pushed his groin toward her as he pulled her face toward it. Despite the frigid air around her Bethie could still smell the odor that she had come to think of as Wade's bad smell. It reminded her of urine, sweat and the dirty clothes hamper all in one. Wade pushed his penis right against her face. Bethie felt the poke of its rubbery texture against her face but she kept her teeth clenched viselike with her lips pressed tightly over them.

"Open your mouth!" came the harsh command. He had too tight a grasp on her head to permit her to shake it so she remained frozen with her face crushed against his privates trying desperately not to breath in the rancid yeasty smell.

Finally, Wade shifted his weight away from her but only momentarily. As he brought himself forward this time he began to pull her hair harder. At first Bethie managed to counteract the pain by clenching her teeth even harder. That way Wade only succeeded in ramming his penis against her sealed lips but as he rocked back and forth he kept increasing the tension he was putting on her hair.

Still she refused to give in. The pain in her scalp seemed only to strengthen her resolve but as she heard and felt the first wretched tearing at the back of her head she could stand it no longer. Her lips parted to omit the gasp of pain that wracked through her and as they did the child's sound of torment were choked off by the salty taste of the skin covering her stepbrother's male hardness as it was rammed into her mouth.

"Ooooh yes, yes, suck me!" Wade moaned.

Still part of Bethie fought back. Wade was now using his hands full of hair to direct the motion of her head forward and backward to meet his moving hips. There was nothing she could do to stop him but she still would not cooperate fully. Gagging continuously, she concentrated on keeping all of the muscles in her face and mouth as slack as possible.

Wade seemed oblivious to her efforts of rebellion. He kept pushing her head harder and faster crushing her lips so hard against her teeth that she could taste the coppery blood from the wounds. Between the repulsive tastes, Wade's frenzied motion and the atrocious smell, waves of nausea began to build in her already boiling stomach. Just as the retching and gagging became unbearable Wade pulled her firmly against his body. As Bethie felt his spasm inside her mouth the rest of him stiffened a warm ammonia tasting liquid filled the back of her throat. That was more than she could tolerate. Wade didn't quite have time to move away from her before she began to vomit violently. She heard him cursing as he shoved her away and she repeatedly heaved emptying the contents of her stomach then heaving even more though there was nothing left to come out.

When the storm passed Bethie pushed herself away from the ground where she had collapsed in a shaking heap. She raised her head and saw Wade standing just a few feet away from her. His look was one of contempt as he reached out a hand grabbed a rough hold on the back of her clown costume and jerked her to her feet.

"Boy are you ever a terrible mess!" He curled his lip as he held out her pillowcase of candy. With automated movements and shaking hands she took it from him. He began leading her back toward the road. Once there he stopped and tried to brush off her clown costume. Even in the poor lighting she could see that the once brightly striped material was now badly soiled with mud and vomit.

Wade guided her over to the opposite side of the road where he stopped just so they were both facing the cold, reflecting black water of the channel. His voice though quiet was very deep and threatening as he spoke. It left no room for the already tormented little girl's mind to doubt his words. Having endured the past half hour with him she knew with calculated certainty that the horror he was describing as a threat to her now was not made idly. There was no margin for her to protest. She would just have to go along with the story that Wade was planning on telling their mother. The consequences of disobeying him were far greater than the recriminations of her step mom. The bleak ebony of the water in the channel reflected the dark sky above it and the helplessness that she felt only served to reinforce his point. She knew without a doubt that Wade would definitely kill her if she did anything to cross him. He even went so far as to remind her that his little brother had drowned and how sad her Daddy would be without her.

It was only a short period later that she stood in the brightly lit hallway of her home and faced the full wrath of her mother's anger. Wade had concocted his story and told it very convincingly. "I just cannot believe that you could have done this!" she yelled. "I worked so hard on that costume and you have completely ruined it!"

"Trick or Treat!" came the call from the door and Bethie breathed a shaky sigh of relief as her mother turned away to answer the happy call. However, when the unhappy child caught a glimpse of the children at the door and heard her mother's harsh words her spirits fell even farther.

Behind the gregarious costumes Bethie recognized some of her new found playmates. She also heard her mother's response to their invitation that she be allowed to go back out trick or treating with them. Her broken heart filled with shame as she heard her mother's response. "I'm sorry she can't go with you. You see she has ruined her costume by rough housing and not minding her brother. To top it off she was such a glutton that she made herself sick from eating too much candy."

The other mothers shook their heads and clucked with pity as they directed their own children away from the door. Bethie once again felt her stomach heave with new found nausea. "I never even ate one single piece of candy!" But she only thought the words in her mind as she turned and fled away from the door. She caught a glimpse of Wade parked on the couch happily pawing through her bag of candy as she ran toward her room.

Time kept on passing despite the lessons taking place in the secret life she was leading with her stepbrother. Thanksgiving came with a flurry of activity. The family went to Bethie's new Grandma and Grandpa's house where she became reacquainted with her new cousins. It had snowed for the most part of the day and the ground was covered with a fresh white blanket of sloppy wetness. All of the children young and older hounded continuously until their parents finally relented and let them outside. Once there they proceeded to turn the pristine white blanket of the grandparent's yard into a continuous contingency of footprints in assorted sizes. They laughed and played until they were frozen, red cheeked and soaked to the skin.

Grandma met them at the door with an armload of towels and dry clothes. They were each clad in grandpa's old shirts, bathrobes and pajamas while their own clothes made the circuit through the washer and dryer. By the time the huge dinner was served they were all once again dressed in their own dry clothes.

The holiday had been a huge success as far as Bethie was concerned. There was a small smile of satisfaction on her lips as she sat in the car on the way home with her head resting against the back of the seat and her eyes drifting closed. Her mother was up front explaining to them all how nice it was to be part of a "really close family."

Something about what she had said made Bethie think of Kaylin and Sharon and suddenly she was became the more she wanted to cry. She contained her tears knowing that they would only make her mother angry. She glanced shyly next to her where Robby sat huddled quietly in his corner of the back seat and to her surprise he draped an arm across her shoulders and let her cuddle next to him instead of telling her to get away the way he usually did. It wasn't long before the fresh air and fun of the holiday caught up with her and she drifted off to sleep.

Christmas time came with loads of excitement. There was a festive bustle of activity both at school and at home. Bethie was so excited that she could hardly contain herself. They were practicing for a special Christmas program at school and she could hardly wait for her parents to see it. One morning before school she mentioned their attending and was rather disappointed at her mother's reaction.

"Thursday is Daddy's bowling night and he'll need the car but if you insist on going maybe you could ride with the Dixons." Her mother was referring to the family of some of Bethie's new friends. Bethie did not dislike the thought of going with them but she really wanted for her parents to be at the program too.

"Can't Daddy miss bowling just once?" she asked.

Her mother's answer was almost scornful. "He wouldn't want to! Your Dad would not enjoy that kind of program at all and if you are going to make that much of a fuss over it maybe you should just stay home too."

Bethie tried to concentrate on eating her cereal and not crying. Her tears always seemed to infuriate her mother and just last night she had witnessed another horrible argument between her parents. Because of this she felt strongly that she should not cause any more problems. When she awoke this morning the night's events had nearly been forgotten but something in her mother's tone brought it all crashing back to her confused memory. She wasn't sure just how the argument had started but by the time she was awake enough to understand the harsh words that were reverberating through the wall separating her bedroom from that of her parents the fight had seemed to be in full swing.

"You don't love me or even want me here!" Her mother had yelled. "If you did you would not let them walk all over me like this!"

Her father's tone had been lower but not any less sharp. "I don't see how having my daughters here for Christmas is letting them walk all over you."

"But Rob, you know they don't like me! I'll just take Wade and go to my sister's for Christmas and you can enjoy it with your family!" Bethie hadn't been sure but she had thought that her mother was crying.

"God damn it Ellen! When are you going to realize that you and Wade are my family too. I'm always hearing you preach it to the kids. Why don't you just believe it?"

"Rob, Kaylin and Sharon are different. They won't accept me. They do everything they can do to hurt me and you just let them!"

"Damn it woman I do not let anyone hurt you!" Daddy was roaring. "Ellen you let them hurt you! You let every little thing someone says blow all out of proportion. Besides that, what they might think, feel or say is not my fault!"

"But you just keep throwing them back in my face!"

"Ellen!" Daddy's voice had boomed through the whole house. "Get a hold of yourself. My kids coming here on a Christmas visit is not throwing them in your face. God damn it, I certainly have not stopped you from seeing any of your family!"

Her tone was acid and quick to retort. "But no one in my family has ever treated you like dirt!"

The argument had seemed to go on forever for Bethie. Her parents went back and forth for hours. At one point her mother would scream how she was leaving and never coming back and then only moments later her Dad would be yelling the same thing. These fights were something that Bethie and her brothers were witnessing regularly but still she could not get used to them. The tears soaked her pillow as she lay there in the dark listening to the emotional firestorm coming from the room next door. Eventually, in the same manner that one slept through a thunderstorm, exhaustion won out and Bethie fell asleep as the argument thundered on around her.

Now as she put her cereal bowl in the sink the Christmas program at school didn't seem as important. She was hoping that Kaylin and Sharon would be coming for Christmas but she was sure this was not a subject that she should bring up with her mother. Perhaps she could ask Robby later.

## CHAPTER FOUR

### Santa's Presents

Despite Bethie's previous worries for the most part her Christmas holidays ended up being a pretty happy and carefree time for her. The family had spent Christmas Eve together at her new Aunt's houses where they had many treats and lots of presents. That night Santa came bringing with him many of the child's wishes. Christmas morning was like a dream come true and later in the day Kaylin, Tim and their baby came to visit. They joined them for dinner along with two of her Mom's sisters and their families.

The vacation days from school went quickly and before Bethie realized it the month was January and her birthday was fast approaching. She had not noticed it but she had been enjoying another vacation of sorts. It had been a vacation from her conniving stepbrother's forced sexual attentions and all too soon her respite was over.

The morning of her sixth birthday dawned crisp and cold with blowing, drifting snow making it hard for the little girl to see out of the windows. It was Saturday so her father was home from work. Her mother had errands to do in town. The roads were slippery because of the weather so Daddy was driving her. Shortly after they left for town Robby went outside to shovel their next door neighbor's driveway. Bethie was in her room playing paper dolls and excitedly anticipating the presents that she would receive later. Suddenly Wade appeared in her doorway. "There's the birthday girl!" he spoke loudly through the lewd grin he was wearing.

Bethie's chest heaved. Her heart felt as if it had quit beating and then when it started again it seemed to pound with such intensity that her whole body quaked with each beat. The child retreated from him as he came farther into her room. She came to an abrupt stop when her back ran sharply into the drawer handles of her dresser.

"What's the matter?" his voice seemed to be whining at her rather than concerned about her. "I wouldn't hurt you. It's your birthday and I just might have a present for you."

"I don't want any presents from you!" The excitement of the day seemed to give her more courage to stand up to Wade even though he was wearing one of his most malevolent expressions. Her tone belied how firmly she had resolved not to let him get near her. "Just go away!"

"Now don't be like that Bethie. You know Mom does not like you to be mean to me and you don't want to get in trouble on your birthday. So be nice and I won't have to tell on you."

Her strong resolve faltered a step as she thought for a moment. She was having some neighborhood girls over for pizza and cake later. She hoped that Wade wouldn't ruin that for her. Her mind was racing as he pushed her bedroom door closed and advanced toward where she was pinned against the dresser. When he was so close to her that his tummy was tight against her chest he stopped.

Grasping at straws she spoke quickly. "You better not do anything because Robby will come in here and see you. Then you'll get in big trouble."

Wade guffawed loudly. "Robby doesn't scare me. Besides we have got lots of time. He just started shoveling and old man Stiles is out there watching. He won't let him off until the very last flurry had been shoveled away. Dad and Mom won't be back for ages either. So ya see there is plenty of time for me to give you your present and nobody to bother us."

His matter of fact tone did a lot to dash her hopes of talking him out of doing what she feared he had in mind. Her vacation from him hadn't been so long that she forgot the horrors that he had demonstrated to her and reflexively her eyes filled with tears that she quickly tried to blink away. Like his mother, Bethie's tears only proved to make him angry and in her own defense she bravely spoke out.

"I don't want to do anything with you! I don't even like you I wish you didn't live here!"

"Fine." He backed off a step giving her a glimmer of hope that he quickly snatched away again. "I'll just tell Mom exactly what you just said and that should put a really big end to your birthday. No party, no cake, no presents and none of your stupid little friends over. Won't that be fun telling them in school on Monday that you are so bad that your Mom canceled your birthday?"

"I'll just tell them what you keep doing to me and you'll be the one in trouble!" the little girl was so filled with her angry obstinacy that she failed to recognize the warning signs of his fury until it was far too late.

All of a sudden he grabbed her by the shoulders and his fingers seemed to pinch her bones together he dragged her out of her room toward her parent's bedroom. "You think that you are a smart little girl don't you?" He was more snarling at her than speaking a coherent language. When they reached her parent's room he gave her a strong shove releasing his grip on her shoulders at the same time. The momentum of his strength sent her directly to the carpeted floor. He threw open the closet door, stepped almost all of the way inside and rummaged for a moment behind the hanging clothes. What he held in his grasp when he emerged from the storage area made all of the air rush out of her as if someone had kicked her hard in the stomach. He turned toward her raising the gun with both hands and pointed it directly at her.

"Do you really want to know what will happen if you open that big mouth of yours?" He jabbed her Daddy's gun towards her as she quickly crab walked backwards trying to get behind her parent's big double bed. She felt as if she were trapped in a slow motion movie. Though her body felt weighted and slow her thoughts were racing so fast that she couldn't even begin to comprehend them all. Mental visions of the events in her short life were flashing before her. She hoped desperately that he was not going to shoot her but yet on the other hand there was a small part of her that entertained the thought of putting an end to her nightmares. At least if he pulled the trigger she wouldn't have to do the nasty things that he always made her participate in. However, when he moved his hands along the gun and made it make a sharp metallic whacking sound she quickly discovered that she was not ready to end her life.

Her tears now flowed in rapid rivers down ashen cheeks. "Please, please," she begged him. "Don't shoot me. Pleeeeeease."

In the relative short time that she had been alive Wade's laughter was the evillest thing that she had ever heard. All of the scary movies and Halloween tricks were joyful compared to it. "Don't be stupid. I'm not going to shoot you right now. I'll just shoot Mom, Dad and Robby when they get back. Then there won't be anyone left for you to tell. They will all be dead. Dead, do you hear me?" he was nearly screaming with his rage.

"It will be all your fault and with them gone I could really do the things I want with you instead of playing these little baby games. I could fuck you anytime I want. How would you like that?"

Bethie was too horrified to do anything other than shake her head back and forth in a timid response.

"Are you still thinking of telling anyone about our secrets?" He demanded and once again the trembling child shook her head. Her response was not acceptable to him this time. "What? I can't hear you."

"No, no. I won't tell anyone! Never!" The child vowed between soul-filled sobs. She knew that she could bear practically anything but the thought of not having her Dad, Mom, or Robby was just too much.

"Good. I'm glad you see it my way." Wade seemed to gloat. He still kept her Dad's gun pointed toward her as he eased to the bedroom window that overlooked the driveway. Cautiously, so as not to be seen, he looked out making sure that Robby was still busy with the neighbor. Apparently satisfied with his observations he turned his attention back to his little sister. "Now take all of your clothes off and be quick about it."

Despite the guilt, shame and other reservations that filled her the little girl obeyed immediately. It was only seconds later that she stood naked before him. Still holding the gun Wade moved closer. When he pushed the gun's cold metal barrel between her legs she couldn't quell the scream that rose in her throat but she did manage to gain control enough that it only came out as a whimper that diminished into silent tears as he began moving the gun barrel back and forth prodding the barrel against her. The hatred rose inside her like a flock of birds taking flight, but she knew from experience that any endeavor to go against his desires could only end on worse terms.

Late that night she lay in bed wide awake listening silently to her parent's conversation in the next room.

"Well I'm sure it was that phone call from Kaylin that upset her." Her mother was saying. "She seemed to be fine before that and you know how Kaylin always makes it a point to mention Kathy to her and Robby. She never forgets to remind them that I'm not their mother and that Kathy still loves them even though she's dead."

Bethie groaned inwardly. Kaylin's phone call didn't upset her or make her act any differently than she had before she had spoken to her. Kaylin had not even mentioned her real mom. She had only called to say Happy Birthday to her and to tell her that she would give her a present when Bethie came to visit the following weekend.

The little girl's emotions were torn. Her loyalty and love for her big sister made her want to burst into the next room and tell her mom that she was far off base. She knew if she did that she would have to explain what was really bothering her. After the morning's events there was no way that she would ever do that. Besides she tried to comfort herself, "If I did that I'd only get in trouble for listening to grownups talk."

The whole problem had come from how she had acted that afternoon when her friends were over to celebrate her birthday. She had tried her best to be happy but after Wade's antics of the morning and the shame she had felt for going along with him the new ice skates and cake just didn't make her feel like giggling with her friends. Now she wished that she had tried harder to at least act like she was having fun because she was now really afraid that her parents would cancel the highly anticipated visit to her sister's house.

The next morning her spirits were even lower but she tried her hardest not to show it. She was going to make sure that she didn't miss her weekend at her sister's.

Her brothers and their friends had shoveled off an area of ice, in front of the house and it made a terrific skating rink. As soon as her mother suggested that Robby would take her ice skating she quickly donned her snowsuit, hat, and gloves then waited patiently as he helped her tie her skates.

Holding tightly to Robby's hand she made her way tiptoeing carefully onto the cleaned ice. This was her first pair of "real skates." Previously she had used a hand me down pair of double bladed shoe skates. Just walking in her new skates proved to be a challenge. As soon as she set foot on the smooth ice her feet flew out from under her and she thumped down hard on her backside.

She could tell that behind the scarf Robby had tied around his face to keep out the cold wind he was laughing. Still she didn't feel intimidated as he firmly grasped both of her hands and helped her to her feet. She was surprised when he didn't let go but instead he skated gracefully backwards and guided her gently in a circle around the rink. As they glided her brother patiently instructed her how she should move her feet.

On their second tour around he let go of her with one hand and they skated slowly hand in hand around another loop. She only fell twice and despite the pain in her knees from landing on the hard ice she got quickly back on her feet to try again. By her sixth or seventh circuit she was skating on her own with Robby skating out in front of her doing fancy pirouettes and skating backwards, showing off, while yelling words of encouragement to her. She fell several more times. One time she struck the back of her head on the ice so hard that it brought stinging tears of pain instantly to her eyes but Robby teased her about breaking the ice so she soon giggled and forgot her pain.

Their time alone on the ice was almost magical. She was very happy that Wade had weak ankles and that it was Robby teaching her to skate. She loved it when she and Robby were alone. Left alone together Robby seemed to treat her as if she were as grown up as him. Sometimes he even told her secrets about how he thought their Mom was mean and how he thought that she and Daddy liked Wade best. Bethie agreed with him and always promised not to tell. She never worried about what the consequences would be if she forgot and gave away their secret. However, they were soon joined on the ice by Wade and two of the boy's friends so Bethie was restored to being just another pain in the neck bratty little sister. The little girl really didn't mind her change in status as she made her way back to the house alone. Robby had said that he would help her skate tomorrow after school.

True to his word Robby skated with her almost every day after school that week. Because of his ankle problem Wade only seemed to go on the ice if his friends were over. Their days began to fit into a pattern where she and Robby skated after school and after dinner he and Wade skated with their friends. Sometimes Bethie watched from the window as they played hockey.

It hardly seemed that time had passed but Bethie found the week was ending. On Friday afternoon when she arrived home from school Kaylin was there waiting to take her to her home for the weekend. Bethie was so excited that she practically danced to her sister's car. Just as she was climbing in next to her young niece's car seat her

Daddy leaned in and spoke sharply. He looked pointedly at the two sisters. "There will be none of your shenanigans when you come home little girl or this will be your last visit." Her father's harsh words seemed to be aimed at her but as he finished the ominous speech his attention seemed to be focused directly at Kaylin. Bethie was confused. She didn't understand what he had meant so she questioned her sister as they drove away. Kaylin told her not to worry about it and quickly succeeded in distracting the child with questions about school, her new friends and her birthday. As Bethie answered she was very careful not to mention Wade.

The weekend passed much too quickly for the little girl and before she knew it Sunday had arrived. As Tim and Kaylin were busy getting ready Bethie stole into the living room for one last look at what she thought of as "the forbidden picture." She remembered the heated argument between her parents after one of their visits to Kaylin's home. She could still almost hear her father's scoffing tone as he explained to her upset stepmother. "Kaylin did not hang those pictures to remind me of Kathy or to hurt you. Kathy is her mother you know and she probably misses her terribly. They were close Ellen. Besides that, I have no say over what she hangs on the walls of her own home."

Bethie closed her eyes and tried her very hardest to find a memory of this woman who gave her life. Every time that she thought that she had a slight inkling of a memory the picture in her mind quickly faded away and she was left with a strange longing inside of her. Opening her eyes, she stared hard at the picture trying hard to commit it to her memory. As she stared at the photo image she was filled with questions. She wondered what her real mother could have done that was so terrible that made her new mother hate her. If anyone even mentioned her real mom's name her step mom would blow up in a rage of anger or leave the room in tears.

Tim appeared in the doorway. "There you are. Come along now it's time to hit the road." His smile faded as he saw the little girl's eyes fill with tears. How she hated leaving them. Their house always seemed so warm and safe to her. "Hey, don't cry." Tim tousled her hair. "You'll be back again before ya know it." He put a protective hand around her as they walked toward the door where Kaylin was waiting to help her with her coat. The little girl threw herself into her sister's waiting arms for a long hug before proceeding to don the outerwear.

They stayed for dinner when they drove her home but it was all over much too quickly for Bethie's taste. She managed to keep her tormented emotions in check as she watched them drive away and was glad when bedtime arrived so she could release her tightly contained tears into her pillow where no one would be the wiser.

Winter passed and along came spring. One day her parents brought home a small red two wheeled bicycle from Aunt Tina's house where they had some things in storage. Her mother explained through tears that the bike had once belonged to her son who had died. Now Bethie could use it if she wanted to learn to ride it.

"Oh I do!" the girl was extremely excited as she climbed on the bike. With her mother keeping the bike steady they started down the road. Bethie pushed the pedals forward as hard as she could. The bike wobbled forward with her efforts but every time her mother tried to let go the bike would tip violently to one side or the other and her mom would struggle to keep her upright. They kept making their way up and down the gravel road. They were taking a short break when Wade came out of the house telling them that Mom had a phone call.

"Take over for me." She told him as she turned for the house.

Bethie was too thrilled with the bicycle to be too concerned with her stepbrother. Wade placed one of his hands on the handlebars and the other on the back of the bicycle seat and once again Bethie started to pedal.

"Stand up and pedal." He coached." It's easier if you don't sit on the seat."

He was right. It was much easier to push the pedals around when she was standing on them but this seemed to make the whole bike even more wobbly. They made one trip down the road and were on their way back with the boy yelling at her to stay standing up when she pedaled.

Bethie didn't like standing up. Mom hadn't made her do it like this. She was becoming more unsteady and scared by the second. She gave in and tried again just to appease him. It was just too much for the child to stand up, pedal, and balance all at the same time. When the bike began to tip precariously she quickly lowered herself back to the seat. When she did she encountered his groping hand waiting there for her and he managed to shove his finger hard through the fabric of her shorts into the crack of her bottom.

Bethie let out a surprised yelp of pain and immediately lifted her weight back off the seat. Wade was only holding the bike by the handlebars so when the child so quickly shifted her weight he was not able to maintain his grip and balance the bike. The bike, the child and almost Wade went crashing onto the gravel road.

White hot anger filled the little girl and she was back on her feet practically the same instant that she hit the ground. She was filled with so much anger she hardly noticed the bleeding scrape that covered nearly her whole knee. Her mother walked back out of the house and headed toward them at just about the same time.

Once Bethie was back on her feet the rage that filled her overflowed. A storm of emotion drove her as she ran at Wade kicking and swinging her fists. His laughter only fueled the fire of anger as he dodged her blows. He was much too fast for her efforts to be successful. The more Wade laughed the angrier Bethie became. She wanted to make him hurt as bad as she was hurting.

Before Bethie could even sense her presence her mother had closed the distance from the porch to her children. She reached out and grabbed the furious little girl from behind.

"Now you stop that." She commanded. Knowing the tone from experience Bethie quickly ceased her struggle but continued to glare angrily at Wade.

Feeling that she had the child's physical anger in check Bethie's mom tentatively released her grip. "Hey there, it isn't Wade's fault that you fell down. Falling is just part of learning to ride a bike." She tried to explain as Wade stood there wearing his usual Cheshire cat grin.

"Oh, yes it is!" Bethie quickly retorted as she noticed and nursed her skinned elbow. "It's all his fault!"

Her Mother's tone was quick to become impatient. "Everyone falls when learning to ride a bike. It's just hard to balance at first—that's all. It's no one's fault!"

"Yes it was! You weren't watching! It was all Wade's fault!" The child stormed. "I don't want to ride that dumb old bike!" Bethie turned away to run for the house but in three quick steps her mother once again grabbed her from behind. This time she gave the child a quick sharp crack on the backside.

"Well if that's how you are going to act young lady you don't need a bike!" She punctuated her words with three more hard whacks then turned and spoke over her shoulder to Wade. "Take little Donald's bike and put it away in the shed," she ordered. Turning back to the little girl her tone became even more vehement. "You had better just get to your room." One more spank accompanied the order and then Bethie was running on her way.

Three days later two of Bethie's friends rode their bikes over and were playing happily with Bethie in her yard. The threesome was giggling merrily over something that had happened when they were jumping rope. Bethie's Mom came outside bringing snacks for them. "See my new bike." Judy spoke up proudly to her.

Bethie's Mom gave the bicycle an approving glance as she talked. "Bethie can't have her new bike because she's too afraid to learn how to ride it" Once again Bethie felt betrayed. Her young friends looked at her in wide eyed wonder and an embarrassed silence fell over the small group. To Bethie's dismay the quiet pall lasted until her Mom once again disappeared back into the house.

Kyleigh spoke up first. "Don't worry about it." The cheery blonde girl spoke with a comforting wisdom that was older than her young years. "It just takes some kids longer than others. My sister Haley still doesn't know how to ride a bike either." With that the uncomfortable moments were quickly behind them and the girls were once again back to the business of playing and giggling. The day flew by quickly and Bethie was sad when it was time for her friends to leave. As she watched them climb back on their bicycles she was cheered by the whispered promise from the blonde girl. Kyleigh put her head close to Bethie's and in a quiet tone promised to teach her how to ride a bike the next time that Bethie visited at her house.

Spring warmed into summer and then school was out. Bethie's Dad had bought a small wooden boat. During the day while he was at work the boys were busily sanding it. Then, at night when Daddy came home he helped them paint it. As the weather became even warmer they all happily anticipated days of swimming and boating.

Bethie's Mom couldn't swim. Robby had told the little girl that she couldn't swim because she was afraid of the water. The idea of anyone being afraid of the water was hard for the little girl to grasp. Again Bethie consulted Robby's wisdom concerning this matter and he was quick to explain. He told her that Wade, his first Daddy and his little brother Donald had all been going across a bridge when the truck fell off the bridge into the water below. Bethie's eyes grew even wider when he told her that both Wade's daddy and his little brother had drowned. She shook her head knowingly as her brother finished his story. "That's why she can't swim and is afraid of the water." After that the little girl never protested when she was told to wear a life jacket unless her Dad was home and swimming with her.

Bethie wasn't quite sure that she understood it all but she couldn't help but wonder sometimes if it had been Wade's brother who lived and he had come to live with them if things would have been different. Most of the time she forgot about it and found that swimming with a life jacket on and jumping off the dock in front of their house wasn't so bad. She especially liked it when her friends came over or if their moms got together and took them to the beach which was only a few blocks from her house.

One particular hot afternoon they had spent the day at the beach. When they returned home Mom went into the house to start dinner and Bethie wandered to the front yard. To her dismay Wade was already there, sitting on the dock and dangling his feet in the water. Bethie quickly switched her course and went and sat on the front porch.

Wade was quick to notice her and gave her one of his sly grins. Bethie resisted the urge to stick her tongue out at him and ignored him instead.

"Hey Mom!" Wade shouted toward the house.

His mother appeared at the window. "What do you want?"

"Can me and Bethie go swimming?" he asked.

"Be careful." came her reply. "Make sure you wear your lifejacket and stay close to Wade." Her mom came to the door and looked seriously at the little girl as she gave the instructions.

Bethie was flabbergast. She hadn't even thought of going swimming. Especially not with Wade. He never did anything with her unless it was bad and no one else was around or else he happened to be showing off for Dad and Mom. That must be it she thought. He's trying to make Mom see what a good boy he is.

"Come on, let's go swimming." Wade called out to her. "I've already got your life jacket."

Very reluctantly the little girl climbed off the porch and headed toward her stepbrother and the dock. She toyed with the idea of calling back to her mother that she really didn't want to go swimming but she didn't want to risk making Wade angry at her. Her Dad had a firm rule that no one could go swimming alone. So if she decided not to go swimming Wade would not be able to and his anger had ways of going unforgotten. Slowly she donned the bright orange jacket and climbed down the dock ladder into the cool water where her step brother was already waiting.

"Come on, let's swim over to the sandbar." Wade indicated an area of shallow water about forty yards away, beyond the dredged boat channel. He then took off swimming. Not knowing what else to do Bethie followed him. Not having any reason to hurry she paddled clumsily and let the life jacket do the work of keeping her afloat. Finally she reached the shallows of the sandbar where she could stand on the hard sand bottom.

"Bethie come over here." Wade issued the command from where he stood waist deep, only a few yards away.

The child froze where she was. She knew the tone of voice he used and the glint in his eyes told her to trust her hearing. She was dumb founded. What was he going to do? They were right outside in the broad daylight. She was sure that her mother was watching them from the kitchen window and some of the neighbors were even sitting outside in their yards.

She felt her stomach do a sort of flip flop as she took the first tentative step in his direction. But when he spoke she felt a little relief.

"Hurry up. I just want to help you learn how to swim so that ya don't have to wear that dumb old life jacket."

When she had nearly closed the distance between them Wade reached out and grabbed her life jacket pulling her closer to him.

Bethie still felt nervous. Her Dad had been giving her swimming lessons and if that was all that Wade had in mind it would be pretty harmless. She kept reassuring herself with her thoughts.

"Roll over and float on your back." he instructed. She breathed a small sigh of relief. This was one of the things that her father had been having her practice. However, with Dad she didn't have her life jacket on. It was much easier this way she thought as she lay back in the water and let her feet rise up to the surface. Once her toes protruded through the surface of the water Wade reached out and put his arms under her.

"You don't have to do that." Bethie was quick to explain. "I won't sink because I've got this life jacket on."

Wade just gave a grunt in response as he moved one of his hands under her buttocks.

"I said you don't have to hold me up," a small edge of panic began to take hold as Bethie tried to explain again. When she looked at Wade's face she knew that the panic wasn't unfounded.

"You just lay there and make it look like I'm teaching you how to swim. If you don't I can promise you will not like what will happen." The tone of his voice alone told her that she had absolutely no choice but just to illustrate his point he put one hand on her chest and pushed downward so that despite the protective jacket her head nearly went under the water. She began to struggle but his other arm was snaked under her legs and she quickly knew that she was no match for him.

Once he was sure he had total control the hand from under her legs worked its way up to her backside and his prodding fingers found their way inside the crotch of her bathing suit. He pushed his finger upward inside of her and she had to bite hard on her lip to keep from crying out.

"There," he crooned. "Doesn't that feel good? You like it don't you?" His olive pit eyes glowed as he grinned down at the squirming girl.

"No! It hurts. I don't like it!" Bethie used her arms and pushed hard against the water trying to propel her body away from him. Her actions only proved to encourage him as he began probing his finger farther inside of her.

"Oh yes you do. I can tell you like it. Just think someday I'm going to put my cock inside there and you'll really love that. You'll beg me to do it to you again and again. Now reach under the water and rub it with your hand so it feels like I put it in there."

"No. Please. Wade, Mom is going to see us and then you'll get in big trouble." Bethie whined.

Wade's laugh was even colder than the water when he replied. "Well, if she does I'll just tell her exactly what you were trying to do to me and how you and Robby do it all of the time. Then who is going to get into big trouble? Mom would probably move out today and then even dad would be mad at you and Robbie both. So you see, you had better make it look like we are just having fun swimming and don't you cry either."

Later as she followed her stepbrother back to shore she couldn't help but wonder if the neighbors who were sitting on their porch enjoying the late afternoon breeze were staring at her because of what she had just done with her step brother or if her mother was lying in wait for her inside the house ready to punish her for her actions. She was so scared that she could hardly propel herself forward through the water. When she reached the dock her knees were shaking so badly that she could hardly climb out of the water. Wade on the other hand disappeared immediately into the house without a moment of hesitation.

Dejectedly the little girl dropped her life jacket on the dock and went back to sitting on the porch where she remained until her Dad arrived home from work and then summoned her in for dinner.

It was only two days later when Wade connived his way into taking her swimming again. This time her mother was sitting right on the shoreline. She and her lady friend were in side by side lawn chairs, chatting amicably and sipping lemonade as they tanned in the sun. It was Robby's turn to do the lawn and he was mowing in the back yard. Her father was in the driveway where he was getting the boat ready to launch. Just as Wade was climbing into the water he called back to him. "Dad, can I let Bethie take off her life jacket when we get over to the sandbar? I'll be careful and watch her closely."

Bethie's Dad spoke sternly. "You stay right by her and make sure that she stays where she can touch bottom!"

"I will Dad." Wade smiled triumphantly as he answered.

Bethie swam as slowly as she could toward the sandbar. She offered little to no resistance to the small waves that pushed against her. Once tired of waiting for her. Wade swam out, grabbed ahold of one of the straps on her life jacket and towed her to the shallows where once again he blackmailed her into doing his bidding.

This time with everyone present she could not control her emotions upon their return to shore. Once she had climbed onto the dock her glance traveled back and forth between her parents and she broke into tears. Her mother quickly got out of her lawn chair and came to meet her but just one more warning glare from Wade inspired her to quickly devise a story.

"I hurt my foot on a rock in the water." Bethie cried. "It hurts really bad."

"Sit down," the concern in her mother's tone made her cry harder. "Let me look at it."

"I really don't see anything wrong with it." Her mother told her as she inspected the foot that Bethie had raised. "I'm sure it will feel better in a little while. Just quit your bawling."

Bethie fought hard to regain control of her emotions. She didn't want to anger her mother. That would only add to the problem. She could also still see Wade glowering at her from where he stood just behind her mother.

That afternoon the boys helped her father launch the boat. Once he had taken it for a ride and checked it over to make sure everything was working properly he returned to the dock to collect the rest of the family.

Both, Robby and Wade climbed on board enthusiastically and were quickly followed by Bethie. Still Mom hung back. It took a lot of coaxing from their father and even more verbal reassurances on their safety before she finally relented and let Daddy help her aboard.

Bethie loved the boat. She thrilled at the wind in her face and the way the boat seemed to skip over the top of the water when they went fast. She was immensely disappointed when she was not allowed to try water skiing along with her brothers.

"It's much too dangerous." Her mother told her. Bethie saw her father start to say something but only cleared his throat and bit his lip instead. "Besides you are too little."

The little girl watched enthralled as her brothers tried to water ski. After a few tries Wade managed to stay on the skis without falling immediately. When it was Robby's turn his efforts weren't quite as fruitful. The harder he tried the angrier and more frustrated he became. After falling for the sixth time Robby slammed one of the skis across the top of the water. "These stupid things!" he yelled. "They are so big they won't stay on my feet!"

Bethie had never saw him so angry and her father's anger was quick to match it. He rose on his feet behind the wheel. "The problem is not the skis!" he roared. "Now you collect those skis and get your ass back in this boat!"

Once Robby was back on board her father wasted no time getting them back to the dock. Everyone was quick to climb onto the dock and head quickly for the house except for her father and Robby. Her father had told him to stay and as Bethie turned toward the house she felt sorry for her brother. It seemed that no matter what he did her father was always yelling at him lately.

Later, when her dad and Robby came in the house she saw Daddy slap Wade on the back. "Good job on the skis out there." She also saw Wade's grin of pride contrasting starkly to Robby's crestfallen expression.

The summer continued, Robbie learned to ski, and Bethie's mom was even getting to like the boat. Many evenings after dinner she would go out in the boat perch fishing with Bethie's father. When Bethie asked to go along with them her mom told her that she was too little to be good for that long and that she just didn't like kids in the boat with them.

Bethie knew that once her mother made up her mind about something she would never change it so she resigned herself to staying ashore. She didn't mind so much the first time when it was Robby who was left in charge of her but the next time it was Wade's turn to watch her. Just thinking of it gave the child a rather sick hot feeling in the center of her stomach. She mentioned the stomach ache that night when she couldn't finish her dinner.

"Perhaps we should stay home." Her dad suggested and Bethie felt her heart lurch with hope. However once her mother felt the child's forehead that set of hopes were quickly sent away.

"She doesn't have any fever. I'm sure it's just a case of not wanting to finish her dinner. She'll be just fine here with Wade." Her mother responded. With that decision made Bethie's stomach hurt even worse. She couldn't help wishing that it was only a matter of eating the food in front of her. Even if it tasted bad she would rather eat it than spend the evening in her stepbrother's care. A thought struck her and she stole a glance across the table at her other brother. Maybe he would stay home too. Wade would have to behave if they were both home! It was only moments later when this small chance of respite was quickly dashed. She heard and watched as Robby asked for permission to go to his friend Joe's house after the dishes were done. The child's eyes fell back to her plate and she absentmindedly pushed a piece of cold pork chop around until her mother yelled at her not to play with her food.

It was only a little while later that the little girl sat watching the boat pull away from the dock. She could hear her brothers in the kitchen finishing the dinner dishes. She knew that when they were done Robby would be the next person to leave and her list of protectors would be deleted. She would be left at Wade's mercy.

She glanced longingly at the boat growing ever smaller on the horizon. If only she had been allowed to go with them. The burning sensation in her stomach increased from a smolder to a full-fledged flame. Suddenly her spirits rose. Perhaps she had spied a safety net. Underneath the large shade tree Mr. Stiles was sitting in his lawn chair next door. Quickly Bethie sprang to her feet and headed in his direction. Wade certainly would not try anything in front of Mr. Stiles.

The kindly neighbor man looked up as she walked next to him. "Hi there, little one." He greeted her with a warm smile.

"Hi." She answered in a small sad voice.

"Hey, why do you sound so unhappy?" His gaze followed her eyes to where the boat had turned into just a tiny speck on the horizon. "Oh I see," he shook his head in understanding. "You wanted to go too."

As Bethie nodded shyly the elderly neighbor's chuckle came out in a deep pleasant rumble. "Well it's like this kid. We don't always get to do everything that we want in life and do you know why?"

He waited while she mulled this over and then answered, "No."

"Let me explain it to you then. It's like this. If we always got to do everything we wanted to we wouldn't appreciate it. Sometimes if you stay at home you'll have an even better time when you do get to go."

Bethie thought to herself that she would have appreciated going in the boat and not having to stay at home with Wade but she couldn't explain that to him so she remained silent. As she sat thinking Robby came out of the house and headed down the driveway toward the road.

Wade came out the front door and glanced around. When he noticed her with Mr. Stiles he headed straight in their direction. "Bethie it's time to come home." He turned his attention toward the elderly man seated nearby. "Good evening sir. I hope she hasn't been too much of a pest."

"Oh, not at all." Came the man's throaty response.

Bethie looked at the neighbor with thanks in her eyes and also a desperate plea that went quickly unnoticed as he continued. "She has just been keeping me company but now it's time for our visit to end. You run along with your brother and I'll see if mother has my dinner ready."

To the rising dismay of the little girl he rose quickly from his chair and headed for his house. There was nothing left for her to do but to follow her brother back into her own yard. Once there she sank down into the velvety grass and began intently studying each individual emerald blade.

"It's time to come into the house Bethie." Wade didn't speak loud but the electric shock that struck through her body couldn't have been any stronger if he had yelled at the top of his lungs. When she failed to respond he spoke two more words. These words were spoken far quieter than the first. Despite the lowered volume they were heard with even more impact. "Or else."

This time she didn't hesitate to obey. She rose to her feet and despite the way she was trembling from head to toe she followed him directly up the steps, across the porch and into the house.

Once inside she had to blink waiting for her eyes to adjust from the brightness outside to the dim interior light. She looked around surprised that her stepbrother had come straight inside and then disappeared into a different room. She was not disappointed with his lack of presence but she was confused.

Wade reappeared quickly enough from the direction of the bathroom. She saw that he was clutching a few assorted items one of which was a jar of Vaseline. He gestured for the girl to follow him and headed for his bedroom. Slowly Bethie followed. She was only halfway to the doorway when Wade stormed back out of the bedroom, grabbed her by the arm and impatiently pulled her into the room with him. He was quick to close and lock the door behind them.

As soon as the door shut he pulled off his shirt and threw it aside then began tugging at the shorts he wore. He told her to do the same.

"I want to go outside and play." Bethie's mouth was so dry that her words barely came out in a croak.

"You can go outside when we are all done." He growled. "If ya do what I say and do it right."

"Please Wade, this is very bad. We're not supposed to do these things. It's not right." Bethie was crying freely now. Bethie's friend Kaleigh's older sister had told them about sex and how it was supposed to happen when you got married.

"This isn't bad." Wade explained. "I'm just teaching you all of the things that you will need to know when you get bigger. If you learn from me all of the boys will really like you a lot. You will be the best fuck around and I'm going to start teaching you how today." He pointed toward her bathing suit top. "Now let me see your tiny tits."

Slowly the little girl obeyed and he was quick to give her more directions. "Reach up and squeeze your nipples."

"Nooooo," Bethie cried wretchedly.

"Just do it or I'll tell Mom and Dad when they come back! They will be really happy to know that you wanted me to take you in my bedroom so you could suck on my cock." Total shame and humiliation filled her as she once more obeyed his orders.

When her parents returned a few hours later they were quite surprised to find that she had already had her bath and was in bed fast asleep.

"Maybe she really was sick." Her dad suggested.

Wade was quick to retort. "I don't think so. I think she was just tired." He didn't want them to awaken the little girl and see how red her eyes were. He was sure that the child wouldn't tell but the swollen red eyes would be pretty hard to explain.

The next time that her parents went fishing after dinner it was Robby who stayed with her. She did manage to confide one thing to him as they were sitting companionably on the swing in the front yard. Out of the blue the girl spoke out vehemently. "Do you know what?" She didn't wait for his answer. "I really, really hate Wade's guts!"

Robby did not even seem shocked by her admission. He just looked her seriously in the eyes and agreed. "Yeah, me too."

Neither of them even considered asking each other the ultimate question of why.

Summer came to an end. Everyone was back in school and getting into a new routine. Even Bethie's mom decided that she needed to get out of the house now and then. She signed up for a ceramics class that was offered on Tuesday nights. She was going to attend these classes with her sisters so Bethie's dad would drive her to the city where he and the uncles would play cards while the ladies took their lessons.

To Bethie's utter dismay the arrangements were made so that her brothers would take turns taking care of her on these evenings. Unknown to Bethie and her parents Wade had presented Robby with a proposal that he had quickly accepted. The two boys agreed that seeing their parents would not be home until around midnight they would never know if the boys extended their usual weeknight curfew until 11:30. So that is how it went and every other week she was left in Wade's care.

Sometimes Robby and his friends came back to the house but more times than not she was left alone with Wade. The first time that Robby left Bethie cried and practically begged him to stay. However, without telling him why she couldn't begin to convince him to miss a night out with his friends. When he closed the door behind him the child threw herself against it and wept uncontrollably until Wade pulled her away by the hair on her head.

"What do you think you are doing?" he asked gruffly. "You do remember what will happen if you tell anyone our secrets? Don't you?" he had pulled her back to the kitchen and he reached out and grabbed one of her mom's sharp butcher knives from the rack on the counter.

He was still holding her by the hair with one hand and with the other hand he pushed the knife in front of her face. "When Robby comes home later I could use him to test how sharp this is. You would like watching that wouldn't you?"

"No!" Bethie screamed. "I hate you!"

"When are you going to face it? You love me and you love all of the things that I've been teaching you." He tossed the knife back onto the kitchen counter and led her to the couch. He was breathing hard as he undid the fly on his pants. "Now, let's pretend that we are married and I'm your husband. Take off all of your clothes and tell me what you want me to do to you."

Still thinking of the knife and her brother Robby who never hurt her she slowly started on the buttons of her blouse. Her fingers fumbled but she still obeyed. She kept her eyes focused on the floor in front of her refusing to look at him in his nakedness or to speak a word.

"Go ahead Bethie," he prompted, "Tell me what you want. Say, Wade please, please fuck me."

Gritting her teeth tightly together she pulled off her shirt still looking down at the floor as she did. Her tears were falling like rain onto the carpet. Wade reached out and pinched her nipple hard. "Say it Bethie! Say it!" He growled as he pinched harder.

When she could stand it no longer, hot shame filled her as she spoke the words. She was crying so hard that they were hardly intelligible but still he went on.

"Go ahead. Say, Wade put your cock inside of me. I want the real thing inside me--not just your fingers." He pushed her to the floor and removed the pants she had been fumbling with in one smooth motion. "Say it!" he yelled and she had to respond.

The little girl was terrified. Wade had been putting fingers, pencils and other things inside of her for quite a while now. He had kept telling her that he was making her ready for having the real thing inside of her and tonight all of her instincts told her that this is what he had been talking about. Tonight he was telling her yet another version of his preparing her for the future as he opened the jar of Vaseline and began to use his fingers to spread it along his penis. He next used his hands to separate her knees and knelt in between them. Her heart was beating a rhythm so hard that it was all she could hear.

Bethie squeezed her eyes tightly shut hoping if she couldn't see him he would go away and leave her alone. At first she only felt Wade's suffocating weight on top of her and a warm pressure between her legs. She tried not to breathe. His usual yeasty cloying body odor was extremely strong. He shifted his weight forward crushing her even more. Suddenly she was filled with a tearing, searing pain which made her scream out loud.

The pain between her legs was so intense that she barely realized that Wade had quickly scrambled off of her and was frantically trying to cover her mouth in order to silence the trilling scream that was still issuing from her.

When she eventually ran out of air and the scream dwindled away to a gasping whisper. Wade let his grasp across her mouth slide away and Bethie realized that he was talking but it took her a few moments before she could focus enough to hear what he was mumbling.

"I'm sorry, I'm sorry." His face was pasty white with red blotches and his eyes bulged frantically. He looked between her legs. "You're not hurt. You are just acting like a little baby! We just popped your cherry—you're going to really like it from here on out." His tone was quickly changing from repentance to scorn. "A lot of girls like me to put my cock inside of them and they don't cry!"

Bethie tried her best to ignore him but he was still kneeling in between her legs staring intently at the spot where they came together. With a finger he once again probed painfully inside of her body. Despite Bethie's lack of response Wade continued. "I was six like you the first time I put my thing in a girl and she only screamed more, more, more. She liked it a lot. She wasn't a little baby like you."

He paused as if to let the little girl think about what he had told her. Bethie was still in too much pain to really care about what he was rambling on about and more afraid of what he would do to her next.

"Your cousins like me to do this to them too." Wade talked on naming the two beautiful older cousins that she had met when her Dad had remarried. "I've been doing this with them for a long time now. But you are too much of a little baby to be like them. We'll just have to do something different." He waited a moment and then called out to the family dog. "Blackie come here."

The little beagle came on a full run. Wade picked him up and positioned him between Bethie's legs. He pushed the dog's nose toward the child's crotch. At first the dog just snuffled but when he started licking the place that she hurt the most the little girl was once again crying out loud.

"You little baby." Wade snorted as he turned the dog to face him. "You're not even fit for the dog."

Soon Wade was moaning with pleasure as the little dog licked him. When he sprang to his feet clutching himself and ran for the bathroom Bethie grabbed her clothes and made her way to her own room.

By the time that Wade returned to give her more of his usual threats she had donned her pajamas and was curled in her bed.

As Wade left her room he paused at the door and turned toward her. His expression was almost kindly but his words only filled her with dread. "I'm sorry that I hurt you but now next time it won't hurt. My cock will fit right inside you. We'll get you all stretched out to fit it then y

ou'll like it. You'll see." He was smiling as he turned and shut the door behind him.

She closed her eyes and tried hard to forget what had happened but it was very difficult. She found herself wondering if what he'd said about her new cousin was true. She didn't think so. She knew that her step brother lied regularly. She had witnessed some of his lies first hand and besides that she just couldn't picture her pretty outgoing cousins doing those nasty things with fat old Wade.

The pattern was established throughout the fall. For the most part Bethie appeared to live the life of a normal first grader. She worked hard to make things look that way. Wade's Tuesday nights of sexual experimentation and exploration left the child not only in physical pain that she could tell nobody about but at times nearly paralyzed her with devastating shame.

Wade was continuously pounding her emotions with a rock solid hammer of guilt. He constantly told her how she made him do the things he did, how much she liked it and how disgusted and ashamed of her their parents would be if they ever found out what she was making him do to her. It was all too much for the little girl but still she trudged forward.

Another change took place in her life. It wasn't a large one but it did contribute greatly to the load of guilt that she carried. On Saturday mornings she was now attending catechism. Her mother was insisting that she would attend the Catholic Church and had signed her up for the classes. She was now learning all about God, his son Jesus, the Bible, The Ten Commandments and sin in all of its forms.

The class instructor never mentioned specifically what she was doing with her step brother when they explained about sin or The Ten Commandments but she was learning enough to realize that her sins were so bad that they were unspeakable. Now when she thought about dying she could only hope to live because she was sure that upon her departure from this world God would send her straight to hell. Never once did she realize that she may have already been a regular resident due to her brother's unwanted attention.

Christmas came with the same ardor as the previous one. On Christmas Eve they left home before dark and headed for Bay City where they visited all of the Aunts, Uncles, Cousins and Grandparents from her step mother's side of the family.

There were many presents and lots of merriment. They didn't travel home until the early, early hours of the morning. All of the way home as Bethie sat perched on the backseat between her two brothers she leaned forward and kept her eyes intently glued to the starlit sky searching hopefully for a glimpse of Rudolph's nose or Santa's sleigh. Robby let her climb onto his lap so that she could have a better view out his window. He pointed out a flashing red light in the sky and told her that he was certain that it was Rudolph's glowing red nose and asked Wade if he agreed.

"Nah, it's just a dumb old plane." Wade grumbled tiredly. "It's so late that Santa has probably already passed right by our house."

"Oh, no," Robby reassured her. "Santa would not do that. Even if he passed our house he would come back later. Wouldn't he Dad?"

"I don't know about that." Her father's deep voice came from the front seat where the dashboard glowed softly and the radio played Christmas carols. "I think it depends on whether or not you have been good."

Bethie's eyes fell from the sky. Even if that light was Santa and Rudolph there was no use watching for him to come her way. Everyone knew that Santa's elves knew everything and they reported directly to the man himself. Bethie was sure that Santa knew exactly how bad she had been. She was glad there was darkness and lowered her face as they drove under streetlights so that the tears that had suddenly sprung to her eyes remained hidden. She did find some comfort however. She figured that Santa would know exactly how bad Wade was too. At least that way he wouldn't get any presents either. Boy wouldn't her parents be shocked when only Robby got presents from Santa she thought as they drove on in silence. "Well at least Dad would know that Robby wasn't always bad," she thought.

Her father guided the car into the driveway and killed the motor. "Now everyone march straight in the house and go straight to bed!" Bethie's Mom ordered as she led her by the hand into the house. What the child saw when they got inside took her breath away and brought tears of joy to her eyes all at the same time.

The kitchen, dining room and living room all ran together as one. The only lights on in the room were the ones that sparkled like a million glistening diamonds on the Christmas tree. The effect was beautiful but not as breathtaking to the little girl as what was under and all around the gaily decorated pine.

The tears that filled the child's eyes spilled over and down her cheeks as she stood frozen with delight drinking in the scene in front of her.

"What the heck?" Wade spoke from behind her.

There was a flurry of activity as their father entered and Robby gave his surprised explanation. "Look, look! Santa came even though we weren't home." His voice was filled with wonder.

Everyone moved forward all at once. Wade was at one side of the tree and Robby at the other. Bethie stood rooted to the spot until her mother gently pushed her from behind. "Go ahead." She coaxed. "See what Santa brought you."

This was all the coaxing that it took to put the little girl in motion. She was on the floor in front ot the tree in a matter of seconds. She couldn't believe her eyes. She had to touch everything as if validating the reality that Santa had really came. Later that morning after she had slept she had run back into the living room to make sure it hadn't been a dream. She was totally delighted that it hadn't been but she still didn't understand how Santa had missed her indiscretions.

Bethie thought about it that day as she played with her new toys. She loved the new doll that Santa had brought and as she watched it ride a little tricycle across the room she thought that perhaps she had it figured out. Maybe Santa knew that she didn't want to do all those bad things. There was only one small problem with her theory. Santa had brought Wade presents too.

When Bethie saw exactly what Santa had brought to Wade her blood seemed to freeze in her veins. The past fall both Wade and Robby had taken hunter's safety. Santa must have known that they had both passed with flying colors because he had brought each of the boys a gun. When Bethie saw Wade holding his she nearly choked. Santa couldn't have possibly known what he had been up to or he would have never brought him a gun. Suddenly the holiday didn't seem quite so bright anymore. The little girl gathered up her new doll and went to sit on her bed until the guests began arriving.

## CHAPTER FIVE

### Bath Time

Winter turned to spring. Bethie was still suffering from Wade's regular Tuesday night liberties. Sometimes he even volunteered to baby-sit so Robby could have the night off. He gave the excuse that he had homework but Bethie had never saw him bring home any books. Everyone was very impressed with his generous offers. Bethie's parents and Robby all marveled at his kind gesture but only Bethie knew the truth. She knew better than tell anyone of his ulterior motives. The consequences were more than she could bear.

About mid-season she was given a break from his unwanted attentions. When Bethie awoke one morning Mrs. Stiles the neighbor lady was at her house. She explained that her mama had gotten sick during the night and that her daddy had taken her to the hospital.

Bethie tried really hard not to cry. She remembered that her real mom had went to the hospital and then she had never come home again. Mrs. Stiles must have noticed the emotions playing across the child's face. She crossed the room and gathered the little girl to her breast in a grandmotherly hug. "It's all right." She crooned. "Your mama will be just fine. You'll see sweet heart."

After she held her for a moment Mrs. Stiles helped Bethie pick out clothes to wear to school and then fed her and her brothers' breakfast. She kept the household cheerful so by the time that Bethie left for school she felt better about the situation.

That afternoon when she got home from school Mrs. Dixon, her friends mom, was waiting at the bus stop. She told Bethie that her dad had made arrangements for her to spend the night at their house.

"When is my mom coming home?" the child was very quick to ask.

"Come and get into my car and I'll tell you all about it." She led the way. Bethie climbed into the backseat with Haley and Kyleigh while Bett, the oldest, sat in front with her mother. True to her word, Mrs. Dixon, or Ruth as she told Bethie to call her explained about her mother. "Bethie your mom has appendicitis and right now the doctor is doing surgery to remove her appendix. If everything goes good she'll probably only have to stay at the hospital for a few days but then she will come home and be as good as new!" She finished the explanation with an encouraging smile and Bethie accepted it readily.

They made a quick trip to Bethie's house so that she could get her nightie and some school clothes for the next day. Then they went on to the Dixon's house.

Most of the afternoon and evening seemed like a huge adventure for her. Bethie was amazed at the differences in their families. This house was full of a continuous stream of chatter and laughter as the entire family pitched in to make dinner. Even the arguments seemed good natured compared to some of the long cold silences that she was used to at her home.

The evening passed quickly for the child. There were brief moments where concern for her mom and a sort of empty and scared loneliness crept up on her. These were counteracted by bright moments of laughter and chatter that managed to drive most of her worries to the back of her mind. However even with the four little girls crammed together in the one small bedroom with the occasional burst of laughter created by girlish mischief she was no longer able to keep her dark thoughts at bay. She was really glad that the darkness and a pillow hid her worries from her friends as unsuppressable tears trickled into the pillow.

Two days later her father met her at the bus stop after school. Bethie saw a silhouette in the passenger seat. "Mom!" she cried as she dashed toward their car. Once she reached the vehicle she used all of her strength to tug open the door opposite her father. She found another surprise. Instead of the familiar form of her mother seated in the passenger seat she found her grandmother. Instead of her mother's dark eyes she was looking into a face that was an older wizened version of her father's. Quickly the woman wrapped the little girl in a warm bear hug and as her brothers climbed into the back seat her father did some explaining.

Their mother was going to be just fine, he told them, but she was going to have to stay in the hospital for a while. Until she came home Grandma was going to help out by staying with them.

Though she was disappointed in not seeing her mother Bethie could just tell that Grandma staying with them was going to be an adventure. Her instincts were proven correct as soon as her father deposited them at home and said his goodnights so he could return to the hospital to be with their mom.

Grandma led them all into the house and to Bethie's delight immediately assigned them each a task to help prepare dinner. Bethie's chore was to put the bread slices into the toaster. Robby readied the table, Wade poured milk into glasses while Grandma quickly set about scrambling eggs and frying bacon. It wasn't long before they were all seated around the table telling the animated white haired woman all about their school day. When they had all eaten their fill Grandma shooed them off to do their homework as she tackled the dishes. Later that evening Bethie snuggled next to her on the sofa as they watched television.

The school week passed quickly and soon it was Saturday. The boys were both off visiting friends and Bethie was in the kitchen helping Grandma bake cookies. When the cookies were done and the mess cleaned up the two sat down on the sofa. Bethie loved having Grandma here. Grandma shared Bethie's big double bed at night and not once had she had an accident nor had Wade come into her room. "Grandma, can you stay here always?" the child asked.

"Oh sweetie, I have my own house and soon your Mom will be well again and she will take care of you."

"I like it better with you here." Came the child's quick reply.

"Why would you say that?" Grandma chuckled as she asked.

Without thinking twice Bethie answered. "Cause when you are here Wade doesn't make me do bad things with him."

"What did you say?" Grandma's question was quick and somewhat incredulous.

Hearing her tone Bethie hesitated. "Nothing." She mumbled.

"I heard you sweetie," Grandma said quickly pulling Bethie into her lap. "I was just surprised is all. What kind of things does he make you do?"

Even though her heart felt like it was going to beat right out of her chest Bethie pushed forward. "He takes my clothes off and hurts me here." Bethie pointed between her legs. "Can you make him stop Grandma. I don't like it."

"You forget all about it honey. I'll talk to your Daddy and Wade won't hurt you anymore."

"Please don't tell Daddy!"

"Why not honey?"

"Wade will kill Daddy then hurt me more." Tears filled the little girl's eyes and Grandma held her closer.

"There, there, child that will never happen. You just forget all about it honey." Grandma put Bethie's head on her shoulder and stroked her hair as she spoke. Finally unburdened the little girl fell fast asleep.

Bethie was scared of what would happen when Grandma told her daddy. Now she felt as if a dark foreboding cloud was following her and that at any moment Wade would take his revenge. The quiet calm of the household only contributed to her fears Even the distraction of her mother's return home did not help calm her fears. Her Grandma stayed a few days longer to help out but as soon as Bethie's mom had regained some strength her grandmother returned to her own home in Saginaw. It was that same day that Daddy and Mom sat Bethie down in the living room to have a talk with her. It was after dinner and the boys were both out with friends so it was just the three of them.

Daddy started the talk. "Bethie, has someone been hurting you or touching you in places they shouldn't?"

Bethie thought that Daddy looked really mad. It took all of her courage to nod her head yes.

"Did Wade hurt you?" Daddy asked but before Bethie could gather the courage to answer him her mother jumped in.

"It was Robby who did that to you wasn't it?" She demanded sharply. Her tone reminded Bethie of Wade's warnings. She didn't want her family to die or her Daddy to be mad at her for driving his wife away. She also didn't want Robby to get in trouble for something he didn't do.

These thoughts drove her to quickly shake her head negatively.

"It wasn't Wade or Robby?" Her Dad asked to clarify.

"No," Bethie croaked.

"Who then?" Mom barked at her. "Why did you tell your Grandma that Wade hurt you?"

Bethie's mind was spinning quickly. "I said it was Markie." She was referring to the retarded grandson of one of the neighbors. Bethie had played with him in their backyard just last weekend while Mom was still in the hospital.

"What did he do to you?" Her Daddy asked.

"He pinched me hard right here." Bethie said indicating her chest. "He said it was a titty twister." She didn't want Markie to be in trouble but, he had really did that to her. When she yelled at him and told him not to do it again he had apologized.

"Did he hurt you anywhere else?" Daddy asked.

"No." Bethie answered a little more boldly.

"See, I knew your mother must have been exaggerating." Mom looked at Daddy as she spoke.

Daddy was still looking sternly at Bethie and she squirmed uncomfortably under his gaze. "No one should ever touch you in your private places Bethie. If they do I want to know." He looked so angry that Bethie had to look away.

That was the end of the talk and Bethie retreated to her room not knowing to be relieved or sad. Evidently Grandma had tried to help her but she could see where it would just cause way more problems if she talked honestly to her Daddy. Still, Bethie found herself missing the matronly woman as her days fell back into the familiar pattern she had known before her mother's illness.

To Bethie's dismay her mother resumed attending her Tuesday night ceramics class. She was given a small extension to her reprieve however when her father insisted that it was not fair for Wade to baby-sit so often and that her brother Robby would have to take his turn.

Almost immediately upon the departure of their parents Robby quickly explained to her that he had friends coming over. He told her that if she wanted to stay up later than her usual bedtime that she had to promise not to tell their parents that he had broken the rules and had company in while they were away.

His blue eyes twinkled totally denying the serious threat he was trying to make. "If you tell Dad and Mom I will never let you stay up late again when they go away. This will be our secret. Okay?"

Bethie giggled with delight as she nodded her agreement. She liked Robby's friends. They always teased her and never made her feel like she was in the way. Not even when she was being an absolute pest. Usually about that point one of them would find something for her to do. "Draw me a picture." Was one of the favorites and Bethie would quickly respond, feeling self important while giving the older boys the space that they needed.

She had a feeling that Robby's secret would not be too hard for her to keep and she even told him so later that night as her hurriedly tucked her in after his friends left.

It seemed to Bethie that winter turned to spring in practically a blink of her eyes. One day she and her friends were playing in the snow drifts that were as big or bigger than they were and only days later the snow turned to a muddy slush. One evening as they ate dinner looking out the bay window they watched the ice on the bay break loose and float away until it was just a tiny white speck on the sparkling blue horizon.

Wade continued his escapades of experimentation with Bethie. The coming of spring only seemed to increase his appetite. Every chance he got to be alone with the little girl he took great advantage.

Bethie cringed as soon as the door closed behind her parents. Wade would watch closely until he saw their car disappear from view and then immediately begin issuing his varied commands. His threats became even more horrifying as his imagination expanded on his sexual exploits. To Bethie's horror her body had even seemed to betray her by sometimes responding to his touch only adding greatly to the frightened guilt she carried.

On one particular summery Saturday night Wade turned from the window and went into the bathroom where Bethie heard the bathtub water start running. She breathed a small sigh of relief. Perhaps he was going to leave her alone for a change. Just as she was turning to make a beeline for her bedroom the bathroom door seemed to burst open and Wade emerged calling out to her.

"Bethie, Bethie it's time for your bath."

She kept her head down and walked quickly toward her bedroom pretending that she did not hear him. If only she could get inside and shut the door before he got there she might be able to keep him away from her.

"Bethie!" came Wade's stern yell. Bethie risked a glance over her shoulder as she turned toward her room. Wade was still rooted to the bathroom doorway with his hands on his hips. Apparently he thought that she would be afraid of him enough to just give up and go to him. The child nearly laughed with delight as she pushed the door to her bedroom open and then closed again behind her. She reached behind the dresser and retrieved the butter knife that she had snuck from the kitchen earlier that day when her mom was in the bathroom.

When she made sure that the door was tightly closed and with her stepbrother still bellowing at her from the other room she shoved the knife blade under the wooden piece of trim on the door casing. That left the handle of the knife protruding out across the edge of the door where it opened so when anyone tried to open it from the outside the knife would hold the door securely shut.

"Bethie! You had better come here right now!" Wade was screaming as the little girl admired her work. She thought it looked the same way that it did the other day when she had watched Robby and his friend do it in order to keep Wade out of their room. Or at least she hoped that it was the same. She would know for sure soon. She could hear pounding footsteps approaching quickly punctuated by his sharp words. "Bethie! You get out here right now! If you don't come here you're gonna be sorry!"

The little girl cringed and backed away from the door. She saw the handle turn and heard Wade's grunt of surprise when it refused to yield.

"What the hell? What have you done now Bethie? Open this door." There was a pause as he seemed to be listening for her to obey him. Instead the little girl backed farther away from the door. With large fear filled doe eyes still glued on the door and her makeshift lock she climbed onto the bed and pulled her pillow to her in a protective hug.

The next thing that she heard was more howl of rage than spoken words. "You open this door and get out here!" Her room seemed to fill with thunder as Wade pounded against the door.

The little girl's eyes filled with tears. Fear and doubts flowed through her. Perhaps she shouldn't have done this. Wade sounded even angrier than she had ever before heard him. She could only pray that the butter knife held true. If Wade got to her now she was not sure that she would survive the consequences of her defiance.

Suddenly the pounding stopped. Her heart gave a leap of hope. Perhaps he had given up. Maybe Wade had realized that he could not get to her and had resigned himself to leaving her alone in her room. She listened hopefully for the sounds of his retreat. When he spoke the sound of his voice startled her so much that she nearly fell off her bed.

"Aw, come on Bethie. Please let me in. I'm not going to hurt you." His tone changed drastically. "I promise."

There was silence as he waited for her response. When no answer came to him he continued on. "I really did not mean to scare you Bethie. I just wanted you to come and take your bath like mom said."

Though the child perched on the bed was as still as a statue her mind was racing in full motion. She was quickly weighing her options against his words. Maybe, just maybe, Wade was not mad at her anymore and she should just open the door before he got mad all over again. On the other hand though she doubted the words he was speaking. Her mother did not usually have her take a bath on Saturday nights! She always had her bathe on Sunday nights so she was all clean for school on Monday morning. Then she thought about how angry Wade had been. What if he was just pretending not to be angry when he really was? She remembered his thunderous wrath from only moments before. If he was still that angry she could not even begin to imagine what he would do to her when she opened the door. His very next words made the decision easy for her.

"Just come out of there Bethie. If you come out here I won't tell Mom and Dad how bad you have been tonight. I'll just help you wash your hair and then you can play."

That was it. She made up her mind. She knew that there was no way that she wanted him to help her take a bath. Mom didn't hardly even help her bathe anymore and she was positive that the kind of help that her stepbrother would give she didn't want. She summoned all of her courage and finally yelled back to him. "I am never coming out!" Though she was terrified to the bone she felt jubilant for finally being brave enough to stand up to him. She couldn't keep from adding in her childish obstinate voice, "And you can't come in!"

On the other side of the door Bethie heard his rage explode with unrestrained physical fury. The walls of the house around her trembled with vibrations as he threw his weight against the door.

Eyes widening with increasing horror she watched as the knife repeatedly took the brunt of Wade's onslaught. There was a splintering sound and then a sudden thunderous crack as the molding that held the knife in place finally gave way under the continuous blows of force.

The child's screams of terror were uncontainable as the door burst open and slammed hard against the opposing wall. In three quick strides Wade had crossed the room and with one hand lifted the hysterical girl off of the bed. His free hand sliced the air in front of him and landed a lightning strike across the little girl's face.

The stinging blow put a quick end to the girl's screams. She could only watch with vigilant dismay as he carried her like a rag doll from what had once been the relative safety of her room and headed back toward the bathroom. He was growling words at her the whole time but the child's shock and despair kept her from comprehending what he was saying.

Once they had reached the bathroom door Wade became even angrier. He turned her to face the room as he shouted. "Now look what you've done!" he screamed. "You little slut you are going to owe me big time now!"

He put Bethie on her feet and dragged her across the small room toward the overflowing bathtub. The floor was completely soaked and Wade slipped and fell dragging her down with him when they were halfway there. Though the fall knocked the breath right out of her the pain was nothing compared to the fear that Wade's demeanor instilled in her as he tugged her across the floor the remaining distance to the tub.

Strengthened with rage he lifted the girl effortlessly and dropped her fully clothed form into the tub. More displaced water sloshed over the tub's rim and onto the floor but

Wade didn't even seem to notice. The hot water had run out but there was still enough to make the temperature of that in the tub tepid. Bethie didn't notice as she watched him reach over her head and turn the faucet controls to the off position.

He was no longer yelling but instead his voice had lowered to a clenched teeth rumble. "I'm going to have to clean this whole mess up before Mom and Dad get home and it's all your fault! You are going to learn a huge lesson girl! You will never ever defy me again!"

Bethie tried to wiggle and squirm away from him but her efforts were futile. He held her firmly by the front of the shirt and as he spoke he pulled her toward him. He leaned over the tub toward her until they were practically nose to nose. "I think it's time that you learn to mind me!" he growled. "Do you hear me?"

Bethie could only nod as she stared into his anger filled bulging eyes.

"Good now you make sure that you listen very closely. You will never ever disobey me again or this is what will happen to you." Before she knew what to expect he pushed her away from him. His strong grip forced her head down under the surface of the water. She tried to plead with him but when she opened her mouth to speak it filled with water. All of a sudden she was choking. She tried to twist and turn out of his grasp but she could not break his iron grip. Panic filled her in a way that she had never known. She needed to breathe. She was filled with a burning need for air and the more she struggled to try and get it the harder Wade held her shoulders pinned to the bottom of the tub. He was going to do it. Bethie knew in her heart that he was finally going to kill her. Her eyes were wide open and through the blur of the water she could still see his wrathful expression.

From somewhere a thought came to her. She was drowning. Drowning just like Wade's real daddy and his little brother. Suddenly a memory came to her. It was of her stepmother. She was crying and when Bethie had asked her why she had explained that it was because she missed her little boy. Now Bethie wondered if her mother would cry when she was dead. Bethie was getting dizzy. Her chest felt as if it were filled with red hot coals. The burning in her lungs was fading as she thought that she would finally meet the blackness that was beckoning to her from her peripheral vision. Then suddenly she felt the pressure on her body being released. She was pulled roughly upward and then tugged over the edge of the tub.

As her body was slammed against the linoleum in another huge gush of water she began to cough and choke. Her chest hurt terribly and it seemed like forever before she managed to intake even the smallest of breaths. She felt her stomach knot tighter and tighter. She barely had a moment to roll her head to the side before she began to vomit. Violently she expelled the water that she had swallowed along with the dinner that she had eaten earlier. At last the heaves subsided and she was able to fill her lungs with ragged torturous gasps of much longed for burning air.

"I warned you! I told you not to defy me! Didn't I?" Wade was panting nearly as hard as she was. He jerked her into a sitting position. "Now you've made even more mess and you are going to clean it up!"

Bethie didn't have the strength to do anything but sit there staring at him in horrified disbelief as he began pulling off her saturated clothing. She was as limp as a rag doll when he tugged and yanked. When it came to pulling off her soggy jeans he jerked her so hard that she fell backwards her head making a hollow thonk sound as it hit the floor behind her. Still she did nothing more than blink in pain.

Her whole body and mind felt frozen. It was like the sensation that she had felt in her mouth before the dentist had pulled her bad tooth. Only this time the feeling engulfed her whole body.

Once she was totally naked Wade pulled her back into a sitting position. She was so weak that he had to lean her against the front of the vanity to keep her upright. Bethie could see his mouth moving and assumed that he must be talking to her but at the moment his words were not penetrating the fog that she drifted in and she had no idea of what he was saying. She watched him reach out and flip the plug on the bath tub. Finally as if it were happening a very long ways away Bethie heard the faint gurgling sound of the water starting to drain and then as if someone had suddenly turned up the volume switch inside of her head her step brother's angry words drowned out the sounds of the tub.

"We could have just taken a nice warm bath together and had a little fun but, oh no, you had to spoil it! Now you are just going to have to take your punishment and believe me you are going to get it."

He pulled her forward and when she slumped toward him he reached behind her putting his hand on her buttocks. He lifted her into a position where she was bent over the side of the bathtub with her backside facing him as he began removing his own pants. She managed to reach her hands out and push off the bottom of the tub keeping her face out of the slowly draining water.

She heard him fumbling with his own clothes behind her but was too mesmerized by the water in the tub to realize what the sounds meant.

His voice still seemed to come to her as if it were coming down a tunnel from a long distance away. The tone of voice he used became more urgent. "You aren't woman enough to take my cock inside of your pussy but you will take it where I put it this time and maybe you'll even like it!"

Bethie felt his hands upon her buttocks spreading them apart. When he drove himself inside of her the scream that issued from her was blood curdling. He repeated his action pulling himself out and then roughly driving inside again as she remained slumped over the side of the tub. The entire time he was growling and grunting out words but the pain was so encompassing that nothing he was saying made sense. She wasn't sure how long before the tearing pain became so unbearable that she finally cherished the meeting with the blackness that had beckoned to her earlier.

The next thing she was aware of was a pounding somewhere in the house. The noise seemed to match the pain that was throbbing throughout her entire body. She slowly opened her eyes blinking at the brightness of the light that was glaring down from above. She was freezing cold and when she turned her head to the side she realized that she was lying on the bathroom floor in a huge puddle of icy water. Abruptly the memories of Wade's assault came rushing back at her. Startled and becoming more aware of burning pain she pushed herself up into a half sitting position. She balanced on her hip not wanting to put any pressure on her throbbing backside then searched the room for Wade's demonic presence.

She felt momentary relief when she didn't find him. Once on her feet waves of pain set her afloat in dizziness. She reached out and grasped the vanity to steady herself. She was so cold that her teeth began to chatter and as she reached into the vanity for a towel to wrap around herself Wade returned.

"That's right." He spoke mockingly. "Get a towel and get this whole mess cleaned up!"

Though she stood on wobbly legs, trembling with cold, she could see no other choice other than to do as he was telling her. He stood in the doorway giving her directions and leering at her nakedness the whole time she worked. Occasionally he got close enough to rub his hands over one part or another of her body as she cleaned. Finally when she was done she deposited the wet items in the hamper and turned toward the door only to find Wade blocking her path.

Roughly he grabbed her by the shoulders and shoved her back against the wall. "Now you listen girl and listen hard." He paused for a moment and then continued. "This whole thing is all your fault! I fixed the trim on your door casing but there is still a big dent in the door that I can't do anything about. When Mom and Dad see it they are going to be really pissed. I will do what I can but I don't think that I can keep you from getting into trouble so you are just gonna have to take what you get."

His voice turned to a threatening snarl when he went on. "And don't you even think for a second about telling Mom or Dad your version of what happened or I will make what happened tonight seem like going to one of your little kiddie parties if you know what I mean!"

The child flinched not only from the paralyzing pressure that he was applying to her shoulders but also from the thought that anything could be worse than tonight.

Finally he released her and she hurried as quickly as her pain would let her toward her bedroom. As she pulled a nightgown from the bottom drawer she found herself wishing that Wade had killed her. Then she would not have to face her parents. As she climbed onto her bed she thought that even burning in hell couldn't hurt as bad as she did right now.

She lay on her bed for a long time. Scalding hot tears burned ragged paths down her icy cheeks. Eventually she fell into a nightmare tormented sleep. She was unsure how much time had passed when she awoke later. Her pain had subsided to a dull ache in her stomach and an extreme burning sensation in her nether regions. She could hear voices coming from the living room.

Her parents must have returned because she could hear Wade explaining. "She turned on the bathtub and forgot about it. I thought that she was in the bathroom taking a bath but she had gone to her room and blocked the door so it would not open. By the time that I realized what was going on the tub was overflowing. Then I had to practically break down the bedroom door to get her to help clean up the mess. I didn't know what else to do! She wouldn't answer me or anything so I pounded on the door until I got it open. When I did she was just playing with her doll. I tried to get her to help me clean up the mess in the bathroom but she just cried and threw a big tantrum. She puked all over the floor and I ended up cleaning up all of that mess too!"

Bethie lay really still as she listened to them. When her mother opened her bedroom door to check on her she feigned sleep. With a building stomach ache the little girl lay awake for a long time after she heard her parents go to bed. She dreaded the arrival of morning. From the conversation she had heard she knew that she was in very deep trouble. She rolled over and tried to sleep but her stomach was beginning to cramp painfully. She threw herself out of bed and hurried for the bathroom. She perched on the toilet just in time for the first assault of diarrhea to overcome her. The pains from her abdomen were excruciating but still not as bad as the burning in her rectum. At last when the spasms passed she tried to use toilet paper to wipe but the pain was unbearable. She could only dab daintily and when she turned to flush the toilet she saw that it and the toilet paper were both full of blood.

There was more blood than she had ever seen before. She was terrified. She began to run to get her mother but a chilling thought stopped her. If Mom saw this maybe she would know what Wade had done and he would blame her. Bethie knew that no matter what she did she would just end up in even more trouble. Instead she reached out and pushed down the flush handle on the toilet. Then she returned to her room where she lay awake waiting for the next onslaught of diarrhea, the inevitable approach of morning and more punishment. Eventually, after two more excruciating trips to the bathroom, she finally dozed.

It had been light out for a long time but still she lay in her bed restlessly listening to her family going through their usual Sunday morning routine without her. Finally her father opened her door and spoke. "I know that you're awake so you might as well get out here!" his tone was stern and one that Bethie knew from experience must never be disobeyed. She climbed out of bed and slowly followed him into the living room. Daddy perched on the edge of his chair and Bethie had to stand facing him.

"Well young lady it seems that you were the cause of quite a big mess around here last night. Do you have anything to say for yourself?"

She opened her mouth to speak but as she searched for the right words she felt her step brother's eyes burning into her from the kitchen table where he sat calmly munching his breakfast. Tears filled her eyes as she pressed her lips together and mustered the energy to shake her head no.

"Very well, but I do have something to say." She saw her father's lips stretch flat the way they always did when he was being stern or angry. "When your mother and I leave you here with someone else in charge you are to treat them the same as you would us. You are to obey that person and follow all of the house rules just as if we were here. Do you understand?"

Tears trickled down Bethie's cheeks as she nodded.

"Come here then. Bend over my knee and take your punishment."

Bethie crossed the room taking her steps in the tiniest of increments. When she finally reached his side it was her father who bent her over his knee. As he doled out her punishment to her already throbbing backside Bethie screamed in painful agony, anger and shame.

Her mother's laughter seemed to echo in the kitchen as she retreated to her room. "Rob," she was saying. "That child should be an actress! From the way she screamed you'd think you had branded her with a hot poker rather than those little slaps you spanked her with."

Bethie spent the rest of the day in her room only coming out when her father made her come to the dinner table. Her stomach had been upset all day and every time she had to use the bathroom she once again found blood, just not as much as the night before. At the dinner table she sat resolutely pushing the food back and forth on her plate managing only to gag down a bite when her mother firmly demanded it. She was still seated at the table when everyone else had left. She watched Wade and Robby as they cleared the serving dishes and plates from around her.

Though her throat seemed so dry that she would choke she finally was able to force down enough of the food to either satisfy her mother or bore her enough to release the girl from the table. Bethie tried her hardest to make the hasty retreat for her bedroom but just as the child was crossing the doorway her mother's words brought her up short.

"Hold it right there girl. You can take a bath and then go on to bed. Get your clothes and I'll start the water!" came the sharp command.

The child understood her mother's no nonsense tone and hurried to obey. Clutching her nightie and clean under clothes Bethie entered the bathroom where she found her mother waiting at the edge of the tub adjusting the water temperature.

Bethie could tell that her mother was still angry with her over the previous night's incident. Her tone was chilly and she spoke no more than was necessary. "Get undressed, climb in and I'll wash your hair." Came the firm order that Bethie hurried to obey. She pulled her shirt off over her head and dropped her pants and underwear to the floor. She stepped toward the tub but a sudden reticence overcame her as she was about to step over the edge into the water.

Upon seeing the child falter her mother reached out and took the girl's arm firmly in her grasp. She guided her over the edge of the tub until she stood rooted to the spot in the steaming water. Bethie didn't know why but her chest was beginning to heave with every breath. Panic filled her with a vengeance as memories of the previous evening came crashing back to her.

As was the usual routine when her mother helped her bathe her mother tried to ease the girl down into the water. However, this time the fear filled memories that all engulfed the little girl forced her to resist. The small sense of reality she still retained told her she should be cooperating with her mom but the memory of her step brother's angry face glaring at her through the choking water forced her to push against her mother's downward pressure.

"What's the matter with you?" came her mother's startled exclamation. "Just lay back and get your hair wet so I can wash it!"

The child could hear her mother's voice but it seemed to be coming to her through a very long tunnel. She knew that she should be following her mother's instructions but the grip of fearful memory held her much too strongly. Wild eyed the little girl reached out and pushed her mother's hands away. In only a fraction of a second she was on her feet inside the bathtub crying hysterically. A sharp stinging slap landed firmly on her cheek almost immediately. Along with the shock of the blow her mother's tone did a lot to quell her hysterics. "I don't know just what you think you are pulling but you'd better knock it off right now!" Her mother rarely yelled loudly. Instead she had a way of lowering her voice and speaking through her tightly clenched teeth which usually got her point across as it did now.

Bethie quickly sat and then laid back down in the water. She in turn clenched her own teeth and managed to keep her emotions in check as her mother washed and then rinsed her hair. At last the chore was over and Bethie once again retreated to the privacy of her room where she curled on her bed.

Slowly a tear trickled from her eye but she knew better that let her mother find her crying so she let her imagination take her away to a place where she never cried. This was her special place where no one ever came.

This was her retreat alone. Wade did not exist here. There was no mother person who she would have to try so hard to please only to fail. Here there was always sunshine off sparkling blue water. Sometimes there were nice people, Kaylin, Tim, Sharon, Robby and various other relatives, and other times she was alone. But always she felt safe and secure here. The people she conjured with her imagination were always kind and smiling.

Sometimes when she was really sad she imagined a loving person who would take her into their arms, holding her close, making all her tears and shame disappear. Sometimes she thought of this person as her "real mom." Other times it was a prince who was so strong that he would beat Wade and banish him from the kingdom because he would know how bad Wade really was without Bethie ever having to speak a word about it. The little girl longed for fantasy to become a reality but, as usual, after she drifted off to sleep she awoke to the same world where her step brother ruled in his secret reign of terror and to her dismay she was surrounded by soaking wet sheets.

CHAPTER SIX

## Bethie's Trophy

Bethie was bored. Winter was long and boring. Mom and Dad bought snowmobiles but she wasn't allowed to ride them. On weekends she was left at home with one of her brothers or she was deposited at the neighbor's house where she was instructed to fall asleep on their couch then Daddy would quietly come in and awaken her and guide her home.

One of her friends would speak up in sharing time and tell the whole class how her whole family had snowmobiles and on weekends they went on trail-rides and raced on their snow machines at assorted snow carnivals. At recess and on the bus rides to and from school it seemed that no one could get a word in edgewise as the child droned on and on describing each ride and race in detail.

After many weeks of this Bethie was feeling very jealous and left out. It was on a Monday morning when she joined her friend in their assigned seat on the school bus. As the little girl started to describe her weekend of fun Bethie felt something take over her. Finally the girl seemed to be winding down and Bethie wasted no time jumping into the conversation. Carefully she spun a tale about how she and her family had gone to a snowmobile race over the weekend. She described how her Dad had allowed her to drive his new Polaris snowmobile and enter a race.

The more that her friend, Caroline, looked at her with her wide brown eyes, the more she felt impelled to embellish her tale. Finally, when she paused her friend asked, "Where was this at?"

Thinking quickly, she remembered the name of one of the places she had heard her father mention and answered. "Hubbard Lake."

This seemed to satisfy her friend and the two moved on to other topics until they arrived at school. Once in the classroom they quieted down and took their seats. The teacher took attendance and welcomed everyone back from their weekend and then announced that it was time for Monday morning sharing.

They listened as one of the boys talked about playing hockey and another said their family had gone to see the latest Disney movie. Then it was Caroline's turn. Bethie started to daydream. She figured that she'd already heard this story on the school bus but as her friend droned on something brought her back to focus. Caroline was saying, "Bethie won a snowmobile race this weekend too, but I think she should tell everyone about it."

Bethie's stomach jumped as her teacher turned her attention to the girl who was now cringing in her seat and said, "Bethie would you like to tell us about it?" Though the teacher was smiling at her expectantly Bethie shook her head no.

"Aw, c'mon." Caroline coaxed and was soon joined by her classmates.

"Don't be shy," the teacher spoke. "Your classmates want to hear about your exciting weekend."

Feeling very self-conscious Bethie climbed to her feet and repeated a condensed version of the tale that she had told Caroline on the bus that morning. She felt sick to her stomach and once the tale was done she slunk red-faced down in her seat.

The school day passed busily and she had practically forgotten the incident until on the bus ride home she overheard Caroline repeating the story to her older brother. Wade was seated nearby on the bus and Bethie hoped that he was not listening.

That night at dinner she found out that he had heard every part of the story. Everyone was seated around the dining room table enjoying Dad's favorite dinner of spaghetti when Wade spoke up. "Boy Bethie sure told a whopper at school today." He was laughing and shaking his head as he went on to relate what he'd heard on the bus.

When he'd finished her mom turned to her. "Is that true? Did you tell that story at school today?"

Bethie couldn't answer. She only looked down at her plate where she found herself pushing spaghetti noodles around randomly.

"Answer your mother," came Daddy's demand.

In reply Bethie managed to nod her head.

"What were you thinking?" Mom asked. "You know lying is wrong." Staring at Bethie she spoke further. "Rob, she needs to learn a lesson from this."

"Go to your room." Daddy ordered.

As she left the room she heard her parent's dinner conversation turn to how she should be punished. Bethie curled up on her bed and wondered about her fate. It wasn't until the next morning that she found out.

When she appeared at the breakfast table dressed and ready for school the next morning her mother spelled out her punishment in complete detail. Bethie wasn't going to ride the school bus with her brothers, her mom was going to drive her to school where she was instructed to tell her classmates the truth.

It seemed like no time before she and her mom were entering the classroom. The teacher had already taken attendance and was getting ready to start class when

Bethie's Mom knocked on the doorframe of the open classroom door then led her inside.

"Well Hello," her teacher greeted with a welcoming smile.

"Bethie has something she needs to tell you and her classmates." Mom spoke up.

Bethie's teacher looked puzzled and said, "Okay, go ahead." She prompted.

Bethie shot a pleading glance toward her mom but found no comfort so she began very quietly. "I lied yesterday."

"They can't hear you." Her mom said. "Tell them again."

Trembling with shame and embarrassment Bethie tried to speak louder. "I lied yesterday."

"Go on," came her mother's voice.

"I didn't win a snowmobile race and I didn't even go to one." She blurted getting it close to what Mom had said she should say. "I'm sorry." With the two final words Bethie burst into tears and made a dash toward her seat. What she really wanted to do was to run from the room but she knew if she did that her Mother's anger would get worse.

The class room was totally silent. The students sat frozen like statues with looks of horror on their faces.

"I'll go now." Bethie's Mom said. "Bethie you are to ride the bus home with your brothers.

Once her Mom had left the room Bethie's teacher walked over to Bethie and squatted next to her. From where she sat with her head buried in her arms Bethie didn't see her but she felt the teacher reach out and put her arm around her shoulders. As

Bethie raised her head the teacher whispered. "Would you like to go to the restroom where you can calm down in private and wash your face?"

Gratefully she shook her head, rose to her feet, and left the classroom. When she returned to the classroom Bethie noticed that none of the students met her gaze. At recess her friend Caroline reached out and took her hand. "I'm sorry your mom was so mean." She said and once again Bethie's eyes filled with tears but this time she was able to keep them from spilling over.

Time continued grinding forward. The routines of the household continued on and adapted to accommodate changes in schedules. Tuesday nights were still ceramic's night for Bethie's step mom and the little girl's brothers still took turns caring for her when her parents were away. Often Wade volunteered to take Robby's night saying that he had homework or a test to study for anyway. To Bethie's dismay Wade's sexual exploits with her continued. Since the night in the bathroom and the next day's punishment Bethie found no courage to resist him. When Wade made demands she checked out—retreating to her special place and let her body function robot-like on auto pilot to do his bidding.

One Saturday morning, when Robby was away with his friends, and their parents were off doing errands. In the living room Wade lay on top of her. He had stripped her jeans and panties down around her ankles and he lay naked, humping and groaning. Bethie was holding her breath trying not to breathe in his smell as he heaved and groaned. Suddenly he roughly grabbed both of her cheeks and growled at her. "Look at me Bethie."

It took a moment for the child to realize he was talking to her. As his bulging eyes came into focus she heard what he was moaning. "Look me in the eyes and tell me you like this. Tell me to go faster. Tell me you love me."

Her scattered thoughts focused and she found herself appalled at what he wanted her to say. She couldn't find her voice to say no. Even though filled with fear her voice wouldn't say the words he wanted either. A small part of her felt happy about this. Wade stopped his grinding into her and pulled away. "Remember what happens when you don't do as I say?"

Bethie couldn't breathe. The anger in Wade's eyes flared up like a newly lit fire. "I told you it's time for you to act like a real woman. Real women like to fuck. They do nice things for their men. Maybe you should do something nice for me."

Bethie didn't have a chance to struggle as he jumped up and pulled her to her feet and began dragging her toward the kitchen. With her pants around her ankles she couldn't take a step and found herself being dragged painfully across the living room carpet toward the kitchen linoleum. About half way there she felt something in her shoulder stretch with burning pain then as she both heard and felt a grinding pop she screamed out in horrified pain. Wade dropped her arm and as she fell back toward the floor he reached around her waist and scooped her into one of the kitchen chairs. "Stay there." He demanded.

Weeping in pain the child had no choice other than to obey. Her shoulder felt as if it were on fire. The pain radiated across her chest and down her arm clear to her fingertips. She watched as Wade walked to the kitchen cupboard. He was still naked and Bethie could see him reaching toward the layered cake that her mother had baked last night and then frosted this morning. Her mom had explained that this cake was dessert for dinner that evening when her cousins came to visit. When Wade turned back toward her she saw that his finger was thickly coated with fluffy white frosting and he was smearing it along the length of his penis.

Suddenly he shoved it toward her saying, "I know how much you like frosting Bethie. Now it's time you do something nice for me."

About two hours later Bethie was in her room, Wade was watching television and Mom was busy putting groceries away and making dinner preparations for their guests. "Who put their fingers in the cake?" Bethie heard her mother ask.

"Good," Bethie thought, "Finally Wade will get in some trouble."

"I saw Bethie messing around over there when you were gone." Even through her closed door Bethie heard Wade's reply loud and clear. Her stomach cramped with fear as she heard her Mom's thundering footsteps heading for her door.

"You get out here." Her Mom bellowed as she threw open the child's bedroom door.

Bethie jumped off the bed and on trembling legs followed her mother to the kitchen. "Did you take frosting off of this cake?" Once there her mother demanded.

Bethie was quick to shake her head negatively.

"I asked you a question. Now you answer me."

"No, I didn't." Bethie managed to squeak out her answer.

"Don't you lie to me." Her mom yelled. "I hate liars and you've been doing quite a lot of it lately."

Bethie couldn't help herself as she thought. "You must really hate Wade then."

"Do you want to try that answer again?" Mom demanded.

Bethie shook her head negatively once again seeming to make her mom even angrier.

"If that's how you want it we'll just have you eat liar food." Her mom growled and turned toward the cupboard where she rummaged for a moment then chose a can and moved toward the can opener where she inserted the can and pushed down the lever.

Bethie glimpsed the label on the can and her stomach quenched sourly in reaction.

"Sit down." Her mother indicated a chair at the table and poured the contents of the can into a small pan she put on a burner.

Bethie stole a glance toward the living room where Wade sat staring toward her. His scowl told her that she had best not mention his name or what he'd done to the cake this morning and she is quick to look down toward the floor. It seems like it's only a few seconds before her mother interrupts her absent stare by putting a bowl and spoon down in front of her. She returned to the stove and carried the small pan back to the table where she filled the bowl with the entire contents from the pan then slid it closer to Bethie.

"You are to sit there and eat this until it's all gone." Her mother said sitting down across from her. "If you insist on letting lies come out of your mouth you will have to put something in it that tastes as bad as lies."

Bethie grimaced when she smelled the pungent aroma of the spinach nestled in the bowl in front of her. Bethie hated the taste of spinach. It was all she could do to gag down the two bites that her mom insisted she eat when they were served it for dinner.

She recalled one evening when she had sat at the table until bedtime still not finishing the bite of green vegetable left on her plate. Robby had swooped into the room and scooped it off her plate and put it in the garbage when her mom was in the bathroom. He then called out. "Guess what Mom?" and before Mom answered he continued, "Bethie finally finished her spinach."

"Get your pajamas on and get ready for bed then." Her mother had ordered as she came back into the room.

This time the child knew there would be no heroic rescue and looking at the dish she hoped her mother was going to get a plate and a fork then put a smaller serving on the plate for her to eat. "You'd better get started," Mom told her, "Or you will still be sitting there when the company gets here."

As Bethie picked up her fork and scooped up a limp spinach leaf her Mother began opening some mail that she'd brought in when they'd came back from town. Bethie looked over the leaf with disdain then popped it way back in her mouth and tried to swallow quickly without tasting. In her mind she tried to convince herself that it wasn't so bad but when she tried to repeat the process she gagged aloud causing her mother to look at her sternly. "That sort of nonsense is not going to get you anywhere." Came her scolding retort.

The child managed to painfully swallow a few more small bites but now her stomach was churning and starting to feel like it did one time when she had the stomach flu. As her mom stood up and balanced the mail against the basket of flowers that sat in the center of the table she looked into the bowl of spinach. With a disgusted snort she spoke. "At that rate you are going to be there all day." With that she grabbed the fork out of Bethie's hand and scooped up a forkful of spinach. "Open your mouth." She demanded.

With reticence Bethie complied and was rewarded with a huge mouthful of spinach. It was far too much to swallow without chewing and her mouth was flooded with the bitter taste. She tried to chew without using her tongue and swallowed as quickly as possible. Her reward was another huge forkful of spinach. In the back of her throat Bethie felt water gathering. She tried desperately to swallow the wad of barely chewed green goo and it nearly worked but, just as it was going down it felt as if a volcano in her stomach erupted. With a tremendous thrust the contents of her stomach spewed forth across the table covering its surface, the mail and splattered over the basket of flowers.

In one quick jerking motion Bethie found herself snatched out of the chair and bent quickly over her Mom's knee. Three sharp spanks landed on her backside accented by her even sharper words. "Now look what you've done! You did that on purpose." She put Bethie back on her feet and shoved her roughly. "Just go to your room and stay there."

Two hours later Bethie still sat in her room all alone. She could hear the clamor of company in the rest of the house but it seemed that she had been forgotten. She fought back the urge to cry because she knew tears only made her mother angrier. It seemed like forever had passed when she heard a small tapping on her bedroom door. Thinking it might be Wade she was afraid to answer until she heard a small squeaky voice saying. "Bethie, let us in."

At the sound of that voice she was off the bed and throwing open the door in a flash. Standing outside her bedroom door were her cousins, Bradley and Jamie, both grinning from ear to ear. She grabbed their arms and pulled them both inside. Bradley was quick to turn and close the door behind them. He turned and looked at Bethie voicing his question as he moved. "Why are you sent to your room?"

Bethie's face fell and Brian was quick to make a funny face. "The last time I was in trouble it was because I put Jamie's doll's head in the toilet and I got spanked with the belt and had to go to bed before dinner." Hearing this Bethie's eyes widened. She was kind of surprised that other kids got in trouble too. "Go ahead, you can tell us. What did you do?"

Gathering her courage Bethie looked at him. Pausing to consider what she could say without making it worse Bethie's wide eyes grew even more serious. Finally she found her quiet voice and tried to explain. "Wade ate some frosting on the cake and said I did it. If I tell on him I'll get in even more trouble." Bethie was looking at the floor and mumbling quietly but the next words came out louder. "I hate his guts."

Jamie's eyes were dark and serious staring at her. Bradley replied. "That was really mean! You should tell on him. He'll be the one in trouble." Jamie shook her head in agreement.

"No! I can't!" Bethie cried out in dismay. Her heart was racing. Wade would use his gun and kill everyone if she told. She knew better than say the words she was thinking so instead she said, "I can't tell on him or Wade will hurt me when Mom and Daddy aren't home."

Now it was Bradley's face that fell. "You better not tell then."

"Don't you tell either." Bethie looked seriously at her cousins.

"We won't." Bradley said looking toward his sister who nodded in agreement. "Now let's play a game."

The three were engrossed in a game of Candy Land when Bradley and Jamie's mom, Aunt Tillie, came to the door and summoned them to dinner. "Come on you three hooligans. Go wash your hands for dinner."

In a little while everyone was sitting around the table eating and chatting. The delicious fried chicken, biscuits, potatoes, gravy and corn were quick to disappear off of plates and soon dinner was over and it was time for dessert. Bethie's mom served the pudding filled cake on little plates. When it was Bethie's turn her mother passed right by her. "Bethie ate her cake earlier." She spoke to the group and gave the next piece of cake to Jamie who was seated next to her.

Bethie's eyes were filling with tears and she was struggling to hold them back when Jamie spoke up indignantly. "No she didn't have cake. Wade ate it and said it was Bethie. That's why she hates his guts."

Bethie wished she could die right there as all eyes turned toward her. Her heart was pounding hard. What should she say? What could she do? Wade spoke up. "Ha, ha," he laughed, "That's good Bethie. Now she's blaming me. What a little liar."

Daddy looked at her as Bradley was staring hard at his younger sister. "Jamie, you promised not to tell."

"Elizabeth, go to your room." Daddy was using her whole name and his stern, angry Daddy voice. She climbed out of her chair and ran quickly for her room. Once there she threw herself on the bed and poured tortured sobs into her pillow.

There she stayed for the rest of the evening. She was laying quietly. Her tears had run out when Bradley tapped on the door, pushed it open a little ways and said, "Bye Bethie. I'm sorry Jamie was a tattle-tale and got you in more trouble."

"I didn't lie Bradley." She said as she sat up. "It was Wade."

"I know," her cousin said seriously. "I saw Wade laughing when they sent you to your room. I hate him too."

"Thank you." Bethie said as he shut the door. After he left she must have drifted off to sleep because it was dark in her room when she woke with a start. It took her a minute to realize that it had been a sound that awakened her.

At first she lay completely still pretending she was still asleep. She was terrified that it had been Wade sneaking into her room. After a moment she let her eyes open to little slits where she peaked through her eyelashes. What she saw there relieved her a little. It was Daddy standing next to her bed. Gently he rolled her to one side and pulled her covers down. She wasn't sure why at first but she pretended to still be sleeping. Then as Daddy rolled her back to the other side of the bed and tucked the covers up around her neck she spoke in her crying hoarse voice. "Am I still in trouble Daddy?"

"No honey," came his quiet reply. "Just go back to sleep." Bethie liked her Daddy's quiet voice so she snuggled back into the covers and was soon back to sleep. Later she was startled awake once again. This time she didn't have to figure out what had awakened her. Immediately she knew the weight shifting on the bed next to her belonged to Wade and this knowledge made her heart stand still. She felt him reach out and pinch her nose at the same time that he covered her mouth roughly with his hand.

She began to panic and thrash. She couldn't breathe and was terrified that Wade was going to kill her.

"Stop it!" came the harshly whispered command. "Just stop your squirming, be quiet and I'll let you go."

Bethie tried hard to calm down and do as he said. She was seeing white lights bursting like fireworks behind her eyelids before he let her go. The first breath that she gasped inside of her made her choke and she had to fight to keep from coughing. She was afraid of making any noise. She didn't want to make Wade angry so he covered her mouth and nose again. Once she was breathing somewhat normally she heard his whispered words

"Just what did you think you were pulling today?" He never gave her a chance to answer before he kept on talking. "What did you tell Bradley and Jamie? Haven't I told you what would happen if you told?" His words were flooding her mind with a myriad of horrifying images and hot, silent, tears began flowing freely from her eyes.

"I didn't tell the bad stuff." She managed to squeak out.

"Right." He said in an indignant tone. "Then what did you tell them?"

"I just said you ate the cake and blamed it on me. I didn't tell anything else!" she explained.

"That was too much." He told her. "You are going to pay for this and this is just the beginning." He pulled her blankets down and positioned himself between her legs after pulling down her panties. "Don't you make a sound. If you do, I'll kill everyone you wake up." He warned her.

In response Bethie squeezed her eyes tightly shut and gritted her teeth as tight as she could. It still hurt her every time Wade did this even though he said that after the first time it would quit hurting her when he did it. She tried really hard to go to her special place but the heaviness in her heart just wouldn't let her. It took all of her concentration to keep from crying out. She really didn't want to wake Robby and Daddy but after the spinach incident she hoped if someone would wake up and get killed it would be her Mom. She felt bad for thinking bad thoughts about her Mom but thinking bad thoughts about her Mom helped her forget the nasty things that Wade was doing to her.

In the morning Bethie's world didn't seem to be any better. When she woke up she found that she'd wet the bed once again. Bethie started to cry as she lay in the warm wetness wondering what she should do. Her Mom was going to be so angry. The last time this happened her Mom had told her that if she acted like a baby she was going to be treated like a baby. Bethie didn't know exactly what being treated like a baby was but she was sure she wouldn't like it. Just as she finished this thought her bedroom door opened and there stood her mother.

"Time to get up." She told her. Bethie sat up quickly hoping that she wouldn't notice the wet sheets but to her dismay she saw that Mom was wrinkling her nose. "Do I smell piss? Did you piss your bed again?" she asked in her disgusted tone.

Bethie found she was so scared that she couldn't answer and she quickly realized that she didn't have to because her Mom stomped across the room and pulled the sheets back. When she did she yelled. "You lazy little brat! Why the hell can't you get out of bed to use the bathroom?" she roared. "You must love the smell of piss! Get those wet clothes off right now."

Bethie obeyed quickly and when she was standing naked in front of her she saw her Mom bend over and pick up her soiled panties and nighty. Because the house was so small the washer and dryer were located in one corner of Bethie's bedroom. As Bethie undressed her mom had pulled off the wet bedding and stuffed it inside the washer. Her mom stood up and yelled "Do you like this smell?" and as she yelled she wiped the wet panties across the little girl's face. Bethie tried to pull away but Mom held her firmly. Once she released her she added the clothing to the wash machine and strutted out of the room. "Stay there." She ordered.

Bethie didn't know what to do. Should she go to the dresser and take out clean clothing or should she just stay there she wondered? Before she could decide her Mom came back and told her to climb up on the bed and lay down. She did as she was told and saw that her mom was carrying one of Daddy's white T-shirts and two safety pins. Bethie felt very strange as her mom folded her Daddy's shirt and wrapped it between her legs and around her hips safety pinning it at each hip.

"I warned you," her mother said, "If you are going to act like a baby you'll be treated like a baby. Now you can wear a diaper."

Bethie was mortified as she followed her Mom from the room and sat down at the table for breakfast with her brothers. They were both already seated at the table and they burst out laughing when Bethie entered the kitchen wearing nothing but her makeshift diaper. She had tried to pull on a t-shirt but her mother had make her leave it behind in her bedroom "Baby." Wade called out and Bethie saw the mean glistening in his eyes before she dropped her chin and started to cry. Robby just looked away as if he was ashamed of her. Bethie didn't feel much like eating the cereal that her mom had placed in front of her.

After taking away her uneaten breakfast Bethie's mom made her go outside in the front yard. It was a hot summery day and boats were going by on a regular basis. Wearing only the diaper and no shirt Bethie felt exposed and embarrassed when the people on the boats looked her way. She made her way to the backyard but once there she saw neighbors outside in their yards and even a few cars drove by. Once she tried to go inside the house but her Mom told her to get back outside. Bethie thought quickly, "But I need to go to the bathroom." She said.

Her mother answered quickly, "Just go in your diapers. That's what babies do."

Back outside Bethie wished she could just melt into the grass so no one could see her. She finally noticed the shed door was ajar and she made her way inside where she found a perch between the lawn mower and the water skis. Robby found her still sitting there a couple hours later.

"Hey there" he said.

Bethie couldn't answer because she was afraid she would start crying.

"I can't believe that bitch did this to you!" Robby's voice was really angry. "When I'm done mowing the grass I'll ask her if you can go swimming with me. Maybe then she'll let you put your bathing suit on." Bethie smiled at him gratefully. "But right now you should get out of here. It is way too hot and you'll get sick. Go sit in the shade in the side yard and I'll mow that part last."

Bethie made her way around to the side yard and found herself feeling much better in the shade. When Robby came to mow the side yard she moved back to the shed until he came to put the lawn mower back away. "Let's go." He told her and she followed him back inside the house.

Bethie was thrilled when Mom said she could go swimming with Robby after lunch. Putting her face under the cool water she held her breath and scrubbed at her face where her mom had rubbed the peed on panties earlier. By dinner time when Daddy came home from work Bethie was dressed in a pair of shorts and a flowered T-shirt and her Mom was acting like nothing out of the ordinary had happened. Later when Bethie was lying in bed, fuming because she had been sent there like a little baby and it was still light outside, she overheard Mom and Dad talking. "Honestly Rob," Mom was saying, "I don't know what I'm going to do with her. I put a diaper on her and sent her outside thinking that she would be ashamed of her behavior."

"Don't you think that was a bit extreme?" Daddy interrupted.

"Goodness, no! She was proud of it. She acted like she was having the time of her life. She strutted around the yard waving at everyone."

Bethie missed her Dad's reply. She was so angry at her Mom for what she had just said she burst into tears. Never before had she felt so ashamed and embarrassed and here her mom was saying that she had enjoyed it. Once again she fell asleep with tears on her cheeks.

## CHAPTER SEVEN

### More Secrets

Bethie sat on the corner of the couch drawing in a sketch pad. She looked across the room where her Mom and Dad stood together. They were both all dressed up and she thought her Dad looked really important wearing a suit and tie. Her Mom had bought a new dress along with matching shoes and a purse. Bethie wished she could go along with them but Daddy had explained that they were going to a wedding in Saginaw and the kids weren't invited. That scared feeling was there in her stomach again but she did her best to ignore it. Robby and Wade were both staying home with her today so she figured Wade wouldn't be able to bother her.

It wasn't until after her parents had left that she found out that her brothers had made special arrangements. Bethie watched as Robby came out of his room wearing his bathing suit and carrying a beach towel. "Can I come swimming?" she asked.

"Ahhhhh, not this time kiddo. I'm going water skiing with my friends. Wade's going to stay with you during the day today and I'll be home with you tonight. Maybe he'll take you swimming." Robby's upbeat and happy tone did nothing to fix the horrible sinking feeling that engulfed her.

As soon as Robby was out the door Wade came into the room from the kitchen munching on a big sandwich. At first, as he took a seat on a chair, she thought it was going to be okay but when he paused between bites to order her to take off all of her clothes her hopes were quickly dashed. She knew better than argue and rose slowly and did his bidding. Wade just kept silently staring at her and eating the sandwich. She became more and more uncomfortable as the silence dragged on. Finally when the sandwich was gone he spoke. "You have a lot to make up for Bethie."

The girl didn't answer she just continued to return his stare blankly. There was nothing she could imagine that he hadn't already done to her but little did she know his repertoire of horror was well stocked. With her arms crossed protectively over her chest and taking very small steps she finally retreated to her father's recliner where she perched on the edge. Perhaps part of her was hoping that something about the chair being Daddy's favorite would protect her. To no avail. Wade spoke again. "Good idea we haven't done it there before."

He rose and quickly undid the snap on his shorts. He then crossed the room and pulled her out of the chair. Dropping his shorts and underwear on the floor he took her spot on the cushioned seat. Reaching out he turned her around to face him and lifted her onto his lap. As he pushed with one foot to recline the chair he used the other knee to pry her legs apart. With the chair reclined he used his grip around her waist to shove her downward and impaled her upon him.

Even though she knew it would make him angrier at her Bethie could not hold back the howl of pain that escaped her clenched teeth. The tears also came hot and instant and Wade was quick to cover her mouth. "Shut the fuck up," He growled.

With Wade still covering her mouth tightly Bethie managed to quell the sound. She sat very still feeling the burning pain of having him so far inside of her and no matter how hard she tried she couldn't stop her tears. When Wade thrust his hips upward she howled again.

"Calm down." He ordered. "If it hurts when I move you'll just have to get used to it by moving up and down on me yourself and you'd better act like you like it."

Along with the pain Bethie was suffering from a myriad of feelings. Shame, humiliation, and hatred were some of the stronger ones. "I can't." she cried when he removed his hand from her mouth.

"Oh yes you can and you will. Let me stretch you out a little" Wade wiggled slightly from side to side as he spoke causing Bethie to cry out once again.

"Nooooo! Stop please!" She managed to quell her sound to a loud whimper.

"I'm just stretching you out so it doesn't hurt." He said angrily. "Now you move up and down."

Bethie with one leg on each side of him felt like she was being ripped in half. Even her leg muscles were throbbing as they were stretched far apart to encompass the width of his hips. When she tried she could not lift herself off of him. Once again he thrust his hips upward driving himself farther into her and in response she screamed aloud. With the sound of her scream Wade grabbed her under each arm and threw her onto her back on the floor. The rough thump of hitting the floor knocked the wind out of her and effectively stopped her from screaming any more.

Once she hit the floor the family beagle Blackie came running to the crying child. Wade got out of the chair and pushed the dog away. Now he raised the girl's knees and positioned himself between them. Bethie was sobbing hysterically and the dog was not liking it. He kept trying to get to the little girl's face to lick her tears away and Wade kept angrily pushing him away. All at once Wade stopped and grabbed the dog under his stomach.

"That's it," he said angrily. "A little cunt like you probably likes dog dick!"

Bethie had no idea what her step brother was talking about but through the tears she saw him position the dog over her chest. Holding the dog with one hand Wade reached under his stomach and began stroking the dog's privates back and forth with his other hand. Still hiccupping with sobs Bethie watched as Wade balanced the weight of the dog between her legs and then felt something warm and gooey drip onto her stomach as the dog arched in a humping motion. Just as this happened Bethie watched in horror as Wade took his own penis in one of his hands then used his other hand to shove the dog backwards. Just like Bethie had earlier the dog let out a screeching howl. While driving his hips back and forth Wade held the dog over top of Bethie. Now the dog's paws were scrambling in the air and Wade was clutching the dog tightly with both hands around his neck which quickly cut off the dog's snarling howl. Bethie watched in utter disbelief as the dog's paws paddled frantically then quit moving. Wade grunted loudly then quit moving about the same time the dog did. Bethie had to close her eyes as Wade dropped the unmoving dog onto the floor between her legs. Before her eyes closed Bethie could see that Blackie's tongue was hanging sideways out of his mouth and his eyes were bulging so far out of his head that Bethie thought of the frog that she and her friend had caught a few days ago.

She tried to drag herself into a sitting position and as she did Wade spoke. "The next time you try and tell on me that is what is going to happen to you. Now go to your room and quit bawling"

Bethie stood on trembling legs, scuttled to where her clothes were laying, picked them up and went to her room as quickly as her wounded legs would carry her. As she tried to pull her clothes back on she saw that Blackie had left long red scratches across her stomach as he had struggled to get away from her brother's grasp. A fresh batch of sobs overcame her and she did her best to hide them in her pillow as she realized that she had just witnessed the death of her beloved pet. Then Wade's words came back to her and she knew that she would never be able to tell on him.

A few minutes later Wade opened her bedroom door and summoned her back into the living room. She saw that he had a black garbage bag clutched in his hand and as she followed him into the living room she saw him scoop up the dog and put him inside of the garbage bag. "Wait here." He told her. He went out the front door and returned momentarily carrying two large rocks from the pile that divided the front yard from the water's edge. He added them to the black garbage bag then squeezed out the air and tied the bag shut. "We are going to go for a rowboat ride and we'll get rid of this. Wade said indicating the garbage bag as he spoke. "Then we will tell everyone that we were outside and Blackie snuck away. We'll pretend to look for him so no one gets suspicious."

Bethie just stared at him through teary eyes. He continued talking and warning her not to tell as he led her from the house and across the street where the rowboat was tied securely to the neighbor's dock. The rowboat wasn't actually theirs but the neighbor who only came up on weekends let the boys use it as payment for mowing their lawn. Now Wade carried the black garbage bag partially hidden under two life jackets. When they got to the boat he lowered his entire burden into the boat then turned and helped Bethie climb in. As she stepped downward he shoved her roughly then caught her by the wrist painfully keeping her from tumbling into the water.

Once in the boat he made her don one of the lifejackets. He untied and paddled out into the channel and then into the marsh behind where he and Robby often went fishing. Once they were a long way from any houses he reached out and clutched the black package. "Just remember," he said, "If you tell anyone the next thing I wrap in a garbage bag and get rid of will be you."

Bethie turned away so he wouldn't see the silent tears streaming down her face. Oh, how she wished that she was in the bag with Blackie. They returned to the dock. Bethie went to the house and Wade returned the life jackets to the shed. From inside she could hear his voice calling, "Blackie, Blackie."

Later when Robby returned from his afternoon of water skiing Wade asked him. "Was Blackie with you?"

When Robby answered negatively Wade continued, "I don't know where he is. He must have snuck outside or something. We haven't seen him all day." He looked toward Bethie for affirmation but she couldn't find any strength to back him up.

After Wade left Robby bounced onto the couch next to her. "Hey sad sack." He gave her an impish grin. "Blackie will come back. He's just probably off visiting his friends or chasing a rabbit."

Bethie started to cry once again and Robby looked as if he didn't know what to do. He let her cry for a few minutes then began making funny faces trying to distract her. Finally he told her that he had invited some friends over later and that he'd let her stay up late if she promised not to tell Dad and Mom. She agreed but found herself wondering just what she could tell Dad and Mom. It seemed that as time went on there was more and more that she was not allowed to talk about. Despite Robby's promise to let her stay up late she found it easier just to go to bed. Her legs and stomach hurt and it was even harder to pretend that nothing was wrong. As she lay in bed crying she wished that Blackie was there wagging his tail and licking her tears away. This thought made her cry even harder.

Mom and Dad returned and the next day they sent both of the boys out to look for Blackie. Bethie didn't talk much and the hollow feeling in her seemed to grow as she thought of where the dog really was. After a few days no one talked about Blackie anymore and one morning Bethie noticed that the dog's food and water dishes had disappeared from the entryway where they had usually sat.

The summer went on without the dog. The boys still took turns on Tuesdays babysitting and in Wade's case fulfilling his warped fantasies. Bethie sometimes still wet the bed, tolerated her Mom's anger and still suffered from Wade's midnight visits. By the time school started she just accepted that this was how her life was always going to be. For Bethie time went on, there were more birthdays, holidays, sessions with her step brother, punishments, lies and brief periods of what seemed like stolen happiness.

## CHAPTER EIGHT

### Walking on Eggshells

When Bethie was in fourth grade the family moved. The move didn't take the family far. Actually it was just down to the other end of the street to a different house. The adult Beth, on her mission of memory, left her car parked and walked the short distance.

This house was on the opposite side of the street and was quite a bit larger than the one they had moved from. Mom had told her it was a colonial style house. Bethie would have a room of her own just across the hall from Mom and Dad's and next to the bathroom. She would no longer have to fall asleep to the sound of the washer and dryer spinning away in her room because this house had a utility room. Robby and Wade would share a room at the other end of the house. There was something called a pantry, a galley kitchen, a separate dining room and the new house had two living rooms. Mom had explained that one was a family room for them to use every day and that the living room was for company only. This didn't make a lot of sense to Bethie but once moved in she quickly learned to follow her Mom's rule that kids weren't allowed in the living room.

Before moving in the new house there was lots of planning and excitement. Dad and Mom spent a lot of time on weekends and weeknights after Daddy got out of work painting and cleaning the new house so it would be ready for them to move in. Wade and Robby were often recruited to help but Mom said Bethie would just get in the way so she found herself spending time with the next door neighbors. She enjoyed having

Mr. and Mrs. Stiles look after her. With Wade busy working at the new house he didn't have any free time to bother her.

Finally, the work was done and it was the weekend they had been waiting for. Many people came to help them. Bethie's Uncles came with trucks and moved the big things like the couch and chairs while her aunts helped mom make the beds and put the towels, wash cloths, dishes and food away. Bethie was told to play outside with her cousins and stay out of the way. Then when everything was put away Daddy cooked hamburgers and hotdogs on the grill and all of the ladies brought salads and desserts out of the coolers they had brought. That night Bethie lay awake in her new bedroom way too excited to sleep. She was thinking that moving day was just like a holiday but then she heard her doorknob turn and knew that her holiday from Wade was over.

The family routines continued along with the secrets. Bethie was now assigned chores along with her brothers. The boys shared the yard chores. One-week Wade would mow and Robby would trim the next week they would each do the opposite. In the winters they would shovel snow instead. Bethie was assigned cleaning the bathtub, sink and toilet on Saturdays and every day after dinner she was supposed to help Robby and Wade clear the table and then she and Robby would wash and dry dishes. Wade didn't have to do dishes because of good grades on his report card. Robby told her they had made him the same offer but not to worry because his grades were not on the honor roll. Whatever that was Bethie thought.

Life in the new house was pretty much as unsettled as it had been in the other one. Even from across the hall Bethie could hear bitter arguments coming from her parent's room. It seemed like Robby was in constant trouble. One-day Mom had found some cigarettes in the boy's room and she confronted Robby about them. Bethie heard Robby tell Mom that she wasn't his Mom and that he wished his real mom was still alive because she wouldn't blame him for everything.

For days her Mom had cried and cried telling her Daddy that they would all be happier if she and Wade just left. Mom walked around the house looking sad all of the time and Bethie cringed when she heard Daddy begging her Mom not to leave. She wondered if there was a way to just let Wade go alone. The whole family, except for Wade, seemed to walk on eggshells all of the time. Everyone seemed afraid to upset the fragile balance and the only time that life seemed normal and happy was when company came over. In times like this Bethie began to realize that everyone seemed to put on their best happy faces when other people were around. She wondered if the family on her favorite show *The Brady Bunch* was like this when no one was watching them.

One good point, Bethie thought was that at this new house they frequently had visitors. Often it was her Mom's parents, sisters and their families which meant her cousins were there too. Her Dad would take the company on boat rides and the kids would fish or swim in the channel behind the house where her Dad parked the boat. Bethie always enjoyed this but wished her sisters would also visit this often.

After one particular family gathering Bethie's new Grandparents, Grandpa Wade and Grandma Betty, took Bethie and her cousin Bradley home with them for a sleepover. Grandpa entertained the two children all the way to their house by teasing them and telling them funny stories while Grandma admonished him for his behavior.

Once there it was nearly bedtime but Grandpa explained that at his house there was no bedtime and he cajoled Grandma into making the two children comfortable in front of the television. She carefully constructed cozy sleeping nests from the lawn chair cushions, soft pillows and warm blankets. Next Grandpa called the two children into the kitchen where he was making his special recipe popcorn in a heavy black cast iron frying pan. Once the snack was satisfactorily buttered, salted and transferred to a large bowl Grandpa led the kids to the living room and helped them find a movie to watch on television.

Grandma said she was tired and hugged and kissed all three of them before reminding Grandpa to make sure the kids were tucked in before he came to bed. She disappeared into her bedroom just a hair faster than the popcorn disappeared from the bowl. Both kids declared it the best popcorn they had ever had. Grandpa suggested that they climb into the cozy nests Grandma had made on the floor and then reminded them to stay awake to see the end of the movie. He sat back down on the couch and neither of the children stirred again until daylight filled the living room.

"How did the movie end?" Grandpa asked while they were eating breakfast at the cheery kitchen table.

The cousins looked at each other quizzically and then Bradley answered sort of sheepishly, "We went to sleep."

"What?" Grandpa asked incredibly. "Did I forget to tell you that there is no bedtime here? You could have stayed awake and watched the whole movie." Grandpa was shaking his head as he continued. "I hope you aren't going to fall asleep on the train ride today."

Once again the kids exchanged glances. "What train ride?" Bradley asked.

"Oh, I must have forgot to tell you that too. We are going to take a ride on the American Legion Train that goes all the way around the lake. I think you two might like it."

"All right!" Bradley cheered as Bethie's grin quickly matched his.

"Finish your pancakes." Grandma ordered.

When breakfast was finished they all helped Grandma clear the table and do the dishes. Next they all walked through the backyard to a street corner about a block away where, to the children's wonder, they were picked up by a real life size train. A gray haired man in a conductor's uniform called "All aboard," as Grandpa urged the cousins up the stairs ahead of him. Grandma stayed behind but they all leaned out of a side window so she could take their picture with the camera she was carrying. When the train completed one circuit around the glistening lake and returned to the corner where they had boarded Grandpa asked them if they wanted to get off or go again.

"Again." Both children agreed in harmony. After the next trip Grandpa urged them off of the train. He explained that they could ride the train as many times as they wanted all day but first he wanted to make sure that they knew how to get back and forth to his house from the corner where the train stopped. He insisted that the children lead him back to his house where Grandma gave them a cool glass of lemonade then he had them lead him back to the corner where he allowed them to climb on the train without him. He told them that they could ride the train for three times in a row but then they must come back to the house to check in.

Bethie and Bradley repeated this process twice and the next time they returned to check in they were surprised that their parents were there. "Do we have to leave already?" Bradley asked and his mother was quick to chuckle and explain that they were staying for dinner and she wanted Bradley and Bethie to take Jamie for a ride on the train. Of course neither child hesitated to comply.

Later, on the way home, seated between her brothers in the backseat of the car Bethie happily chatted about how much fun the sleepover had been. She told her parents all about not having a bed time, the movie they'd tried to stay up and watch, how wonderful the popcorn had tasted and the cozy beds that Grandma had made for them on the living room floor.

"I guess you really like your new Grandparents." Her mom observed.

Bethie agreed and Wade spoke up with a possessive tone to his voice. "I am named after Grandpa Wade. He taught me how to make popcorn that way."

For some reason his statement seemed to tarnish the glow that she'd been feeling after the sleepover. Eventually the excitement of the sleepover caught up with her and Bethie leaned toward Robby and fell asleep with her head against his arm. When they arrived home Wade elbowed her sharply in the ribs to wake her up and Bethie cried out.

"Stop that whining." Mom demanded as she climbed from the front seat.

Bethie was quick to follow Robby out of his side of the car keeping as far away from Wade as possible. Once inside she went directly to her bedroom where she changed into her nightgown and climbed into bed without being told. Bethie was so tired that she drifted right to sleep. She was awakened some time later but she wasn't sure how much later or what it was that had awakened her.

She lay as still as she could but her heart was pounding so loud she couldn't be sure if the noise she was listening for could really be heard. It seemed like forever before her heart beat slowed and focused on the sounds in the room around her. The room remained silent and Bethie figured that she had been imagining things. Just as she started to relax and gazed around the dark room an even blacker figure rose up from the dark next to her. Heart beat escalating again she opened her mouth to scream but just as she did her mouth was covered firmly. No sound issued from her and Wade's voice spoke close to her ear.

"Be still." Came his order.

Bethie wasn't sure if she was glad it was Wade or if she'd rather have faced the monster of her imagination.

Wade's hand was covering both her nose and mouth so when Bethie began to squirm he spoke again. "Promise you'll be quiet and I'll move my hand."
She shook her head as much as the pressure on the front of her face would allow and she was grateful when he slowly eased his grip.

"I missed you last night." Wade whispered. "But we can make up for it tonight. Remember if you make a sound there will be consequences." He had pulled down the pajama bottoms that he was wearing and climbed over top of her until he was straddling her with her arms pinned tightly to each side of her body by his legs. As his penis flopped toward her face she turned her head.

With both of his hands Wade firmly forced her head to face him. "Open your mouth." He demanded, "Sorry no yummy frosting this time." He was chuckling as he moved forward. Bethie squeezed her eyes shut tightly but the tears still leaked out leaving wet paths down both of her cheeks. Soon she was fighting not to gag and about the same time Wade was ready to finish she surprised him by wriggling free and pushing him backward with all of her might. Distracted by what he had been doing she caught him off balance and she managed to get away. She jumped off the bed and opened the bedroom door in one quick motion. She left the room and went into the bathroom where she just managed to lift the lid on the toilet before she began to gag and vomit.

Deep racking heaves shook her body. She wasn't aware of when her Mom came into the bathroom until she heard the faucet turn on. Finally, when the violent storm calmed she managed to reach out and flush the toilet. Her Mom moved closer and reached out toward her. She brushed the hair back from the child's forehead then wiped her face with a cool wet wash cloth. "Are you okay? Do you hurt somewhere?"

Bethie couldn't speak but she managed to nod her head affirmatively.

"Where do you hurt?" Mom asked.

Bethie pointed to her stomach and her Mom quickly opened the medicine cabinet. She took out a familiar pink bottle then said, "Wait here a minute."

Bethie heard her mom rummaging in the kitchen silverware drawer then her attention was drawn toward motion in the hallway. She saw her step brother quickly step out of her bedroom then with a warning glance toward her he quickly retreated through the living room toward his own room. It was only seconds later that her Mom appeared, measured out the prescribed dosage of the mint flavored medicine then sent her back to bed.

Once again her step brother had escaped without detection. Bethie didn't know whether to be disappointed or relieved. As she lay back in her bed another emotion filled her. Tears of shame soaked into her pillow and it was light out before she ever fell back to sleep. This seemed to establish the pattern of life in the new house. Any observer from the outside would see an average loving family but on the inside of Bethie's world there was a myriad of fear, shame, confusion and pain intermixed with sporadic moments of love and happiness. One of the new neighbors told Bethie that her deep brown eyes were far too young and beautiful to always reflect such seriousness.

## CHAPTER NINE

### Who is the Bad Son?

Bethie found herself thinking long and hard. She couldn't ever remember Wade being in trouble before. At least, she thought, this didn't have anything to do with her, so he couldn't use this as an excuse to punish her in some new and terrifying way.

It was spring time, Wade was now in twelfth grade and getting ready to graduate. She had been all set to enjoy a week-long vacation from him but her respite was soon to be over five days early. Last night Mom and Dad had received a phone call from the police and then another from one of the teachers who were chaperoning Wade's class graduation trip to Washington. After that Wade himself had called.

Bethie got to hear the one sided phone conversations along with her parent's entire conversation that followed because she had been close by in the family room. She had been lying on the floor quietly drawing a picture in her big sketch pad. Her parents had forgotten about her as they took the phone calls then sat at the dining room table and discussed what had happened to Wade.

It appeared that Wade and two other kids had sneaked out of their hotel room and gotten drunk. Wade was caught by hotel security sneaking back in with booze and they called the police. Now Wade was being sent back home. The police were going to bring him part of the way and Dad and Mom were meeting them. In a subsequent phone call Wade told Mom that he hadn't been drinking but was really sick from his ulcer and the booze belonged to the other boys. When Mom repeated this Daddy burst out laughing.

Robby's reaction was much the same as his father's had been when his little sister repeated the story after their parents had left to pick up Wade. "Yeah, right," He had laughed then continued. "At last the golden boy's image has been tarnished. Ellen will never be able to blame this one on me!"

Bethie's eyes widened at her brother's use of her Mom's first name. The last time he had called their Mom by her first name Daddy had grounded him to his room and told him not to come out until he could be respectful and apologize. For three days Robby had got up, refused breakfast, went to school, came home, returned to his room, came out to sit silently through dinner only pushing food around on his plate, when Dad had excused him he helped clear the table, washed dishes while Bethie dried, then returned to his room once again. At dinner on the fourth day Robby finally gave in. "I'm sorry for being rude and disrespectful Mom."

Relief flooded through Bethie when she had heard her brother's apology. Even though she saw how sad his eyes were and knew how hard it was to apologize she really wanted Robby to be back to normal. Usually while they did dishes together her brother teased and cajoled her. Sometimes they actually argued over the nonsense things that brothers and sisters disagreed about. However, since Robby had been grounded he remained silent and sullen. This quiet seemed to make the chore last forever.

Robby's next words brought Bethie back to the present. "Don't look so shocked Bethie! You know she thinks Wade is a saint and she only tolerates me and you because of Dad. Whatever she can do to make us look bad to Dad the better she likes it." Bethie thought he was right but she would never find the courage to say it out loud.

Robby looked at her and smiled. "So I think we should have some fun. Dad said that he and Mom will be gone for at least 11 to 12 hours. How would you like to go spear some carp with Joe and me?"

Bethie's eyes widened and she could barely speak, "Really?"

"Sure."

"But Dad and Mom will be mad." Bethie answered.

"They'll never know unless you tell them." Came her brother's reply. "You can even use Wade's spear. We'll be done long before they get home."

Bethie was filled with excitement as the two now dressed in shorts and carrying spears walked down the road to the marsh behind their house where Robby's friend Joe was going to meet them.

Robby and Joe had each speared a carp and Bethie hadn't even got close to one. The heavy spear she balanced on her shoulder like the older boys. She was holding it in place with one hand. Robby had explained to her that when she saw a carp nearby she would have to stand very still until it came toward her. Once the fish got close enough she had to carefully raise the spear and bring it down into the water where it would stab the frolicking fish.

The boys decided to move to the other end of the marsh and Bethie was following a few feet behind Robby. The three were trudging through the water. The boys being taller had no problem walking quickly through the knee deep water but Bethie found the water a hindrance and had to practically run to keep up. Twice she tripped nearly falling forward but managed to retain her balance at the last minute. The third time she caught her foot on an underwater root and found herself plunging forward.

The spear also slid forward off of her shoulder. The momentum of her fall carried the spear on a direct path toward her brother's leg. She hit the water face first and the spear accelerated by its own weight careened on.

"Aaaaaahhhhhhh," Came her brother's pain filled cry. Joe who turned and took in the scene grabbed Bethie by the back of the collar and returned her to her feet.

Bethie, spitting and sputtering, looked toward her brother and immediately began to cry. She could see the water around her brother's leg was quickly tinging red with her brother's blood. Robby was trying to balance on one foot while leaning on Joe so the two could get a look at the wound in the back of his calf. The stream of obscenities flowing from her brother's mouth did nothing to calm the little girl. "I'm sorry Robby, I'm sorry" came her repeated apology. Then when she caught a glimpse of the long diagonal bloody trenches cut across the muscle on the back of his calf her words changed. "Oh, no. Don't die Robby. Please don't die."

Seeing how upset the girl was Robby's friend once again took charge. "He's not going to die Bethie. We just need to get to shore and my mom will patch him up. She's a nurse you know." Joe spoke as he reached down into the water and found the offending spear. Rather than return it to Bethie he handed it to Robby. "Here take one in each hand and you can lean on them to get to shore." He then turned to Bethie. "When I crouch down you climb on my back and I'll give you a piggy back ride. We'll go faster that way."

Bethie did as instructed and the three were soon standing on the bank of the marsh. Once on shore they all looked more closely at Robby's wound. Blood was still gushing freely so Robby took off his t-shirt then knotted it around the wound on his leg.

The threesome quickly made their way to Joe's house where his mother was quick to help out.

Joe's mom inspected the wound and mentioned stitches and a tetanus shot. Robby explained that he'd had a tetanus shot about two months earlier when he'd gotten a fish hook stuck in his thumb and that stitches were out of the question because his parents were out of town with no way to contact them. He showed her the scar. She said her main concern was the shot so she cleaned the wound and bandaged it. Bethie sat by wide eyed with tears flowing and watched the entire process.

Her patient cared for, Joe's mom turned her attention to Bethie. She had the boys reassure her that they knew it was an accident and no one was mad at her. This made Bethie feel better and by the time Joe's mom had fed them lunch, reminded Robby to clean the wound and change the bandage regularly, and Joe's dad had allowed Joe to take the car to give them a ride home the little girl was smiling again.

Once at home Robby explained that she shouldn't mention what happened to Mom and Dad or they would probably get in trouble for going carp spearing. Bethie agreed and as the boys settled in front of a baseball game on television Bethie found her sketch pad and began drawing pictures of the lily pads and cat tails that she had saw growing in the marsh.

Bethie was in bed fast asleep when her parents returned but she was awakened later by their raised voices. "Ellen, you wear blinders. You don't need to take him to a doctor. Honestly, the policeman said he hadn't seen him vomit any blood. He was vomiting from drinking too much and he's not sick. He's just hung over."

"You know Wade has an ulcer. If he tried drinking with his friends it probably hurt his ulcer."

Bethie heard her father's guffaw before he said, "Haven't you ever noticed that Wade's ulcer only acts up when things aren't going his way?"

"What are you saying?" came Mom's response.

"I'm just saying that it's time to quit coddling him Ellen. He is going to graduate in a month and probably go to college this fall. He has to take responsibility for his actions."

"I don't coddle him."

"Yes you do." Daddy said. "And you're not doing him any favors."

"Well you aren't either by making him out to be some kind of alcoholic."

"Ellen, be reasonable. I never said he was an alcoholic. I said he got what he deserved. He went out and tied one on and now he deserves to have a sick hangover. Nothing different than what most people do when they first start drinking. Hopefully he learns from this experience."

Bethie figured that this really wasn't a major argument and she felt very sleepy. Just as she began to drift off to sleep she was suddenly reawakened by a rapping at her door. "Bethie, get up and come out here." Came her father's command from the hallway.

Many thoughts crowded her mind as she bolted from her bed into the hall then toward the lights that were on in the dining room. "What is going on? Am I in trouble for something?" she wondered. Then she remembered Robby's leg and she was suddenly filled with guilt. She knew that Robby would explain her spearing him was an accident but they would both be in deep trouble for going spearing. Her thoughts were following this path when Daddy told her to sit down. She saw that her brothers were both seated silently with their Mom at the dining room table. Both boys were silent and staring at the tablecloth so Bethie turned her gaze to her mother. Mom was sitting in her usual dinner place but now Bethie noted that her face was wet with tears and she was firmly clutching a wad of tissues in one hand. Daddy was standing in the doorway to the dining room half leaning against the door frame. Bethie also observed that Daddy looked very upset and serious. He finally spoke. "Ellen, your mother," he quickly clarified' "feels that we don't want her here anymore and is planning on leaving with Wade."

Bethie's heart skipped a beat and she felt like shouting out until she saw her Daddy's eyes filled with tears. He continued. "I love them both and I know both of you do too. It would destroy me if they left. Please talk to your mom."

Daddy looked so sad and serious that Bethie found herself searching her mind trying to find something to say. Glancing toward Robby and feeling something of a traitor she chirped out. "I love you Mom. Don't go."

Surprise filled her as Robby's voice joined hers. "Don't go Mom."

"There," Daddy joined in. "You see Ellen? We all love you and want you to stay."

Mom's response was somewhat of a hissing sob as she rose from the chair and stumbled toward Dad where he enfolded her into a bear hug where she continued to cry against his chest. Motioning toward the kids at the table Daddy spoke, "Go back to bed you guys. Everything is fine."

Lying between her sheets once again Bethie was more confused than ever. When she'd first been called to the dining room and Daddy said that Wade and Mom were leaving she had felt excited and happy but after seeing how sad her Dad was she couldn't help but speak up. Robby had done the same even though just that morning he had spoken to her about just the opposite. "People are so confusing," she thought. That was her last thought until the sun was filling her room with bright light. Bethie jumped out of bed thinking that she was late for school then she giggled with relief when she remembered it was Sunday.

The family always ate breakfast together on Sunday mornings. Rather than cold cereal they ate something that her mom and dad cooked together, Bacon, eggs, fried potatoes, toast and orange juice was on the menu this morning. Everyone was gathered around the table acting like the events from the night before never happened. Even Wade who Bethie expected to be at least grounded for his recent stunt seemed carefree and easygoing.

Mom and Dad's breakfast conversation centered on the fact that Wade was graduating in just three weeks and that his graduation party was only four weeks away. They discussed the hall that had been reserved, the menu and the guests that were invited. Bethie couldn't hide her amazement but in all the excitement of party planning no one noticed anyway. She couldn't believe that Wade had just got in so much trouble that the police made arrangements for him to come home from his senior trip and now they were rewarding him with a party.

Wade didn't have to go to school that week because of the senior trip so that Tuesday when Mom went to her ceramics class he went along to hang out with the guys when Mom and her sisters went to ceramics class. Bethie was glad that Robby was staying home with her. After dinner when they pulled out of the garage Robby summoned her to come with him into the bathroom. For just a moment her stomach jumped but then she heard what he was asking. "I have to change this bandage. Will you help me?"

She agreed and watched as he brought out peroxide, and some gauze bandages from the first aid kit that was kept under the sink. He peeled back the existing bandage that Joe's mom had put on three days ago and what Bethie saw made her stomach flip. The skin around the trench-like wounds was hot, red and very swollen. The trenches where the spear had grazed them were filled with a yellow scabby and runny substance and Bethie found herself gagging. "I think it is infected." She told her brother. "It looks like my friend's knee when her mom took her to the hospital. You need to show Mom and Dad."

"I can't do that." Robby replied. "Do you know how mad they would be? After the other night we don't dare rock the boat around here." Bethie agreed and Robby told her to pour the peroxide over the wound as he balanced his leg over the toilet.

As she was pouring the peroxide she remembered something. "Hey Robby, do you remember when I got the rake in my foot?"

"Yeah."

"Daddy cleaned the hole in my foot with alcohol and said that it would kill any infection." Bethie explained. "Maybe we should use that."

"Yeah, I remember." He told her. "Go ahead, get the alcohol."

Bethie retrieved the bottle from the medicine cabinet, opened it, warned her brother that this was going to hurt and began to pour the fluid over the wound. The horrendous groan that came from between her brother's teeth made Bethie pause in pouring. She clearly remembered how bad the alcohol had hurt when Daddy cleaned her wound with it.

"Just a second." Robby spoke as he grabbed a wad of gauze and used it with soap and water to scrub away the yellow pus from inside the wound. "Now pour the alcohol on it one more time."

Bethie followed directions, the whole time admiring her brother's courage and strength. She held the gauze in place as Robby taped around the edges once again covering the wound. She hoped that the infection would go away. She didn't want to get in trouble but she would rather face her parent's anger than have Robby get really sick. She told him this and he told her not to worry about it.

The next day Robby stopped her as she got off the bus and started walking toward home. He told her to tell Mom that he was going to Joe's house to help him move something heavy in his garage and would be right home when he was done. He said it shouldn't take too long and Bethie was surprised that her mom wasn't upset. Later when Mom was outside talking to the neighbor lady Robby explained that he had allowed Joe's mom to look at his wound and bandage it again. He said that Joe's mom said it was going to be okay. "She told me I could take off the bandage in a couple days." Bethie felt relieved.

That weekend was one of the first really warm weekends of the season. The family went out in the boat. Robby was getting ready to water ski and Mom got a glimpse of Robby's wound. "Oh my God what happened to your leg?"

Bethie turned and felt her heart jump into her throat "It's nothing." He said. "I was moving some stuff in the garage and got scraped by one of our spears when it fell off the hook."

"Let me see that." She demanded. Robby turned his leg in her direction but didn't go any closer. Bethie could see the thick brown scabs now covering his wound and there was only a little redness around the outside.

"That looks like it was deep." Mom commented. "Look at it Rob."

Dad looked at the wound then at Robby. "It looks like it's healing just fine. Are you sure you want to ski with it?"

Robby nodded then dove into the water and Daddy handed him the skis.

Wade's graduation party came and went without major event. They were now planning on Wade going on to college this fall. Mom and Dad had took him on a college visit then he spent two days at some sort of thing called orientation. Bethie wasn't quite sure what that was but she was very glad that it took him away from home. She normally loved summer vacation but she found herself wishing this one quickly away so Wade would leave for college. He was constantly making excuses to be alone with her and forcing her into one of his "special goodbyes" as he was calling them.

His most recent goodbye occurred in her father's car. Mom had sent him to pick up some things from their aunt's house in Bay City and on the way home he drove down a dirt road. When they came to a wooded area he pulled the car down a shaded path where it couldn't be seen from the road. As he turned off the engine but left the radio on he told her that he was going to teach her what happened when boys and girls went on dates.

"I thought they went to the movies." She replied quietly and he laughed.

"They do sometimes but I'm going to show you what they do after the movie or instead of the movie." He had an evil grin as he said. "I find this much cheaper." Wade reached out and he pulled her very close. He kept making her kiss him and even used his tongue which made her gag. Eventually he was reaching up under her shirt then undid the top button on her shorts. Every time she tried to protest he would say something like. "That's right baby you are supposed to say no but you really don't mean it."

Eventually he pulled her into the back seat and by that time she was practically naked. When he climbed on top of her she closed her eyes tightly and tried to breathe through her mouth so she didn't have to smell him. Finally he pumped on to his grunting finish and allowed her to pull her clothes back on then return to the front seat and they continued on their way home. On the ride home he chattered to her about his going to college and other such nonsense. He acted as if nothing was wrong and they were the best of friends despite the fact that she never even acknowledged that he was speaking. This time she was deep in thought about dating and if that was how it was she was never going to go on one.

The special goodbyes lasted through the rest of summer. Mom and Dad went fishing or out with friends frequently leaving Bethie at his mercy. Several times Bethie managed to thwart his plans by having friends over to spend the night but eventually he found his way around this too. One night Mom had given special permission for the girls to sleep on the floor in front of the television in the family room. They had stayed awake watching an old movie, whispering and giggling until neither of them could keep their eyes open any longer.

It took Bethie a moment to remember where she was when someone awakened her by shaking her by the shoulders. When she started to speak her mouth was covered and Wade leaned over her and put his mouth to her ear issuing instructions. Bethie got to her feet and followed him quietly out to the garage where he walked around the car and assumed his perch on the seat of the snowmobile.

The light streaming in the garage windows from the mercury lights outside lit the room dimly. Anyone who might have opened the door that attached the house to the garage would not have been able to see them because of the car parked in between. Wade explained in detail what he wanted and when Bethie tried to protest he told her he would go back in the house and get her friend. Then he would do it to both of them but he'd have to kill her friend so she wouldn't tell. Bethie gave up any inkling of protest, took off her clothes and bent over the seat of the snowmobile exactly as he had told her to. Once again she endured until he grunted his release then issued his usual threats before letting her tiptoe back to the house. Once back inside she lay down on the floor next to her friend. She jumped in alarm when her friend rolled over and asked her where she had been. "I went to the bathroom." She quickly thought of the lie.

"In the garage?" her friend asked.

"No, I just made sure the door was locked when I came back from the bathroom." Bethie countered. "Wade just got home and I didn't know if he locked it."

"Oh," her friend replied and Bethie lying awake was relieved when she realized the girl had accepted her explanation and went back to sleep. Her relief lasted through the next morning until her friend once again brought it up at breakfast. It was Sunday so the entire family was gathered around the table when the bright eyed girl asked Wade why he had woken Bethie up to lock the garage door in the middle of the night.

Bethie thought she saw Wade actually jump in his seat before he answered. "I didn't wake her up to make her lock the door. I asked her why you guys were sleeping there instead of in her bedroom." Came his quick retort. Bethie was thankful when her friend shook her head and let the subject drop. No one else seemed to question the situation whatsoever.

Two days later when her parents were away and Robby was out with friends, Wade made her pay for her friend's question. "What the hell were you thinking telling that girl I woke you up to lock the door?" he asked without allowing her to answer. They were in the living room at home and Wade was jerking her shirt off of her as he spoke. "You know better than say anything about me to anyone don't you?" Another question he left unanswered. He took in the new undergarment she was wearing and went on with his torment as he pulled it off of her. "Ha, you are wearing a training bra." He announced with a laugh. "I don't know what you are training because you don't have any tits." He pulled her forward and held her arms to her sides as he painfully bit and sucked at her nipples. She tried to pull away but he held her firmly until he had become bored with this and proceeded to peel off the rest of her clothes then made her stand in front of him touching herself where and how he instructed her to. Embarrassment and shame filled her almost making it a relief when he roughly pulled her to the floor and spread her legs apart so he could drive himself inside of her. Bethie couldn't wait until he left for college.

Three weeks and several of Wade's "special goodbyes" later the awaited event occurred. As Wade, Robby and Daddy were loading the trunk of Daddy's car Mom was pacing back and forth between the garage and the house occasionally adding items to the trunk but often just watching them work and swiping the tears that were escaping from her eyes with a tired wad of tissues. Every time Daddy caught a glimpse of her he would chuckle and say something like, "Geez Ellen. The way you are carrying on you'd think that he was going off to be a soldier in the foreign legion and not going to college to be an electrical engineer."

Finally the heavily laden car pulled out of the driveway and disappeared down the road. Bethie and Robby watched from the garage window until it disappeared around the corner, "All right!" Robby cheered and Bethie felt the smile spread across her face. "No more Wade in the stink pool and a room to myself." He added and along with that he said to his sister, "I think we should celebrate."

Bethie looked at her brother quizzically and he was quick to describe his plan. "We'll have a swimming party." Robby had then went on to explain that he would call some friends and they would all gather and swim in the back yard. He made a few phone calls then the twosome climbed into the jalopy that Robby had bought with the money saved from two years at his part time job and the money he got paid from mowing lawns. They made a quick trip to town and bought a variety of chips and pop. Once back home she helped her brother haul his stereo speakers out to the back yard then string the speaker wires outside through his bedroom windows. In the garage they retrieved a cooler and filled it with pop and ice. Robby said to leave the cooler in the garage out of the sun and then instructed her to give him a hand. They gathered lawn chairs, beach towels, swim rafts and other summer paraphernalia and hauled it out to the back yard. It wasn't long after they were done that Robby's friends began arriving hauling a variety of coolers along with them. One of the boys brought a small grill and hot dogs. Another friend had brought buns and one of the girls helped Bethie retrieve ketchup and mustard from the kitchen.

In no time the back yard was filled with pretty bikini clad teenage girls and summer sun darkened boys. They were hopping and bopping along with the music coming out of the speakers. Many times individuals would disappear to retrieve paper cups of pop and ice from the garage cooler or their assorted vehicles. Eventually they were diving in the water and there was lots of splashing and screeching.

Bethie was by now a very good swimmer and Robby's friends were very willing to keep an eye out as she swam with them in the channel that bordered their back yard. They stayed with her until she felt secure in swimming across the width of the channel where they then helped her to climb one of the large willow trees that grew there. At first she was afraid but with patient coaxing Robby and one of the girls taught Bethie to climb to a horizontal branch of the tree that was located about 20 feet above the water where some of them were happily diving and doing cannonballs. Daddy had been teaching her how to dive and now Robby talked her into applying her skills from this new perch in the tree. The first time she did a rather awkward belly smacker but the mouth full of water and brief pain did nothing to dissuade her from trying again immediately. The next time she cleanly cut the water fingertips first. The thrill of this filled her and she dove again and again barely paying attention to Robby and his friends. Eventually the crowd thinned. Robby's friends returned to their homes and Bethie was quick to help her brother restore order to their yard.

Everything else was taken care of and the two were carrying the speakers back into Robby's bedroom. Bethie was feeling giddy with the excitement of the day and grateful to her brother for including her. Once both speakers were deposited on his dresser Bethie reached out her hand and stroked Robby's groin.

Robby jumped as if electrified. "What the heck are you doing?" he asked.

"I just thought that you'd like me to rub it to say thank you like Wade makes me."

"What did you say?" Came Robby's incredulous question.

With Wade gone to college she was feeling a bit more courageous. "When Wade does something nice for me he makes me say thank you by rubbing his thing."

Robby's blue eyes widened with anger and disbelief at his sister's words. "Bethie, you don't ever have to do that to anyone! That is not the way to say thank you and you should never touch your brother or step brother like that!"

Robby's anger was very apparent and his tone put Bethie on edge. She had to calm him or Wade would find out that she'd told!

"Does he make you do anything else Bethie?" Robby's next question filled her with shame and fear. She could do nothing but drop her head. She couldn't face him. She watched as a lone tear fall from her eye and made a raindrop splash on the top of her foot.

Robby squatted down in front of her and took her hands his voice was quieter and less angry now. "Bethie, it's okay. You can tell me anything."

"Please don't tell Robby, Please." She cried. "He'll hurt all of us. Please don't tell."

"He has done other things to you hasn't he." Robby was staring at her knowingly.

"Robby, promise—don't tell." She managed to avoid answering before her tears nearly overwhelmed her completely.

"Calm down and look at me."

When she raised her eyes to his she could see that he already knew the answer. Tears were now threatening to spill down his cheeks. "He has hurt you."

"You can't tell Robby. Not ever, ever, ever. You don't know what he'll do." She shuddered and her tears flowed freely.

"Okay, I won't tell but only if you promise me one thing. Can you do that?"

"What?" She sputtered.

"You have to promise me that you'll tell me if Wade tries to do anything to you" He dashed his arm across his eyes and stared at her intently.

"You won't tell?" Her tears were slowing.

"Not if you promise to tell me."

"Okay." She answered quietly.

That night Bethie went to bed and for the first time in as long as she could remember she went right to sleep and slept the whole night through. She hadn't awakened and lay there waiting for the quiet whoosh of her bedroom door sneakily opening; or felt the hand covering her mouth; or the bad dreams that often awoke her and she had to wonder if it had been a dream or was it really happening. She had just slept the entire night through feeling peaceful and safe.

As she walked into the kitchen she was greeted by mom and the neighbor lady drinking coffee and chatting at the dining room table. They both greeted her brightly before Mom started asking probing questions.

"Bethie, what did you and Robby do yesterday when we were gone?"

"We went swimming out back with some of Robbie's friends. They all swam by me and taught me how to swim across the channel and dive out of the tree." She knew Mom was always concerned when she swam in the deep channel but they had followed the rules. Bethie was never allowed to swim alone in the channel.

"What else did they do? What were they drinking?" This gave Bethie an idea of what she was getting at. Robby had gotten grounded a few weeks ago because he had come home drunk.

"Robby bought some pop and put it in the cooler and some of the kids brought some too." She replied. "Oh, yeah," she added. "We ate hot dogs and chips too."

"They weren't drinking beer?" Mom asked pointedly and Bethie adamantly shook her head negatively.

"Did anyone go in the house?" Mom asked.

"Just to use the bathroom and one of the girls chopped an onion up for hot dogs then helped put the hot dog stuff away when everyone was done eating." Bethie didn't tell Mom that she had seen Robby kissing the girl in the driveway before she climbed in a car with her friend and drove away.

"No one went in the bedrooms?"

"No.

"What did they do with the empty cans and stuff?" Mom asked.

"We put them all in a garbage bag in the garage just like you do." Bethie answered.

"Show me." Mom demanded then told the neighbor that she'd be right back.

Bethie led her mom into the garage and pointed to the shiny black garbage bag. Mom quickly opened it, rummaged through it, then returned to the dining room.

"Just pop cans and paper plates." Mom directed her comment to the neighbor as she refilled their coffee cups and Bethie poured cereal into a bowl and topped it off with a splash of milk then sat down at the table to eat her breakfast.

The two women kept talking as if Bethie wasn't there at all.

"I could have sworn they were drinking Ellen." The neighbor said. "The music was blaring and they were dancing and singing. Then they were screaming and splashing in the water."

"So what?" Bethie thought, but she knew better than to be that rude and disrespectful out loud. From the conversations she heard between her mother and this neighbor she also knew that because of her mother's constant complaining the neighbor lady didn't like Robby and was always watching for him to do something wrong.

The reason behind the neighbor's dislike was easy. Bethie had witnessed many such visits between the two ladies when Mom frequently told her what a "troublemaker" Robby was, how she was sick and tired of his bad behavior, and how she wished he could behave more like Wade. The day she'd heard her Mom make that statement she nearly guffawed out loud and had to leave the room thinking to herself, "I'm sure glad he doesn't!"

Later in the day when Robby was mowing the lawn Bethie heard her Mom telling her Dad that the neighbor lady claimed Robby had a loud drunken party yesterday afternoon. Mom said the lady claimed they were drinking beer and couples were going into the house hugging and kissing constantly and mom did a pretty good imitation of the neighbor's voice when she said "The Lord only knows what they did in there."

Daddy replied, "You know what a busy body she is. Don't listen to her. You didn't find any evidence. Robby is seventeen years old he is entitled to some fun." This made Bethie feel better. The previous day had been fun and it would be sad if Robby got into trouble for it.

Later when Dad and Mom went out perch fishing Bethie found her brother sitting in his room listening to one of his albums. She reported the events of the morning. She told him about the conversation between Mom and the neighbor, how Mom had searched through the garbage bag, and then what Dad had said when she told him.

"That lady is such a bitch!" Was Robby's response. "I'm glad I had Joe take all the paper cups and throw them away somewhere else."

Bethie didn't know what he was talking about but now her suspicions were aroused. She also knew no matter what Robby and his friends had been drinking she would never tell their parents.

## CHAPTER TEN

A new school year began. Bethie was in fifth grade, Robby was a senior, and Wade was gone! Bethie felt greatly excited as she climbed the steps and joined her friends who were already seated and chatting excitedly on the bus. She had high hopes for this school year. Last week she and Mom had went shopping and she loved wearing her new school clothes and carrying the bag that was filled with new pencils, pens and paper. Bethie liked school. At school she knew exactly what was expected of her, there weren't any secrets and when she was there she could forget about all her worries at home.

This year she would change classrooms. She found that different teachers taught different classes and she would even get to take choir. She loved to sing and their teacher said that her class would record an album. At dinner that evening she couldn't wait to tell her parents. When she mentioned the choir class and the album her mother's response quelled her happiness. "You aren't going to sing are you? Nobody would want that album if you are. You couldn't carry a tune if it were in a bushel basket."

Bethie fell silent and no longer felt like sharing her day. Robby kicked her foot under the table and winked at her when she looked up. This helped to lift her spirits a bit and by the time they were doing dishes together she was smiling as Robby told her stories about some of her new teachers.

Another school year routine was established. After dinner Bethie and Robby were supposed to sit at the dining room table and do their homework. Once homework was done Robby was free to go out as long as he was home by his curfew and Bethie could enjoy some free time until her 8:00 bedtime. She strongly resented this bedtime. When she questioned other students in her class she found that some of them said that they didn't have bedtimes or they were later such as 9:00 or 9:30. She was happier when a few of the students also protested their 8:00 bedtimes. It was her sister Kaylin who unknowingly helped to find an acceptable compromise. She and her family had come for a visit and she had brought Bethie a gift of some of the Trixie Beldon books she loved. Kaylin knew Bethie hated her bedtime because she had complained to her when they had managed to catch a private moment together. As the family sat chatting after dinner Bethie once again thanked her sister and brother-in law for the books and Kaylin said, "I always like to read in bed for a half hour before I go to sleep." She said. "Maybe you could do that."

"Can I?" Bethie asked looking between her Dad and Mom.

"Well, you'd have to go to bed a half hour earlier." Mom said.

Daddy answered at nearly the exact same time. "Sure, I don't see why not."

Now Bethie looked confused until Daddy added. "She goes to bed so early now she probably just lays awake at least that long just waiting for it to get dark."

"I guess it would be okay." Mom said. "But, the first time we have a problem getting you up in the morning that will be the end of it."

Bethie nodded grinning from ear to ear wanting to jump up and hug her dad and sister but resisted knowing it would anger her mom. "You won't."

As time went on Bethie figured out that it was pretty easy to read as late as she wanted. If someone opened her door to check on her she just let the book fall to her chest and pretended she had fallen asleep reading.

The first couple weeks of school were uneventful. Wade called home to talk to Mom frequently and many times the dinner conversation between her parents focused on the fact that Wade's ulcers were bothering him and he really hated his classes. According to what her mother explained he was arguing with his teachers. Mom explained that he already knew the stuff they were trying to teach him and that one of his teacher's hated him because he could do the math faster than him.

When Robby heard this he looked knowingly at his little sister and rolled his eyes.

Daddy said, "He's just homesick. Give him time. He'll get over it."

One Friday when Bethie got home from school she was pleasantly surprised. "We are going to a football game tonight." Mom announced. "Your cousin is on Homecoming court and she may even be elected Queen."

This sounded exciting to Bethie. She really liked her pretty cousin and she loved watching the cheerleaders at football games. Bethie hurried to gather the warm clothes that Mom had instructed and was ready to go in no time.

The football game was very exciting for Bethie. She loved the marching band and baton twirlers who marched on the field before the game and during half time. The cheerleaders who were calling out random cheers, doing cartwheels and keeping the crowd involved were often the center of her attention until the halftime ceremony. Bethie gasped as she saw the beautifully gowned girls who were led on the field by smiling young men and she even shed a tear with her Aunt when they announced her cousin's name and placed a sparkling crown upon her head.

That night she had wonderful dreams about beautiful princesses but the next morning she heard some very bad news. When Bethie sat down at the table after pouring her cereal she realized that her Mom and Dad were both busily bustling around as if getting ready to go somewhere. She overheard her father saying something about being a man and an incredible waste of money. When she enquired where they were going Daddy explained that Wade had called late last night asking them to come and bring him home. He was leaving college because his ulcer was too bad. Bethie thought that Daddy sounded angry but she wasn't sure and didn't want to ask. Daddy explained that Robby was still asleep but knew they were leaving and that he was supposed to stay home with her today. "If you need something you can wake Robby." Dad explained just before they climbed into the car and pulled away.

Bethie didn't bother waking Robby. She just dumped out her uneaten cereal in the garbage and went to sit in a chair in the living room without even turning on the television. That's where Robby discovered her when he arose about an hour later.

Robby saw her sad expression and took a seat across from her. "Hey kid!" he said, "It looks like you heard the bad news." He tried to lighten her mood with a joke. "How do you think I feel? I have to share a room with him." He made a funny face as he spoke.

This time they didn't celebrate with a party. The twosome watched television. Robby made one of their favorite lunches of macaroni and cheese but the major part of it went into the garbage along with Bethie's cereal. At dinner time neither of them were very hungry so, trying to change the mood Robby suggested, "I think we should eat ice cream for dinner."

Bethie peered at him with surprise.

"Why not?" he asked. "No one will know we ate dessert for dinner. We might as well have some fun before the creepy Wade in the water comes home."

This made Bethie giggle she liked the fact that Robby had used their special nickname for her step brother and she joined him in the kitchen.

By the time Dad, Mom and Wade came home they were both once again in front of the television. "Wade doesn't feel well." Mom declared as she entered. "You two get out there and help unload the car."

That night as Bethie lay awake in her bed she once again had a midnight visitor. She feigned sleeping but he shook her shoulder and said, "I know you missed me." After Wade left with his usual warning she knew that she would have to break the promise she had made to Robby. If she were to tell him what Wade had done there was no telling the amount of hurt and heartache that would fill her family.

For Bethie time once again seemed to drag on measured in shame and repeated sexual encounters with her step brother. Just before Thanksgiving Bethie brought home her school pictures. She proudly handed the packet to her mom. When Mom opened it she exclaimed. "Oh my, look how fat you are. You are so fat I could wallpaper the dining room with just one picture. You are starting to look just like your fat cow sisters. You better watch what you eat or you'll be just like them." That night, when clearing up after dinner, Bethie took the packet of pictures and slid them into the garbage. As far as she knew no one ever missed them.

Christmas, New Years, and her birthday all passed. Nothing had changed in her relationship with her step brother. Daddy had helped Wade get a job at the foundry where he worked. It was a Tuesday, just before Easter when she came home from school and found a policeman sitting at their table. Bethie wide eyed, looked at the man. Mom was quick to send her to her room and called out to Robby who had come inside and went directly to his room.

Bethie had dawdled on her way to her bedroom. She couldn't help but wonder why the policeman was here and what it had to do with Robby. She heard the low rumble of the policeman's words but she had to tiptoe back down the hallway to understand what he was saying.

"Young man," the policeman said. My name is officer Fitzor. Your mom found some things in your room and is concerned about your safety and health. Do you know what this is or where she found it?" The policeman asked. Bethie didn't hear Robby's answer so she assumed that her brother had nodded his answer and the policeman continued. "This is paraphernalia used for smoking marijuana and she tells me she found it in your top dresser drawer when she was putting away laundry."

Bethie still didn't hear a response. "Robby," the policeman continued, "Do you smoke marijuana?" Again no answer. "Are these your rolling papers and pipe?"

This time Bethie heard Robby answer, "No."

"Robby, I'm not really concerned about busting you with a little bit of weed, or this pipe and rolling papers. My concern is eliminating suppliers. Where do you get your weed?"

"I don't have any weed." Robby said, "And that's not my stuff."

Bethie figured she'd heard enough and better get to her room so her mom didn't catch her eavesdropping. "Wow," she thought, "Robby is in deep trouble this time." She didn't know if Robby smoked marijuana or not but she did know he smoked cigarettes. She had caught him one night when he was babysitting her. When she spoke up that night he'd had her take a puff off of his cigarette so that way she couldn't tell on him for smoking or he'd tell on her.

That night Mom and Dad had everyone make a sandwich for dinner and they spent a long time in Robby's room. From the kitchen Bethie could sometimes hear their raised voices and other times there seemed to be silence. When they came out Robby went to the kitchen and made a sandwich, Wade left for a date and their parents left for the city because it was Mom's ceramics night. Bethie could only imagine the story that her Mom would tell her sisters as they worked on their ceramics together. Though she didn't like the thought of Robby being in trouble she was happy that he was the one left to stay with her.

Once her parents left Bethie couldn't help but ask her brother, "Are you okay?" Robby looked both pale and sad at the same time.

"Yeah," he answered. "Mom and Dad might send me away to a juvenile home." He said. Before Bethie could ask her brother continued. "Honest Bethie that stuff wasn't mine and it wasn't in my drawer last night when I took a shower. I might smoke now and then but I'm smarter than that. I don't keep anything like that here in our house."

"How did it get there?" she asked.

"Either Ellen wants me to look bad or Wade put it there. I have no idea but Dad is madder than I've ever seen him. He told me I'm grounded until graduation. I don't know what to do. I hate them both."

She knew that Robby was referring to Mom and Wade. "Me too," Bethie felt guilty for agreeing with him but she couldn't help it. Her brother Robby was the only person she could really trust in this house so, if he hated her Mom and Wade, she did too.

It was only a few weeks after Easter when Robby came home from school with his big news. He waited until dinner to deliver the news. He had recently celebrated his eighteenth birthday and he had decided that when he graduated he was going into the Navy.

When her mother gasped "No, Robby." It was 1972 and Americans were full of talk of the draft and the Vietnam Conflict.

"It's just talk Ellen." Dad said reassuringly.

"No Dad, It's not. I've been talking to a recruiter." Robby explained. "He gave me this information to give to you guys." Bethie gaped in awe as Robby produced a handful of papers that he'd stashed under his chair. She wasn't really sure what this meant but she knew from hearing adults talk and glimpses of the daily news that young men were dying in the war and now it seemed that her brother, Robby, wanted to join it. The only person at the table who seemed unconcerned and kept on eating carefree was Wade.

Questions and answers seemed to fly across the dinner table and Bethie watched intently as Daddy took the papers from Robby and the discussion continued. Bethie noted that Mom was no longer making an attempt to eat her dinner and that Robby and Dad seemed to be sizing each other up as each took turns speaking.

Mom started to cry as Wade finished his dinner and launched himself away from the table, saying that he had a date, and leaving his plate for Robby and Bethie to clear later. Bethie's head swiveled from speaker to speaker trying to comprehend what was happening. Did this mean that Robby would be moving away? She didn't want him to leave and even more she didn't want him to die in some stupid war. Bethie too started to cry.

"Calm down both of you," Daddy directed toward his wife and daughter. "This isn't as scary as you two think." He explained. "We all know that there is a good chance that Robby could be drafted and if that's the case he could end up in the army on a front line in the jungle somewhere. At least this way he will be on a ship and farther away from that type of action." Bethie didn't really understand what he was saying but his calm and logical tone seemed calming and Mom's tears seemed to be slowing too.

Bethie reflected on an earlier dinner conversation that had taken place when Wade had quit college. At that time the discussion started with the news that one of Wade's friends from high school had been drafted and Mom voiced her concerns about Wade. At that time Wade was quick to contribute that he had already checked and he would be exempt from the draft due to his ulcer and flat feet. Now, Bethie found herself wishing wholeheartedly that it was Wade who wanted to go in the Navy and Robby who had flat feet--whatever they were.

The conversation dwindled and dinner ended. As Bethie and Robby cleared the table and did the dinner dishes she asked Robby lots of questions. "Where will you live? What will you do? Why do you want to go?"

Robby was patient and told her that going in the Navy would help him get a good job later on, he'd get to travel and see new places and then he jokingly added, "Besides, if I go in the Navy I won't have to do dishes anymore."

"Thanks a lot. I'll be here doing them all alone." She tried to joke but she found that tears sprang to her eyes.

The time went quickly. Robby graduated and they had cleaned and decorated their garage where they gave him a combination graduation and going away party. Before she knew it Bethie had joined her parents at the Bus Station watching her brother climb aboard a large shiny bus for 6 weeks of training at the Great Lakes Naval Academy. Mom hugged and kissed Robby, Bethie hugged her brother and got back into the car as Dad instructed. Next, Daddy shook Robby's hand and said "I'm proud of you son." Mom was crying incoherently and Bethie couldn't help but wonder why she was behaving like this after all the complaints that she'd heard her Mom voice about Robby. She expected her mom to be happy to see him leave. This life is so confusing she thought as she sat forlornly alone in the back seat. She too felt like crying.

Summer wasn't quite the same without Robby but she did find some consolation. Her cousin Bradley loved to fish and he was coming to spend a week at her house. Dad found fishing poles for both of them and a small tackle box. He also equipped them with bait, a stringer, instructions and strict safety rules. Soon the pair of cousins were the best of buddies. They would wake up very early about the same time as Bethie's Dad got up to go to work. They would grab their fishing gear and spend the morning fishing along the channels and sometimes in the bay casting their lines out from the shoreline of the neighbor's yard across the street.

The week quickly ended and the cousins begged both sets of parents for another week. To their delight the visit was extended. It was during the next week that they made some new friends. Across the street and two doors down was a shoreline cabin that had been for sale for quite a while. One morning Bethie and Brad came outside to see a bright orange moving van backed into the driveway and as they stood blinking in the bright sunshine two kids, one boy and one girl, came out of the back of the truck each wheeling a bicycle.

Bethie was shy but Brad was quick to inspire her. "C'mon let's go talk to them." he suggested and didn't wait for his cousin to answer so she found herself quickly following him down the street, up the driveway and then standing in front of the two newcomers.

Bradley introduced himself as Brad and his cousin as Bethie brat and soon found out through their giggled responses that their names were Lydia and Darren. Before they could gather too much information the kid's parents called to them to keep unpacking so Bethie and Brad offered to help. They wheeled the bikes into a garage then helped them unload and store an assortment of beach toys and fishing equipment. When this part of the chore was done it was time for the cousins to leave but they made plans to meet their new friends later. At this time the twosome had no idea that this was the beginning of a friendship that would last throughout the rest of their school years.

That evening was the day that Brad (he had explained to Bethie that is what he wanted to be called) caught the biggest fish either of them had ever seen. At this time of day the cousins liked to fish in the bay. They would cross the street to a vacant lot and cast as far out into the bay as they could. They always carried their fishing gear along with a big net in an old radio flyer wagon that the neighbors had discarded. They casted out quickly and in just a short time Brad brought in two catfish and Bethie landed a small perch. Brad was prone to good natured banter and storytelling. He was teasing Bethie about the size of her catch compared to his when Lydia joined them.

She sat down on the ground between them and the threesome began to get further acquainted. Suddenly during mid-sentence Brad quit speaking. The fishing pole that he had been casually holding doubled in half and he had to grab tightly as he climbed to his feet exclaiming, "Oh my God! Oh my God!"

At first Bethie thought he was pretending in order to tease them but it didn't take her long to see that he was truly excited and struggling hard just to hold on to the fishing pole. The two girls now on their feet, nearly as excited as Brad, were loudly shouting advice, "Hang on tight, don't jerk the pole, don't break the line, let him get tired."

"Help me." Brad countered, "My arms are killing me."

Bethie moved next to him and put a hand on the pole just above where Brad was gripping tightly. She was amazed at the strength of the tugging and quickly understood why her cousin was just leaning away from the water and doing his best to stay on his feet.

Once again Brad spoke, "It's too big. We need your Dad Bethie. "Go get Uncle Rob."

"Okay," she agreed and let go of the fishing pole. When she did Brad was jerked about three steps toward the water.

"Whoa," he yelled. Bethie turned back to help but Lydia countered.

"I'll help him. You go get your dad." As Lydia grabbed on to the fishing pole Bethie turned and ran as fast as she could toward her house.

When Bethie returned with her dad following closely she was glad to see that the fish was still on and hadn't broke the line. Both Brad and Lydia looked tired. Bethie turned toward her dad as she heard him start to chuckle, "Looks like you got a big one there kid."

"Uncle Rob, I can't even reel him in." Brad gasped.

"No, you have to tire him out a bit first."

"He's tiring me out." Brad countered. "Can you pull him in?"

Brad's question shocked Bethie. She realized just how tired he must be or he would never offer to give up a fishing pole with a fish on the line.

Bethie's father shook his head laughing again. "No way, you caught that beast so you have to bring him in. You just need to work him a little bit and tire him out." He explained.

"Oh, yikes!" Brad exclaimed. "I can barely hold him. How do I do that?"

"Calm down." Came the authoritative reply. "Do exactly as I tell you."

"My arms are killing me." Lydia explained. "Bethie?" She looked for support and Bethie quickly traded places with her.

"Okay," Dad ordered. "Bethie, get a firm grip on that pole with both hands," She obeyed quickly. "Bradley, you put one hand on the reel of the fishing pole." When the grips had been adjusted he continued. "When I count to three I want you to steadily raise the tip of the fishing pole up above your heads be sure not to jerk it. Once you do, you need to take two quick steps forward then Brian you have to reel very quickly to take the slack out of the line. If you take too long he'll throw the hook and the fish will get away."

Here Dad paused. "Ready?" the kids both shook their heads and Dad counted. "One, two, three."

The twosome strained on the pole and then hurriedly took the steps. Bethie braced the pole and Brad reeled frantically. When he'd reeled in all of the slack Dad waited a beat then counted once again. "One, two three." And with Lydia yelling words of excited encouragement the whole process was repeated again and again. Finally, with the fish still tugging and the kids with the fishing pole now located at the edge of the shoreline Bethie's Dad picked up the net and climbed down the rocky seawall where he stood poised waiting for the fish to break water. He instructed the kids to raise the pole slowly and take a couple steps backward. As they did the fish in turn broke the surface. They all let out startled gasps as Bethie's Dad scooped with the net.

Bethie heard him grunt with effort as he turned toward them with the net extended forward. Inside the mesh with the head hanging out one side and the fish tail hanging out the other side lay the curved body of the largest fish any of the three kids had ever seen.

"All right!" Brad cheered. "We did it! We got it!" He turned to Bethie and Lydia then raised his hands quickly and high fived both of them.

"Who's going to take this monster off the hook?" Dad asked.

Brad sprang into action and approached the spot where the net was laid out on the ground and the giant fish lay across the net frame with gills pumping rapidly. As he bent toward the fish with his outstretched hand the fish flopped mightily and Brad jumped back. He laughed right along with the others. "What kind of fish is it Uncle Rob?" he asked as his uncle reached out and restrained the fish. "We should get lots of meals out of this."

"Not going to eat this guy," his uncle responded. "This is a carp."

Brad's face fell as his uncle went on. "This kind of fish doesn't taste good. Though it was fun to catch, it is a junk fish."

"Oh," Brad replied sadly.

"Hey," Bethie's Dad saw Brad's crestfallen face. "We can still take some pictures and measure him up."

Brad's expression became brighter as he backed away from the fish. He had the hook that he'd removed held carefully between his fingertips. "Cool, let's go show it to Aunt Ellen."

Together the three kids loaded the fish into the wagon that they usually used to haul their gear. Lydia and Bethie gathered the fishing poles, net, tackle and bait boxes while Brad proudly took charge of pulling the wagon. Their first stop was the garage where they measured the 46 inch carp with a tape measure. This chore done, Brad went to the doorway and called his Aunt into the garage to admire his catch. They took some pictures of the fish, both laying in the wagon and suspended on a stringer between the three kids.

Back in the wagon the fish went and the next stop was Lydia's house where her family was summoned to see the catch that was longer than the wagon it lay in. Lydia's younger brother then joined the group as they continued down the road and back until one of the neighbors who lived in Detroit but owned a weekend cabin approached them. "Hey, that's one heck of a fish you got there. Who caught it?"

The girls pointed at Brad but he was quick to explain, "They helped and Uncle Rob netted it."

"Yeah, a fish like that is not a one person catch for sure! What ya going to do with it?" The old man asked.

At the question Brad's face fell. "Uncle Rob said it's not good for eating."

"Nah, you don't want to fry up a carp that's for sure. But ya could smoke it."

"Really?" Brad asked. "I don't think we know how to do that."

"You are in luck because I do." The man retorted. "I have a proposition for you. I'll buy your fish from you and smoke it. Then I'll make sure that you get to eat some of it."

Brad thought seriously for just a moment. "For real?"

"Of course. How much do you want for it?"

Once again Brad paused in thought. He looked at the three kids gathered around him. "Four dollars." He answered.

"Not enough." Came the bantered reply. A fish like this would cost me well over $20.00 in Detroit. I think I should give you at least $15.00."

Brad's smile of delight was answer enough and the man continued as he dug into his wallet. "Now if you'll be kind enough to deliver that whale to the picnic table in my backyard I'll get it cleaned up and ready to smoke."

When the kids returned to the house with the empty wagon in tow Bethie's dad and mom gazed in disbelief as they told the story of selling the fish. When the story came to an end Bethie's dad turned to her mom and said. "We'll have to make sure to thank him."

Bethie started to wonder about this but was quickly distracted by Brad's next question. "Uncle Rob, can we walk down to the stand so we can buy ice cream cones with our money?"

There was a small snack shack located about a few blocks away on the edge of the public beach that served ice cream and snacks. The kids often walked there during the day to get a treat and they were now delighted that, with strong orders to stay together and not to go anywhere else, they were granted permission to go. They stopped at Lydia and Darren's house to get their parent's permission then they were off enjoying the grown up feeling of being allowed to go at the dusk hour.

That night before drifting off to sleep she thought that today had been one of the best days ever. That thought stuck with her until she was awakened by her step brother silently shaking her shoulder.

Brad returned home with the promise of returning for one more week before school started and Bethie couldn't wait until his return. Lydia's parents had purchased their cabin for weekend and vacation use so when they too left for their home Bethie found herself feeling lonely. Many days she would call her friends who lived closer to the public beach to meet her for bike riding or swimming. When Bethie explained to them about her cousin and new friends they were quick to want to meet them.

As summer waned toward its close Bethie's mom took her school shopping and when they were done Bethie was delighted to meet her Aunt and Brad at a restaurant for lunch. As they exited the restaurant Bethie and Brad were both surprised when her

Aunt opened her trunk and removed Brad's suitcase then loaded it into the trunk of Bethie's mom's car. Brad was going to spend one last week with them before school started.

## CHAPTER ELEVEN

### Birth Control

A new school year started. Sixth grade meant a new school and lots of changes for Bethie. Enrollment was up at her school so the district had started what was called split shifts. The middle school and high school students shared the same building but attended school during different hours. The high school students started their school day at 6:45 and were released at 12:15 while the middle school students started their day at 11:30 and were released at 5:00.

Another change that took place was that Bethie's dad had been assigned a new shift at work. He was now working second shift. This meant that he would leave for work about 3:00 in the afternoon and not return until midnight. With the change in schedules Bethie's mom would now cook a big dinner around 2:00 and they would eat dinner at that time of day. Bethie's mom would save a plate that she would warm in the microwave at 6:00 when she got home from school.

This new arrangement had two effects on the little girl. While the freedom of warming her own dinner and taking charge of herself made her feel very grown up, yet sitting alone at the dinner table left her often feeling lonely. She wasn't alone in the house, her mom was sitting in the living room quietly crocheting or watching a television show so her feelings didn't seem to make sense to her.

Just a few weeks after school started Robby graduated from boot camp. Bethie wanted badly to go with them but Mom said this was not a ceremony for children. Bethie missed her brother terribly and knew that after this Robby had to go on to California for more training. It would be Christmas before she saw him again. After that no one knew when he'd get to come home again. Worse yet, Bethie was supposed to stay home with Wade. Mom and Dad were leaving early on Friday morning and not coming home until Sunday afternoon. This thought terrified her so badly that as she waited for the school bus she broke into tears. She turned her back and stepped away from the group of waiting kids, so no one would see, but it was very difficult to keep from sobbing out loud. She wished she didn't have to go home from school today. She knew that Wade would be there waiting for her.

Usually the Friday school day seemed to drag on forever but for Beth, as her sixth grade teachers called her, this day flew by and with a sinking feeling in her stomach she found herself climbing on the bus to go home. The bus dropped her off and she walked as slowly as she could but to her dismay she saw Wade's white car coming down the road toward her. When he pulled up next to her he rolled down his window and said, "Hey, will you be okay at home by yourself for a while? I am going to pick up my girlfriend, Lindy, and we'll bring back pizza for dinner. Otherwise, if you are scared you can come with me."

Beth remembered the last time he'd taken her for a ride in this car. It had been the first day he had it and he had insisted she come for a ride with him when she tried to decline he even offered to buy her ice cream. Her mom had encouraged her by saying, "Your brother is proud of his new car. You don't want to make him feel bad. Go with him Beth." At this Beth saw no way out of it and much later when she'd returned home, hair mussed, clothes disheveled and threw the melting ice cream cone she'd been clutching in the garbage no one even questioned her.

Now Beth was quick to reply. I'll be fine at home and if you and Lindy want to go out go ahead. I'll make a sandwich."

"Are you kidding? Mom and Dad would kill me if I left you home alone. I'll just pick up Lindy and a pizza then be right back."

Beth gave a quick, "Okay" and Wade put the car back in gear and drove off. She quickened her pace and entered her home quickly feeling as a prisoner with a delayed sentence. As she put her things away and turned on the television she wondered about Wade's girlfriend. She couldn't help but hope this turn of events would make him leave her alone. She had suffered too many disappointments in this area so she tried not to get her hopes up too high and settled in to watch her favorite program.

Staying home alone really didn't bother her she told herself especially if the alternative was staying home with her step brother. True, she was almost 11 but in her mind she could pretend that she was all grown up and this was her house. She enjoyed choosing what to watch on television and that she could go to the fridge and select a can of pop without having to ask permission. This is pretty cool she thought then she heard the car turn into the driveway.

Wade entered carrying a pizza box followed closely behind by a short blond girl that he introduced as Lindy. Wade set the pizza box on the cupboard, retrieved some plates and served the pizza and instructed Beth to retrieve each of them a pop from the fridge. They took their plates and drinks to the family room where they ate in front of the television. To Beth's surprise Wade was nice and didn't change the channel when her favorite show, *The Partridge Family,* came on despite the fact that he proclaimed to hate David Cassidy and thought that the character named Lori had a stick up her ass.

The last part made Lindy giggle out loud and Beth thought that her laugh sounded kind of fake.

Once they were done eating and the show ended Wade said, "Beth, I'll give you a dollar if you go clean up the kitchen."

"You don't have to pay me," she replied very quickly and started from the room. She made it a point to avoid taking anything from Wade and she was not about to change her ways now. As she threw away the paper plates and put the leftovers in the refrigerator she heard low murmuring punctuated by an occasional giggle coming from the family room. Once she was done she retreated to her room.

She had seen the look in Wade's eyes when he'd offered to pay her to clean up and she was really happy that his shining gaze had been focused on Lindy and not on her. Still as she shut her door she wished that there was a lock on her door handle but she knew it would do no good. Her closet had two doors on it. One that opened into her bedroom and at the other end of the closet a door opened into the formal living room. Even if she could lock her door Wade could still get in through the closet as he had been doing on a regular basis so her parents wouldn't catch him entering or leaving her room in the middle of the night.

She put on her pajamas and sprawled on her bed. She picked up one of her library books and tried to lose herself in the story. A while later she heard whispered voices in the hallway outside her room then the slight squeak of her parents' bedroom door as it opened and closed quietly. She thought to herself that her mom wasn't going to like this but didn't focus on the thought and retreated once again to her book. At some point she fell asleep and when she awoke in the morning and went out to the hall she noted that her mom and dad's door was closed tightly.

Beth proceeded to the bathroom carrying her clothes. She preferred changing in the bathroom where she could lock the door when it was only she and Wade in the house. She showered quickly, brushed her teeth and was combing out her hair when she heard a knock on the door accompanied by Wade's voice. "Hey, Beth can you hurry up? Lindy needs to use the bathroom."

She continued brushing her hair as she opened the door where she found Lindy wearing one of Wade's shirts and not much else standing in the hallway. "Hey," Lindy said as she indicated the brush in Beth's hand, "Do you want me to style your hair? I am going to beauty school."

"Okay, I guess." Beth answered not knowing what else to say. She was traveling in a strange world. Never before had Wade brought a girlfriend home and Beth was afraid of suffering Wade's wrath if she did something wrong.

"Great," came the girl's reply. "Let me get dressed and I'll do your hair." Lindy disappeared into the bathroom as Wade stepped into the hallway from their parent's bedroom.

"Lindy and I fell asleep on the couch last night and I was way too tired to drive her home so I let her spend the night in Mom and Dad's room." He explained with his eyes gleaming and an expression that dared her to challenge his explanation. Instead Beth just turned away and walked toward the kitchen.

After Lindy had used her Mom's blow dryer and curling iron to style Beth's hair she and Wade climbed into his car and drove away. Wade had told Beth that she could invite a friend come over for the day and that he'd be back later.

After they left Beth took him up on his offer and called a friend to come over. Before the friend arrived she went into the bathroom and washed her hair. She hadn't been quite sure that she liked the bouncy curls randomly scattered on her head and didn't want to have to explain to her friend who had styled her hair or the situation of her brother's girlfriend spending the night in her parent's room. Her friend arrived shortly after and the two decided to bake cookies. They scoured the kitchen cupboards for ingredients only to find there weren't any chocolate chips but they did find plenty of peanut butter so they didn't have to change their plans. Once the cookies were baked, the kitchen restored to order and their stomachs full and queasy from eating too much raw cookie dough the two girls decided on taking a bike ride to see some of their other friends. Beth left a note on the table in case Wade returned and wondered where she had went. She was being very careful not to do anything that Wade could get her in trouble for.

Later that afternoon her friend returned home and Beth had returned to her own house she found herself at a loss for something to do. She tried the television but on Saturday afternoon she found mostly sports and nothing that caught her attention, she thought of fishing behind the house but without Brad it just didn't sound as appealing. Finally she decided on a book and retreated to lay across the bench seat of the wooden glider swing in the front yard. She was deeply engrossed in the book when Wade's white car swung into the driveway.

Looking up she noted that there were two people in the car. Relief flooded over her when she saw Lindy again stepping out of the car. The evening progressed much like the previous evening with Beth once again retreating to her own room to read her book and Wade entertaining his guest alone in the family room. This night Beth was asleep and didn't hear her parent's door close but the next morning she once again noted the door was shut tight and when she tiptoed to the living room and saw Wade's bedroom door open and his room empty she figured Lindy had once again spent the night.

She was at the dining room table, munching toast with jelly on it, when Wade and Lindy entered the kitchen. "I'm going to take Lindy home. I'll be back in an hour or so." He explained as they traveled through the room and out the door. True to his word Wade returned quickly. Beth was in the family room watching a repeat of *I Dream of Jeanie* when he came in slamming the door to the garage behind him. "Get up and come help me," he ordered. Knowing she had better not anger him she followed him to the doorway of their parent's room. She hesitated at the entrance and he was quick to reach out and drag her inside. "You are just going to help me make the bed so Mom and Dad don't know anyone stayed here." She started to feel relieved but then he continued. "After I show you what Lindy and I did last night."

An hour later Beth stumbled on shaking legs from her parent's room and entered her own. The bed was now made, she had been severely threatened not to share the details of the weekend with anyone and her heart felt heavy with the humiliation and shame of what had just taken place in her parent's bed. She had hoped that Wade having a girlfriend was going to make her life easier but it now appeared this was only going to give him more ideas and ammunition to use against her.

The days continued, the holidays had come and gone. Robby had been home on leave and this thrilled Beth but his visit went much too quickly. Shortly after the holidays Robby had to return to Long Beach California where he was set to sail on a ship named the USS Ashtabula. Beth had heard much talk from the adults about this voyage. It seemed that a famous lady psychic, Jean Dixon, predicted that the ship would sink during this voyage. Even though the adults around her spoke reassuringly and insisted that the lady really couldn't predict the future Beth still harbored a huge fear that she would never see Robby again. Standing in the airport watching her brother's disappearing form as he walked down the long hallway that led to his plane she found herself crying silently and for the first time ever she realized that she really did love her brother.

Another birthday passed, so did Easter, and toward the end of a school year Wade and Lindy made an announcement. Despite several breakups and makeups throughout their dating period they now announced that they were to be married in the fall. Once again Beth harbored hope. Perhaps once Wade had a wife he would leave her alone but she soon discovered that his engagement did nothing to change his desire for his step sister. Wade had now discovered that Beth had begun menstruating and he made it a point to note the dates of her cycles so as not to impregnate her, he had explained. When Beth failed to report the dates or if her periods were irregular as they often were he would become very angry and force her to perform oral sex on him or do other things for him that she found gross, humiliating and sure not to cause pregnancy.

That summer was filled with wedding plans and preparations. Lydia and her family spent time at their cabin frequently and the two girls were becoming very close friends. Brad once again came and stayed with them for a few weeks and in turn Beth spent a week with Brad and his family. Beth loved the time spent with her cousin. Brad's carefree nature and her new friend, helped her to put aside, at least temporarily, some of the shadows in her own world.

The wedding plans progressed not without hitches. Beth's mom had taken a dislike to Lindy's family and, Beth even suspected from some of the things that her mom had said, to Lindy herself. Secretly Beth suspected that no matter who Wade married her mom would disapprove. Her mother's animosity kept the household in turmoil on a regular basis. Still the plans went on and the couple even found a place to live.

To Beth's surprise Wade and his fiancé were purchasing the house down the street that her family had previously lived in. The family who had bought the house from her father were moving back to the city where they had come from. Still there seemed to be arguments and discontent between the families. It seemed to Beth that the arguments focused on wedding traditions and costs.

One of the major arguments that Beth had witnessed had been about the rehearsal dinner and where the couple would spend the night before the wedding. Beth's mom was insisting that even though the two had been staying together at their new house that Wade would spend the night at home in his room. That night Beth heard her closet door open and stiffened in her bed as her stepbrother entered. "You are getting married in the morning." She protested.

"Even more reason to show you how much you still mean to me." Came his quiet reply. Tears filled her eyes as her brother pulled her covers back and slid his hand between her legs with his body crowding her in her single bed. She squeezed her eyes shut and wished that her heart would just quit beating and she would die. To her dismay this didn't happen and eventually the October morning came and Beth found herself walking down the aisle as a bridesmaid.

As she listened to her stepbrother and Lindy exchange their wedding vows she once again hoped that Wade would finally leave her alone. Then she snickered along with the rest of the congregation as the bride and groom knelt to pray and they caught a glimpse of the bottom of Wade's shoes. The night before, on the bottom of his shiny black shoes in bright red nail polish, her mom had painted two words. The bottom of the left shoe clearly said the word HELP and the bottom of the right said ME. The bride and groom then looked at each other with puzzled glances causing even more laughter. Beth smiled wryly to herself thinking that the message should be on the bottom of Lindy's shoes and not those of her stepbrother.

The newlyweds began their married life just down the street and at first Beth didn't see much of them but just after the Christmas holidays Lindy took a job at a local factory where she worked second shift. Wade was working with her Dad who had been switched to a day shift at the same factory and the two took turns driving back and forth. Often Wade just came home with their dad and had dinner with the family. On these occasions it seemed that nothing had changed and on Tuesday nights when Mom went to her ceramics classes Beth was sent to Wade and Lindy's house to spend the night. In this aspect nothing had changed. Beth was dropped off at Wade's door and he was quick to take advantage of his time alone with his step sister. He even made excuses to her about how Lindy was too tired from working nights to do any special favors for him and how Beth should help him out so he wouldn't have to cheat on his wife. Beth was starting to like Lindy and this only added to her guilt and humiliation.

When Lindy was home she often invited Beth over to bake cookies or play board games. At first she resisted the invitations but both her Mom and Wade were quick to admonish her and encouraged her to accept. Sometimes Lindy would even invite her younger sister to join them and a friendship between the two girls started to bloom.

That Spring Beth's mom had not been feeling well and ended up in the hospital for two weeks with a stomach ulcer. During this time Beth was sent to stay with her step brother and sister in-law. Lindy was still working nights and Wade was making daily use of his step sister. Beth tried her hardest to persuade him not to touch her. She begged him to leave her alone; told him that he was being unfaithful to his wife: that he would go to hell for what he made her do but nothing had any effect on him. He even started using condoms in order to make sure that she wouldn't get pregnant and on a weekend night he even snuck into the guest room when Lindy was home. Sound asleep Beth was startled awake when he reached between her legs and inserted his finger into her vagina. She screamed with pain and shock. From the hallway they heard Lindy stirring and Wade was quick to open the door and tell Linda that Beth had been having a nightmare and he was just checking on her. Finally, her mom got out of the hospital and Beth was allowed to go back home.

She was now in seventh grade and there were middle school dances. Some of her friends were now finding boyfriends. Boys were now walking girls to their classes while discreetly holding hands in the hallway. What should have been a fun and exciting time in her adolescent years only added to Beth's self-degradation. What would her friends think if they knew the types of activities that she had already participated in? Even worse what boy would ever want to be her boyfriend? Thanks to her step brother she was now what her father would call damaged goods. Some days she felt so bad she considered just running away or better yet taking the razor that her father had in the medicine cabinet and cutting her wrists until she bled to death. Often she took the razor out of the medicine cabinet and just looked at it with contemplation but something inside her always made her return the instrument to the shelf where her father kept it.

Finally, school got out and Brad was coming to stay with them so Beth had something to look forward to. Lydia too was winding up her school year and Beth found out that her family was going to spend the entire summer at their cabin. With glee she thought that this summer was going to be the best summer yet.

That night Wade came over and announced that he and Lindy wanted Beth to go on a camping trip with them for two weeks starting the next Saturday. Beth's heart fell as she heard Wade broaching the subject with her parents. Finding all of her courage and trying not to sound rude she spoke up. "Thanks for the offer Wade, but Brad is coming here to stay and I really want to hang out and go fishing with him."

Wade turned to her with a look of anger. Beth felt a tremor start deep inside her. Now she had angered Wade and next her Mom spoke up. "There'll be other times when Brad will visit. I really think you should go."

Beth was swallowing tears but knew she couldn't hold them back much longer. That was when her father chimed in. "Ellen, don't you think Brad will be bored here without her? Maybe she could go camping a different time. The kids made the plans for Brad's visit a long time ago."

Beth wanted to spring from the chair where she sat and throw her arms around her father but knew she should hold back her excitement. Instead she focused her energy into finding an acceptable answer that would appease everyone. "Yeah, maybe I could go next time." Finally, Wade left and Beth felt as if she had just run across a busy highway and dodged all of the oncoming cars safely. "This time." She told herself with relief.

The summer was everything the young girl had hoped. Brad spent most of it at her house and she had spent a week at his house and a week in the city with Lydia and her family. Though she was forced to suffer through a few traumatic encounters with her step brother she also had quite a bit of vacation time from him. They were also treated to some good news. Robby was coming home on a three week leave and she couldn't wait to see him.

Beth accompanied her father to the airport to pick him up. She stared intently watching the people coming down the gangway and through the gate from the airplane when all of a sudden there he was looking tall and handsome in his white sailor uniform. Heart swelling with pride for her brother she called out, waved happily and soon the three of them were hugging and talking all at once.

"Where's Mom?" Robby asked.

Beth looked nervously at her Dad as she recited the white lie they had rehearsed before leaving home. "She had a headache so I came with Dad instead."

All the way home the three chatted with Robby asking questions about family and friends and in turn answering the questions that Beth and Dad asked about his life in the Navy. Robby explained to them that his ship was now stationed in Hawaii and that there was a good chance that he would take a few voyages to the Philippines and Guam but for the most part he would not be going back to support the Vietnam effort. He explained that on his previous voyage his ship had brought back many Marines who had served on the front lines there and for the most part the U.S. was withdrawing all of the troops who had been sent there. When they turned on to their road Beth was surprised at the closed and vacant look of their house.

Dad pulled into the garage and he helped Robby grab his large duffle bag and small carry on from the trunk. Dad then led Robby into the house calling out to their Mom as if he didn't know she was waiting in the back yard. "Out here." Came her reply and Dad gestured for Robby to go out the back door first. He opened the door to step out and was greeted with a great roar of "Surprise!"

Robby's face lit up and he turned back to look at his Dad with eyes wide with astonished wonder and Beth thought maybe even a tear. The smell of Barbeque drifted on the air as Robby stepped out the door and was greeted by a huge assortment of friends, neighbors and family. Brad stepped forward and told Beth how Lydia and he had made arrangements with all of the neighbors to hide all of the cars in order not to give away the surprise. The party went on late into the night and Beth thought that she'd never saw Robby look so happy.

As it had the last time, Robby's leave ended much too quickly and at the airport Beth hugged her brother tightly and tried not to cry. "At least this time no one is predicting my ship to sink." Robby told her trying to make light of the situation. It wasn't until many years later that Robby told them what had happened during the predicted doomed voyage. During the voyage the ship had a major mishap with a forklift. Robby explained to his family that the forklift had mistakenly been driven off of the main deck and landed in a holding area three decks below. The forklift had landed on a pallet of highly explosive shells. He said it was very lucky that none of the shells had detonated because the tanker had been loaded to the gills with oil and explosives and a detonation would have surely sunk the ship. Beth was very grateful to Robby for saving this story until long after his term of service had ended.

## CHAPTER TWELVE

### Bleak and Cold

Eighth grade went a lot like seventh grade. Beth preferred school to being at home when Wade was around. Lindy was no longer working nights, Wade no longer worked with their dad and Dad was back working second shift. Now that she was getting older her parents allowed her to stay home alone when they were away for an evening. She now took neighborhood babysitting jobs and to her delight it seemed that her parents had forgot her bedtime altogether. Beth tried out for cheerleading and made the squad. This often meant staying after school for practices and games then being driven home by her friend's older sister or her mom who took turns picking up the girls with two other parents who lived nearby.

Beth highly enjoyed her new freedoms and responsibilities. Some of them even gave her good excuses to avoid her step brother and visiting his house. One night when she returned from cheerleading practice she found a note on the table. Her dad was once again working second shift and the note explained that her mom had caught a ride with him when he went to work and he had dropped her off to visit with one of her aunts. If she needed something she could call her mom there, otherwise she would be home when her dad returned from work around 1:00 a.m.

Beth kept the back door, front door and external door to the garage locked when she was home alone. Her parents would get in by using the electric garage door opener so she felt safe and secure.

Beth made herself a bowl of soup and turned on the radio. She sat at the dining room table and began doing her reading for English class as she ate her soup. It was dark out and she thought she heard a noise. When they had moved in this house her dad had bought her mom a small bull dog as a birthday present. When he began barking she turned down the radio and listened. Not hearing anything more she spoke soothingly to the dog. "It's nothing Pit, go lay down."

She got up from the table washed her soup bowl and the pan that she had used to warm the soup, then made a quick trip to the bathroom. While she was in the bathroom she thought she heard the dog bark again but when she opened the door and came out he was once again laying in the dining room. She returned to her homework and was busily scribbling notes in her notebook with the radio playing in the background when she felt a hand on her shoulder.

"Ahhhh!" she screamed and nearly jumped out of the chair but she was pushed back down firmly. She was so frightened that it took her a few moments to process the fact that the laughter she was hearing from over her shoulder belonged to Wade.

Once she caught her breath and could speak again she nearly shouted, "How did you get in here?"

He reached a hand into his pocket then held his hand out in front of her holding out his key chain. "Did you forget I have a key?" He was still laughing and Beth noted the familiar gleam in his eyes.

"That wasn't funny she stammered."

"I thought it was. Besides, I told mom I would stop by and make sure you weren't entertaining a boyfriend or anything like that." He said.

If Beth hadn't been so leery of him this would have made her laugh.

"What are you doing?" he asked.

"Homework."

"Don't you want to take a little break?" he asked.

"No, I've got too much to do." Beth replied quickly.

"Aw, c'mon." he cajoled. "I've missed you and I'm sure you miss me." He was now rubbing her shoulders from behind. He started out rubbing her shoulders with a soothing tempo but the longer Beth tried to ignore him the rougher he was.

By the time she could stand it no longer he was digging and pinching into the muscles of her shoulders so painfully she was sure he would leave bruises. "On your feet." He ordered then grabbed her by the hand and led her into the living room where he was quick to push her to her knees on the floor and unzip his fly. "Get to it." He said as he freed himself from his jeans and shoved his hips toward her face. "Lindy thinks I came to check on you then pick up some things from the store. If this takes too long the store will be closed and you will be in big trouble."

When he was done Beth sprang to her feet and ran into the bathroom where she locked the door and stayed until she heard his car start and pull out of the driveway. Gagging she brushed her teeth and gargled several times but nothing could erase the dirty feelings that enveloped her.

Afterward, she returned to the table in the dining room but she could no longer concentrate on her homework so she packed up her book bag and went to bed. There she lay wide awake until she heard the electric garage door open then her parent's hushed conversation in the hallway outside her door. She closed her eyes tightly when she heard the doorknob twist then the door opened and she feigned sleep until whichever of her parents who had checked on her pulled the door shut in satisfaction. The next day at school she was so tired that she found it hard to keep her eyes open.

This became the pattern for the school year. Usually on Wednesday or Thursday nights Beth's Mom would go to the city with her Dad to spend the evening with one of her sisters and Wade would be instructed to check on her.

Beth even tried to thwart one of his checks by calling Lindy when she got home and telling her she was home and safely locked in. She claimed she had a bad headache and was going to bed early so Wade wouldn't have to check on her. This worked even better than Beth had planned because Lindy had insisted on coming with Wade to make sure she was all right. Unfortunately, the next week Wade made her make up for it by fulfilling all sorts of his warped fantasies. "I've got all night." He had explained to the girl as he posed her naked in front of the hallway mirror. "Lindy thinks I'm helping a friend wire his garage."

Beth formed another plan to keep Wade away from her but it was to no avail. She asked her parents if she could have a friend over to study rather than be home alone but neither of them thought that having a friend visit on a school night was a good idea. Her mom did suggest that if she felt lonely home alone she could always spend the night with Wade and Lindy. Beth rapidly declined this idea.

Many mornings Beth found herself walking to the bus stop with nothing but gloom in her heart. She hated her world and was no longer finding anything to look forward to. On the bus she barely spoke and often tried to catch up on some of her reading assignments. In class she focused on her assignments but hardly ever spoke up. She also tried to do as much of her homework as she could in class because she was uncertain whether or not she would be able to complete it at home. Her parents didn't attend teacher's conferences or go to any of her cheerleading events but they were always concerned about her report card and whether or not she made the honor roll. Beth still preferred being at school to being at home.

As the holidays approached Beth helped her Mom fill a large box with homemade baked goods, cookies, candies, a bottle of wine and personal items for Robby because he would be onboard his ship for the holidays. This helped to alleviate some of the gloom. Beth couldn't imagine being so far away from home on Christmas and focusing on Robby helped her forget her own worries.

Holidays no longer seemed to be that bright for Beth. They were a time of stress. Her mom would insist that Christmas was the only holiday that she hosted and she required everyone to be there. Beth often felt bad for Lindy because she wanted to spend the day with her family and she also knew that it was hard for Kaylin and Tim to haul their three children the hour's trip between Tim's parent's home and her own house. Beth was always thankful that they did. She loved seeing Kaylin, Tim and their growing family. The love that filled her when they were around was completely unshadowed with regret or secrets.

The holiday season passed and life went on in basically the same pattern as it did before the holidays. Beth took to balancing a shovel or other such implement against the garage door when she was left home alone so when Wade would unlock and open the garage door the shovel would fall over. In turn the dog would hear the noise and alert her of his entrance. When he questioned her about this she pretended to be unaware of what he was talking about and after a few weeks she figured different ways to booby trap the door so she would be forewarned. Random fishing poles, empty boxes, the metal garbage can and other such items served the purpose. This did nothing to dissuade him from his intentions but at least he wasn't sneaking up on her.

Mid-February arrived cold and bleak. Beth suffered through life as usual and on one particular Saturday she found that her entire family along with Lindy's family were all invited to Wade and Linda's house for dinner. Beth really didn't want to go but could find no way out of attending. Once everyone was there Wade and Lindy made their big announcement. In September they were going to have a baby. They wanted Beth to be the child's Godmother and Lindy's brother, to be the Godfather.

Everyone cheered and offered up their congratulations. On the ride home her mother stressed that it was a great honor to have been chosen to be the child's Godmother and that she should feel proud to have had this honor bestowed upon her by her step brother. Beth bit back the thoughts that she wanted to voice and instead tried to look as if she were listening respectfully while her mind was busy wondering what the price Wade would charge for this bestowment. As she wondered the voice inside her head was sarcastic and cynical.

Winter went on bleak and cold. Beth felt frozen in time functioning more like a robot going to school, completing assignments, and serving her step brother's needs. She treasured the rare weekends when her friend Lydia and her family came to stay at their cabin for the weekend. These visits served as a tiny splash of color in the darkness that she wandered through. No one ever seemed to notice how unhappy she was.

Finally a break came. Her sister Kaylin had called and made arrangements for her to come and stay for the weekend. Beth was going to babysit for her two nieces and one nephew while she and Tim went out for a few hours on Saturday night. Beth counted down the days until Friday when her sister would pick her up.

"I just have to make it until the weekend" she told herself as she suffered through another visit from her step brother.

In the car on the way to her sister's house Beth felt as if a huge weight had been lifted off of her shoulders. Walking into her sister's home upon their arrival the girl felt as if she had just arrived home after a long stay in a different world. Tears filled her eyes and she had to blink rapidly to keep them from spilling over.

Too fast the weekend passed. It was Sunday. Beth's parents were coming to dinner at Kaylin and Tim's house and would take her home afterward. Her parents arrived and Kaylin made it a point to draw her aside and ask, "Are you okay?' she asked. "You look like you are sad or something."

"I'll just miss you guys." Tears sprang to her eyes as Beth replied. Later in the backseat of her father's car Beth closed her eyes and revisited her sister's words, "We'll visit again real soon. Don't worry." Next she imagined that she was still embraced in her sister's warm hug and fell asleep with a tear trickling down her cheek.

## CHAPTER THIRTEEN

### The Godmother

With Lindy's pregnancy it seemed that Wade was finding more and more reason's for Beth to visit. Lindy had been sent to bed because of some complication. Wade's requests were frequent and varied. Could Beth please come and run the vacuum, Lindy was suffering boredom and loneliness could Beth come and play scrabble, Lindy needs someone to help with laundry and as the list went on Beth's mom was very quick to volunteer her. Of course most of the arrangements were made as sleep over visits and her step brother took total advantage of the situation.

Finally when Beth couldn't take it anymore she mentioned to her father that when she was busy doing housework and favors at Wade and Lindy's she didn't have time to get all of her homework done. Beth was smart enough to know not to go directly to her dad and complain. She just made it a point to wake up especially early at Wade and Lindy's house then walk quickly back to her own house. It took her three mornings to do this before it worked. At 5:30 a.m. on the third try Beth's dad awoke to use the bathroom and found her bent over her books at the dining room table.

"What are you doing up so early?" her father asked.

"My homework."

"Why on earth at this hour?" Dad questioned again.

"Well I don't get time at Lindy and Wade's house." She explained.

That night when she got home from school she was surprised to find Lindy ensconced in her bedroom. Her mom informed Beth that Lindy and Wade would be staying with them until Lindy was feeling better. That way Mom would be able to take care of her and Beth wouldn't have all those extra chores to do.

Terror filled her. She figured that Wade would think of horrible repercussions for what she had said to her father but to her surprise Wade never mentioned it during the times he managed to steal with her while staying under the same roof. Most of these occurred on weekends when Mom and Dad were able to go out and Wade was home to take care of his wife. Once he woke her from where she slept on the sofa and dragged her into the utility room and twice when her parents were gone he'd made the excuse to Lindy that he was taking Beth with him down the road to their house to water her plants and check their mail. Lindy never questioned this in any way.

This situation didn't change for about three weeks but then one early spring day Beth came home from school to find her mom glowering as she sat alone in the family room. What's the matter? Beth asked. Her mom was quick to explain calling Lindy names, such as ungrateful little bitch, as she elaborated on the situation. It seemed that Lindy complained about something Mom had done and Mom had become very angry. The two had argued and Wade had got involved and took his wife's side.

Her mother ended the explanation with the words "And I don't care how desperate he is I don't want you going to their house to help out no matter what! Let them see what it's like not having anyone at their beck and call!" At this Beth's heart soared with glee! The rest of the school year was going to go terrifically but to her dismay Wade still seemed to know when Beth's mom was gone for the evening. He still managed to use his house key to make his sexual visits. Beth had tried to reason with him saying "You need to leave. Even Mom is mad at you and don't want you here."

"That's fine." He snorted, "You go right ahead and tell her and I'll just have to kill all of you." That night as he raped her he covered her head and face randomly holding a pillow firmly so she couldn't breathe then relaxing it just as her vision would start to blur. She would be allowed to gasp in a few burning breaths then he'd increase the pressure on the pillow once again. The more she squirmed and tried to get away the harder he pushed into her. Beth found herself hoping that he'd forget to remove the pillow so she'd just die and this would be over. Still thinking along this line the next time Wade lifted the pillow she tried hard not to take a breath. She froze with her eyes unblinking, her chest unmoving and her lungs burning like she'd inhaled pure fire.

Wade must have figured that he'd held the pillow down too long because he quit humping, watched her closely, then threw the pillow aside and slapped her face firmly. The stinging pain made her gasp and the autopilot of her brain took over the task of air intake. As she took in the gasping breaths he laughed sardonically and continued grinding into her until he held his breath then finished with his eyes bulging and a growling grunt. He rolled off of her then peeled off his condom and handed it to her to throw away. He always made sure that she wrapped it in tissue and flushed it down the toilet. As she pulled her clothes back into place and trudged to the bathroom her heart was filled with pure hatred.

She shut and locked the bathroom door behind her and waited until she heard the door to the garage close. After giving it another minute she figured it was safe to come out. When she opened the bathroom door she jumped in surprise. Wade was standing there grinning evilly. He grabbed her under the chin and slammed her against the door frame. "I couldn't leave without saying goodnight." He sneered as he spoke.

"Goodnight little sister and don't you forget. If you ever tell I will kill everyone you have ever cared for. There will be no one left who even knows your name." He shoved her head against the wood trim of the door a couple times. He seemed to be punctuating his words with his actions. Then he bent towards her and kissed her lips. She gritted her teeth firmly when he tried to insert his tongue. This inspired one more firm push with a head bang included. He then turned away, walked through the house and continued out through the garage leaving the door open behind him.

Summer came again and Beth thrilled. Brad came to stay for weeks at a time. Lydia and her family were spending the entire summer at their cabin. The threesome were inseparable. Lindy, Wade and her mom seemed to get over their differences and several times Wade managed to seclude Beth and pursue his desires but with her best friend and cousin close by it was more difficult for him to gain opportunities. This seemed to infuriate him making what encounters he managed to created even more rough and kinky.

Lydia spent the night frequently. The kids would stay up late playing various card and board games or staying up most of the nights watching late movies and munching popcorn. Brad would sleep in Beth's room and the girls would make nests out of blankets and sleep on the floor in front of the television. It became a game to see who could stay awake longer with the person falling asleep first being the victim of some funny and harmless prank. Shaving cream, seaweed, felt tip markers were just some of the tools used and laughed about for days.

It was agreed that the best prank of all was when Brad who had basically survived for two days without sleep in order to pull pranks on the girls finally fell fast asleep. With Brad finally in a deep sleep the girls used yarn to spider Wade him in the bed by weaving the yarn from the bedposts and other furnishings in the room. When they were done it took all of their restraint not to burst out laughing and wake him up. The girls set an alarm clock in order to awaken early in order to lay wait outside the bedroom door to be first hand witnesses to his awakening.

They finally got their reward when Beth's Dad, recruited as an assistant to the prank by the giggling girls, opened the bedroom door and called out to the sleeping boy. "Hey, Brad. Do you want to go fishing?"

Brad tried to spring up but was immediately deflected back on to the surface of the bed. "Ahhhhhh," he said. Then as he looked at the spider Wade of yarn just above him he joined in the laughter of his uncle, cousin and friend. Sliding carefully to the edge of the bed then rolling onto the floor he was able to crawl carefully to the doorway. Once in the hallway he stood up looked at the two girls and said seriously, "If you guys are going fishing with me and Uncle Rob you'd better get this mess cleaned up quickly."

That summer passed too quickly. Another high point was Robby's return. He had fulfilled his duty to the Navy and was home for good. Beth was amazed by the changes in her brother. He had left as a fun loving teenager and returned a serious man. He was quick to find a job, buy a car and began to reconnect with his friends. Early one summer evening Beth, Brad and Lydia were walking together when they spied Robby's car turn into his friend's driveway. He left the car running and went into the house. The three kids enjoyed being pranksters and found this a perfect opportunity to practice their skills. Following Beth's lead they climbed into the backseat of the car and ducked down just before Robby and his friend came out of the house and also climbed into the car.

The car started to move as the three gripped each other's hands tightly and wide eyed looks passed between them. They stayed quiet as the two in the front seat chatted and the car traveled onward. When Beth could stand it no longer she gave her friends a signal and then sat up. Using the deepest most gravelly voice that she could muster she spoke, "Hey pull this crate over and give me all your money."

"What the fu…." Robby exclaimed as he hit the brakes and the three kids behind him were thrown against the front seat.

His passenger turned with a startled expression as the three burst out in hysterical giggles Robby pulled the car to the side and put it all together. "Jesus!' He exclaimed then turned toward his friend. "It's just my sister."

He started to angrily confront Beth but when the kids just kept right on giggling both his friend and Robby joined in. However, he did threaten to make them walk back home which would have been a good two miles. It was going to get dark soon so, rather than make the kids miss their curfew, Robby turned the car around and gave them a ride. All the while telling the kids what a bad joke they had pulled and how lucky they had been that neither of the adults had carried a weapon.

Robby had stayed at home in his own room for a while but when Mom tried to assign him a curfew and always wanted him to check in he was quick to explain he had been on his own too long to be treated like a high school kid. It was only a few weeks later that he moved in with a friend and only came home to visit occasionally. Beth's mom seemed angry about this and she'd overheard her mom saying to her father that Robby was just going nowhere and would end up drinking and drugging himself to death. Beth was glad when she heard her dad's reply of, "Christ Ellen he's a man not a child. He just spent a whole tour of duty, on his own in the Navy, of course he doesn't want to live under his Mom's thumb."

The season ended and Beth started her freshman year of high school. She stayed busy. She tried out for cheerleading and made the squad and to her delight she had time in her class schedule for a drama class. As a freshman she now went to school during the early morning hours then would stay after school for cheerleading practice or other extracurricular activity. Sometimes she would catch a ride home on the middle school bus or with a friend. The second week of school she auditioned for the latest drama club production, *Jane Eyre,* and received a role. This was the point in life where she fell in love. This love affair was not with a boy, even though she had experienced several crushes, always secretly, unrequited and from a distance. She was far too shy and ashamed of her life to really get close to a boy.

The love affair was with theater and everything that went with it. She loved acting, stage make up and every aspect of being a member of the drama club. When on stage she never worried about her past, who would be there when she went home from school or when her step brother would make more demands of her. On stage she could be another person and fill herself with their life. Reflecting back as an adult she realized her puppy love had grown into a lifelong affair.

At the end of September Wade and Lindy's baby was born. It was a boy and as his designated Godmother Beth held baby Michael in church as he was christened. As she stood in the church, holding the infant wondering why there wasn't lightning strikes raining down upon her or her stepbrother from the heavens above she asked God to forgive her sins and please to make her brother leave her alone now that he had a family.

The memory of what her brother had done to her the day that Lindy and the baby had come home from the hospital lay heavily on her heart. She knew that even God couldn't help her. There was nothing that would ever change her step brother. She couldn't wait to grow up and move as far away from him as possible.

As the school year went on Wade found many ways to be alone with his sister. When Beth brought home her first report card from that school year her accumulated grade point average qualified her as an honor roll student. However, as her father looked at the piece of paper in front of him he noted that she had earned am unforgivable, by her father's standards, C in Algebra.

This was the lowest grade that Beth had ever scored and her father was very upset. "Perhaps," he said, "You should give up Drama or Cheerleading. It appears you don't have enough time for your studies."

"Oh, please don't make me quit." She pleaded. "I just don't understand some of the work. I have time. I'll try harder."

It was Saturday morning. Beth and her parents were seated around the dining room table. Wade and Lindy were going somewhere that day so Beth's mom was going to babysit. The couple entered in the middle of the conversation and Wade quickly volunteered to tutor his stepsister two nights a week until her Algebra grade came up. At this Beth winced with revulsion but her parents were quick to take him up on his generous offer.

This set the pattern for the school year. Now Wade had even more access to his step sister. On tutoring nights, he seemed to consistently find reasons to send Lindy to the store or to arrange for Beth to spend the night, and in his uncanny way he still seemed to always know when the girl was home alone for an evening. By now Beth was old enough to be developing an understanding of relationships and sex. She couldn't help but wonder how her sister in law could be so clueless to her husband's actions.

The weeks wore on and on. At school, cheering for sporting events and being on stage were the only bright points but then she had to return home to what was beginning to feel like a world of darkness. One evening she decided to put into action the plan she had been toying with. She came home from school, reticently ate her dinner, gathered her book bag and told her mom she was walking to Wade and Lindy's house for tutoring.

Beth left the house as usual then, when she was out of the sightlines from the windows of her house, she ducked up the driveway to Lydia's house and circled around to the front of the cabin. It was October, chilly and dark out. The cabin was empty but there was a matching pair of mercury lights that lit the deck which extended across the front of the cabin. Once there she perched on one of the benches and pulled out a heavy beach towel that she had stuffed into her book bag. She draped it across her lap, pulled out her math book and started on her homework.

During her tutoring sessions with her step brother she was unable to focus or comprehend. She was always too busy worrying about the price of each lesson. Instead she had recruited her own tutor. Her self-appointed tutor was a very bright girl in her class who always did well in Algebra and was also involved in Drama Club. The girl was glad to help her during play practice when neither of them were on stage. With her help, and not Wade's, Beth's grade was getting better. She hoped that when the next report card came out in January her parents would allow her to quit the tortuous tutoring sessions.

Math homework finished she checked her watch and saw that she'd best spend a little more time before returning home. She killed about fifteen more minutes by studying her lines for the upcoming Drama Club production then feeling very stiff and cold she packed up her belongings and headed home.

She had just crossed the driveway and was reaching for the doorknob to enter the garage when her step brother stepped out of the shadows and grabbed her by the hair. "Stay quiet, you stupid little bitch." He growled dragging her into the shadows between her house and the neighbors. "Where the hell have you been?"

"Nowhere."

"Mom was worried sick." He was still dragging her farther into the shadows. "Have you been out fucking some boy?"

"NO!" her indignant voice came out loud and clear.

"Shut up." He now had her pinned in between his body and the neighbor's house. "Now tell the truth. Where were you?"

"I just did my homework."

"Yeah right. Whose house were you at?"

"No one's." she replied. "I just stayed outside and did it. I didn't want you to hurt me."

"Just great. Now you are in even more trouble. You didn't show up at our house so I called Mom. She told me you'd left a long time ago so I came looking. Lindy's not home so thanks to you I had to pack up the baby and come out here looking for you. I don't know what her punishment will be but I know what it will be next time I get you alone." His threat came out as a snarl. He reached inside her pants and roughly shoved two fingers inside of her. This made her cry out in pain and he retaliated by pulling out his fingers then shoving them back in farther. "Now it's time for you to face the music." He withdrew his hand, licked his fingers and began leading her back toward the door of the house.

"Where did you find her?" His mother asked when Wade pushed her into the family room.

"She was walking up the road." He answered then added. "I think she may have been with some boys. I'm not sure what they were doing." He added with a wicked tone.

Beth gasped and exclaimed at his words. "I was not! I was all by myself! There was no one with me. I just went to Lydia's and sat on their porch. I wanted to prove that I could do my homework by myself!" Beth, driven by anger, thought quickly and knew that Wade would punish her worse for being obstinate but there was no way she wanted her mom to think she'd been out doing who knew what with some boys.

"Sure you were."

Ignoring Wade she turned toward her mom with her plea. "Mom look in my planner and math book you'll see today's assignment and that it is done. That's all I did. Honest!" Though trembling and very close to tears Beth managed to control them. Both

Mom and Wade both abhored tears and she knew if she cried the situation would worsen quickly. While speaking she dug in her book bag for her planner and math book.

After she showed her mom the finished homework her mother handed the papers to Wade and asked. "Do you have time to check this Wade?"

He took the paper and asked for a pencil from Beth. She retrieved one from her bag and he sat down on the sofa with her math book and homework balanced on his knee. He glanced slyly at his sister as he sporadically drew huge exes through her problems. Finally, he spoke. "You have a couple of these right but you are still making major mistakes. I can't stay and help tonight but I'll help you tomorrow night at my house. Right now I have to get this baby home or his mom will get there first and wonder if something is wrong." Wade took the baby from his mom and gathered up a diaper bag and blankets before retreating out the door.

Beth still stood in the family room and as she turned to go to her bedroom her mom spoke. "Hold it right there, girlie."

She turned back as her mother kept right on speaking. "I hope to hell you are telling the truth about where you were tonight but from now on I'll be driving you to Wade's house. Tonight you showed me that I can't trust you so I'll just have to treat you like a baby until you earn my trust back."

Beth thought about how ridiculous it was that her mom would drive her the half a block down the road to her brother's house. When her mother eventually dismissed her to go to bed she started from the room. At the doorway she turned back and spoke. "You don't have to drive me. I'll go straight to Wade's and straight home. I did tell you the truth tonight."

"We'll see." Came the stern reply and Beth continued on to bed.

That night Beth never slept a wink. All night she lay awake and wished to die. Her thoughts were dark and lonely. She hated herself and wanted the pain to be over. If she would just die Wade couldn't hurt her anymore and would have no reason to hurt her family. She was still lying awake staring into space hating her world when her alarm clock went off. She just lay there letting it ring on and on until her father opened her door and said. "Get up and shut that thing off you lazy bum."

On autopilot Beth arose, turned off the alarm, chose school clothes, showered and dressed for school. After donning her shoes, she grabbed her book bag and stepped out into the garage ready to walk to the bus stop. All at once her attention was gripped by an object lying on the table next to the chest style freezer. For the past week her dad had been repainting the trim and shutters on the outside of the house and scattered on the table were the assorted tools he used for the project. Her eyes were drawn to the razor blade window scraper lying next to a mixture of paint brushes, and trim tape. Lying next to the tool was a small box of extra razor blades.

Beth didn't hesitate once or even think about her actions. She grabbed one of the razor blades, peeled off the protective paper covering and drew up her left sleeve. She gripped the blade firmly between her right thumb and forefinger. Applying pressure, she swiped the blade across her left wrist. She watched without emotion as a white line opened behind the blade then filled with oozing red blood.

At first there was no pain but in just a moment there was a stinging sensation. She shook her arm and blood spattered around her some of it landing on the white cover and front of the freezer in fine red spray which gathered into bright paint splotches. She braced her arm against the freezer not wanting to look at the wound and as she did her attention was drawn back to the front of the freezer then toward her arm.

From the wound she saw that every time her heart beat there was a fresh gush of blood. It was running down the front of the freezer and pooling on the floor. As she reached toward the wound with her right hand she saw she was still gripping the razor blade. In a panic she dropped the blade behind the freezer and then the thought hit her. "What have I done?"

She tried to think rationally. She pulled down her sleeve to hide the ugly wound. She needed her dad. He could stop the bleeding. But what would he think when he found what she'd done? "Oh God this is terrible." she thought. Then the light coming through the window in the walk through door caught her attention. Her gaze traveled to a small gardening shovel hanging on a hook on the wall. Quickly she grabbed the shovel and slammed the handle of the shovel through the window just above the door handle. Her mind already started to compose the story.

With a wad of paper towels wrapped around her wrist she found herself standing outside her parent's bedroom door. "Dad, Dad, I've cut myself." She called out with her voice trembling. She heard mumbled voices then the door opened and both of her parents sprang forward into the hallway looking concerned. Her father took in the blood soaked paper toweling then shoved her into the bathroom under the bright light. Her dad pulled the crimson soaked paper away and looked at the wound.

"It's not as bad as it looks." he said to her mom who was busily pulling things from the medicine chest. "How did you do this?"

Beth recited her quickly compiled story. "My shoe must have come untied and I tripped going toward the garage door. I put my hand out in front of me to catch my balance and my hand went right through the window."

When she finished she held her breath unsure whether or not she wanted her dad to accept her story. "I think you are going to need a few stitches." He said "This is still bleeding pretty hard. It may have nicked a vein." He turned toward Bethie's mom. "I can run her into the emergency room then drop her off at school if she feels up to it."

Her mom quickly agreed and Beth was surprised that she didn't insist on going along too as she had years ago when Wade had cut himself opening a can of dog food. Her Dad took a few minutes to get ready then they were on their way to the emergency room.

The nurse at the hospital complimented her father's bandaging skills and the white clad doctor confirmed her dad's belief that there was a slight nick in her vein. "You are a lucky young lady." The Doctor said as he stared Beth in the eyes. "Just one eighth of an inch farther and that piece of glass would have made an even bigger mess and I would have had to call for a mental health evaluation."

The doctor still stared at her and Beth felt like squirming under his intent gaze but she kept the urge in check and met his gaze directly. She was relieved when the Doctor took his focus off her and turned toward her father. "We have the broken window to prove it." Dad said chuckling. "I'm sure she doesn't need that."

Seemingly satisfied the doctor gave Beth two shots, one to prevent tetanus and the other to numb the wound. Once it was numb he pulled the wound closed with clean precise stitches then added a protective bandage he gave them both instructions to keep the wound dry and return to their family doctor in two weeks to remove the stitches.

Beth followed her dad back to the parking lot and climbed back into the passenger seat of her dad's car. As she wondered in amazement that neither the Doctor or her Father had noticed that her shirt sleeve wasn't torn her dad consulted his watch and then asked. "How would you like to join me for breakfast before you go back to school?"

"Sure." Beth answered.

Seated across from her dad in the restaurant Beth still felt on edge and finally he approached the subject that worried her. "Why didn't you go to Wade's house last night like you were supposed to?"

"I just wanted to see if I could do the homework without him." Beth explained.

Her dad thought this over for a minute then spoke. "I think I want to see your report card and then decide if we should continue the tutoring. Until then make sure you keep your appointment and that your mom always knows where you are at. Got that?"

She dropped her gaze in order to hide the tears that filled her eyes and nodded her agreement. Her Dad reached across the table and raised her chin with two fingers. "Bethie, what's the matter?" he asked.

"Nothing," she lied. "My arm just hurts."

Her dad nodded and then made a suggestion. "Maybe I'll just take you home and you can have the day off today."

At this Beth started calculating. Perhaps if she didn't go to school today she wouldn't have to go to Wade's house tonight. With that thought she tried not to smile as she replied. "Okay."

That evening as she lay on her bed reading a novel from her favorite detective series she heard the phone ring and her mother answer it. In just a few moments her mom was at her bedroom door. "Hey, Wade is waiting for you for your tutoring session."

"Oh," Beth replied. "I don't have any homework because I didn't go to school today so I thought I didn't need to go today. My wrist still hurts can I go tomorrow instead?"

Her mom thought for a minute then replied. I told Wade that and he suggested that you two just go over the problems that you got wrong in yesterday's work. He said it shouldn't take long and I'll drive you down there. He said Lindy went to her friends for a while so I'll watch the baby while he helps you."

At this last statement Beth felt like jumping for joy. "There'll be none of Wade's funny business tonight." She thought to herself and bounced off of the bed, grabbed her book bag and followed her mom out of the door.

Beth had called a friend after school got out and checked with her on the answers from the previous night's homework. They always corrected them in class and with her classmates help she found out that Wade had just marked her problems wrong to be mean. She had got all but two of them right and she was quick to find the mistakes on the other two problems.

The friend had also given her the assignment that she had missed and Beth had read over the assignment and did the problems. Seated at Wade's kitchen table with her mom across the room playing with the baby she explained this, She showed Wade the homework that she had done the day before without mentioning that he'd incorrectly marked her paper then showed him the current assignment.

Beth was pleased that with their mom sitting across the room he was quick to help her find a couple small errors and then declared the assignment complete. However, when her mom left the room to change the baby's diaper he had grabbed her bandaged wrist, squeezed it roughly and whispered. "You may have got off easy tonight little girl, but I have not forgotten what you did last night."

Wade squeezed the tender wrist again and this time Beth couldn't control the yelp that escaped her. Her mom called out from the other room? "That doesn't sound like homework."

Wade answered her as she entered the room. "Nah, we're all done. Beth just hit her sore arm on the edge of the chair as she was putting her stuff in her book bag."

"I swear Beth," her mom commented as she handed the baby to Wade and gathered her coat and shoes, "You are the clumsiest person I know."

As they left the house Beth figured the days. Tutoring days were usually on Mondays and Wednesdays. Today was Thursday so if luck was with her she would not have to return to this house for four entire days. Unfortunately, she wasn't that lucky.

Early on Sunday morning Lindy and Wade stopped by as Bethie and her parents were having breakfast. They explained that Lindy had been invited to a baby shower that afternoon and she didn't want to take the baby with her because he had a slight cold. Wade added that he really needed to get some yard work done and could Beth please come and stay with the baby?

At once Beth tried to decline by saying that she had planned on asking her friend over that afternoon but Lindy was quick to counter. You can have your friend come to our house if you want. If that were the case Beth could handle babysitting. With a friend over Wade wouldn't be able to get Beth alone. She chuckled to herself as she made the phone call and arranged for her friend to come over.

The two girls met at Beth's house then continued down the road to Wade and Lindy's. When they arrived Lindy was just leaving. She quickly showed them where all the baby supplies were and gave instructions. She reminded the girls that Wade was right outside cleaning the shed and burning leaves if they needed anything.

Lindy had just pulled out of the driveway when Wade appeared in the house. "Haley," he addressed her friend. "Can you keep an eye on the baby for a few minutes? I need Beth to hold up a shelf while I put up the bracket."

Beth's friend was quick to agree. It felt as if someone had knocked the breath out of her as she followed her brother out the door and into the shed where he quickly slammed the door behind them. He jammed a board under the door handle so no one would walk in on them and quickly grabbed his sister by the shoulders.

"What do you think you are pulling?" he asked.

Beth tried to back away but his grip on her shoulders only tightened. "Nothing." She replied trying her best to act nonchalant.

Wade was having no part of it. "You need to learn a lesson." He said. "You cannot avoid me Beth. Take your pants down and make it quick."

Wade seemed to be shaking with rage as she struggled with the zipper and snap on her jeans. He finally took his hands from her shoulders and undid her jeans himself then ripped both jeans and panties down around her ankles. He quickly returned his hands to her shoulders, spun her around and bent her over a pair of sawhorses that she later figured he had positioned strategically in the middle of the floor.

She heard him unzipping his own pants and it was only seconds before he painfully rammed himself into her from behind. "Jesus Christ," he complained, "Real women get wet for their lovers but not you. It hurts my dick when you are this dry." He withdrew momentarily, spit in his hand, rubbed the spit along his erection then returned to driving himself into her. His hands grasped her hips tightly and every thrust drove her midsection hard across the saw horses pinching her midsection painfully where her shirt had pulled up. It seemed like forever before he gasped aloud, quit the motion, stepped away from her and zipped up his jeans. "Get dressed and get back in the house." He ordered. "This is only part of the lessons I owe you. I'll see you at tutoring tomorrow."

Beth's entire body seemed to be quaking as she struggled with her clothes and walked out of the shed with tears streaming down her face. When she walked past her stepbrother he took one look at her tear drenched face and warned. "You better tell your friend that a paint can fell off the shelf and hit you on the head." He warned her. "Because if she gets wind of this I'll bring you both back out here. We'll just have a little fuck party and then I'll kill you both."

When she walked back into the house her friend called out to her. "Hey, you're back too soon. I was hoping to get this little guy all to myself for a little longer." Beth looked at the clock hanging on the wall opposite her and knowing what time she had arrived to babysit she realized she had only been outside with Wade for about fifteen minutes.

When her friend caught sight of her she cried out, "Oh my God! What happened?"

Unable to think of a better story she stuck to the paint can story and felt even worse when her friend handed her the baby and went into the kitchen where she rifled through drawers, opened the freezer, then returned with a makeshift ice pack that she instructed Beth to put on her head. As Beth traded the baby for the ice pack she couldn't help but think that there were other places on her body where she'd much rather have the comfort of the ice pack only one of which was her stomach that had been dragged back and forth across and pinched between the rough wood of the saw horses.

Later when her strength had returned and the trembling of her body had quieted she went into the bathroom. When she pulled up her sweatshirt and got a good look at her stomach she saw a bright band of red across her abdomen which was shattered with purpling scrapes with even more bruises forming in the shape of handprints on her hips. "Good thing that it's not bathing suit season." She thought to herself then crumpled to the floor and buried her sobs in a hand towel. When she was able to gain control she climbed back to her feet, scrubbed her face with cold water noting that she didn't think it was working to erase the evidence of her tears but still she opened the door and returned to the living room where her friend had just finished feeding the baby his bottle.

In order to distract her friend from her appearance Beth declared fighting against the hoarseness in her voice, "Okay you fed him so I suppose I have to do diaper duty." By the time Beth had finished the chore and tucked her nephew into his crib for a nap she felt together enough to return to her friend. The two girls turned on the radio and spent the next hour or so playing a fast paced card game pausing every so often to tiptoe into the nursery to check on the baby.

Wade had come into the house a couple times to use the bathroom but never paid attention to the girls until Lindy returned and she told him it was time to pay them. He then made a huge fuss about having to pay them and kidded that his son was so good that the girls should be paying them for the honor. Beth's friend giggled but it was all Beth could do not to grimace. When Wade handed them each a five dollar bill the two girls scurried out the door. Haley didn't notice that Beth walked slowly. She just automatically slowed her pace to accommodate that of her friend.

When they reached the corner where Haley would turn to go home Beth asked. "Are you sure you don't want to come back to my house for a while?"

"I'd better not. My mom said to come straight home when we were done babysitting. But I'll sit with you on the bus tomorrow morning."

"Okay." Beth agreed. "Thanks for coming with me," She added before her friend turned the corner toward her own home. As she trudged the rest of the way home Beth felt relieved that she wouldn't have to spend the rest of the day trying to be entertaining.

"How'd it go?" her mom asked as she entered the house.

"Good," she replied quickly. "But I need a shower. The baby spit up in my hair and it stinks." This was not an entire lie. The baby had spit up but it had been Haley whose hair was soiled. However, Beth thought that this was a good excuse for her to be able to get in the shower without arousing suspicion.

She undressed and climbed into the shower where she adjusted the water temperature to as hot as she could stand it on her scraped and bruised body. She next proceeded to try and wash away all traces of her step brother. Finally, she toweled dry and pulled on some clean clothes. When she bent to gather her dirty clothes off the bathroom floor she saw the mixture of blood and semen gathered in the crotch of her panties.

She cringed as she crumpled the soiled undergarment and took it too her bedroom where she stashed them away at the back of a bottom drawer with two other pairs. Wade hated wearing condoms so if Beth had recently had a menstrual cycle or if she was currently on her period he would go without a condom or bareback as he called it. Per Wade's instructions she saved this type of soiled garment to wash when her mother was away. "That way mom won't find the evidence of what we do." He had explained.

Beth, hearing his words, was so filled with revulsion that she gathered her courage and spoke out with disgust. "Don't you mean what you do? I don't want to do any part of that." Her belligerent statement earned her a round of giving him oral sex just after the round of sex that had just created the mess in her panties.

Beth tried to shove these thoughts from her mind as her mom called to her to help set the dinner table. Robby was bringing his girlfriend Joy to dinner that evening. Beth was really excited to meet her. Her brother had recently confided to her that he thought he had met the girl he wanted to marry then he'd made her promise not to tell anyone.

Beth liked the girl at once but after she and Robby had left her mom ranted and raved about the fact that the girl's parents had let Robby sleep in their basement and what kind of morals was that displaying? Beth had to bite her tongue because she wanted to scream out, "What kind of morals does it take for a step brother to constantly force sex on his little sister?" The unfairness of the world she lived in never ceased to anger Beth but she couldn't speak out in defense of her brother or she would be in trouble.

The next morning Beth thought about her brother and his new girlfriend. She remembered the smile on her brother's face and the glow in his eyes as he had eagerly introduced Joy to the family. No matter what her step mom might think it was great to see Robby so happy. As she walked into the garage and caught sight of the window that her father had replaced with some sort of safety glass a bleak darkness crept into her thoughts. She searched for something nice to look forward to but then remembered it was tutoring night and her world got darker.

Mondays at school usually dragged on forever but before she knew it the school day and play practice were over and she was riding home with her best friend and her mom. Once at home she dallied at heating and eating her dinner. When she could avoid it no longer she went into the family room where her mom sat crocheting. "I'm ready to go to Wade's did you want to drive me or shall I walk?" She asked her mom timidly.

"You can walk but have Wade call me and let me know as soon as you get there." She replied sternly.

"I will." Beth agreed and repeated their mom's request as soon as she arrived at her step brother's house.

"Well you and I have some serious business to take care of before I do anything else." He replied. "Lindy took the baby with her to see his Grandma Williams so we have the house to ourselves."

"Mom is waiting for you to call or she will think that I didn't show up and come looking for me."

Wade laughed sardonically. "Well then you'd better be quick about making me happy, cause you certainly don't want that to happen. Now get over there and take off all of your clothes." He ordered.

As a thoroughly trained automaton Beth went to the spot that he indicated and began stripping off her clothes. When Wade caught a glimpse of her bruised and scraped midsection and hips he exclaimed. "You didn't show that to anyone did you?"

"No," was the girl's flat reply.

"Well you damn well better not! If someone does get a glimpse of that you'd best think of a good excuse. You know the rules!" His tone was firm and his gaze unflinching.

Once she was completely undressed he grabbed her shoulders and drove her to her knees in front of him. Once he had her positioned just the way he wanted he began issuing instructions. If she didn't follow the instructions just right or not fast enough he punished her by taking his foot and forcing it between her legs.

Finally when it was over he made the phone call. Beth could interpret the entire conversation just by his responses. "No, she has been here for a little bit but I was busy putting the baby to bed. Sorry to scare you." Beth was gathering her clothes when he returned the phone to its cradle. She was surprised when he allowed her to leave the room and retreat to the bathroom in order to wash off the seamen that he had left dripping down her hair and face.

When she came back into the room he spoke, "Now let's see that homework."

"I already did it when I was at play practice." She retorted.

Wade wasn't satisfied with her response until she pulled out her planner and the completed assignment. He looked over the paper so quickly that she knew there was no way he even worked one of the problems. He shoved the paper back at her and said. "Okay, just get out of here."

Beth quickly gathered her things together and just as she got to the door she turned and said, "I can't come on Wednesday because I have to cheer at a basketball game."

"You better not be lying." She heard him retort even through the closed door. "There will be big consequences if you are."

With his words Beth turned and began to run. The thoughts in her mind were screaming. "I'm not lying you jerk!" then her pounding footsteps began keeping time to the chant that began beating through her mind. "I HATE YOU! I HATE YOU! I HATE YOU!" With each step she seemed to be pounding out her frustrations and shame.

She barely noticed her heavy book bag on her back as she turned a corner running away from her house. The force of her emotions propelled her forward and she just kept running. When her leg muscles first started to burn she barely noticed. The rasping sound of her breathing didn't even register to her consciousness. All she wanted was some sort of escape from the horrors of her life and it seemed that her running steps were just what she needed so she pushed herself farther and faster until finally her energy abated.

When her steps became faltering causing her to stumble and fall she finally realized that she had nothing left. No energy, no anger, no rage, and at the moment not even enough energy to hate. Surprise filled her when she realized that she had ran two blocks beyond her bus stop. This led her to thinking about how long she'd been gone and her mom looking for her. She struggled to her feet, reseated the book bag on her back and started walking back toward her home as fast as her trembling tired legs could carry her. In a few moments she had recovered enough to jog.

She was still winded when she entered her house. When her mom questioned her she just explained that she had jogged home trying to get some exercise. This satisfied her so Beth said Goodnight and retreated to take a shower and get ready for bed. Standing under the steaming water she was surprised that the uncontrollable sobs did not overtake her as they usually did when she showered after one of her encounters with Wade. This time she didn't have to hide her strangled sobs in the flowing water. This time all she felt was a distant form of hurt and shame but she no longer felt the paralyzing pain. It was sort of like the numbness that occurred in her mouth after the shot and before the dentist filled a painful cavity. There was pain but it was not all encompassing.

Finally, the day she had been waiting for came. It was opening night of her play and Beth was very excited. The play would run for three nights in a row then conclude with a cast party after the Saturday night performance. Beth rushed home from school that afternoon rather than wait for the middle school bus. Once there she spent some time with her script gathering her make-up and costume and then nervously paced the house until it was time for her friend to pick her up.

During her frantic pacing she had paused to ask her mom if she and her father would be attending on Saturday night when her dad wouldn't be working. The answer she received filled her with so much disappointment that her nervousness disappeared. Her mom explained that her dad really didn't like attending plays so the two of them had made plans to go out to dinner with her aunt and uncle. Her mom explained that they would drop her off at school on their way out of town and Wade would pick her up that evening after the show. When she heard her friend pull into the driveway she rushed out of the door swiping her eyes so no one would get a glimpse of her disappointed tears.

After the show during curtain call with the entire audience on their feet applauding loudly Beth realized that she had been so disappointed that her parents would not see the show she totally disregarded the fact that Wade would be providing her with transportation on Saturday night. After the curtain closed for a final time and she walked off stage giving and receiving congratulatory hugs from other cast and crew. Everyone just assumed the wetness on her cheeks were tears of joy.

Later lying in bed that night she pushed away the bad thoughts and tried to relive all the feelings she felt on stage. What mystified her the most was the feeling that had enveloped her just as she walked on stage for the first time. All the worries and fears of being herself disappeared and for that two-hour time span she truly became Georgiana Reed one of the lead character's in the musical. This was a feeling that she had never experienced before and she couldn't wait to immerse herself in the feeling again.

Beth found that the Friday night performance was just as much fun and filled her with even more love of performing. She loved every aspect of the experience. The camaraderie in the makeup room as everyone got ready, the nervous excitement of actors and actresses backstage waiting to make entrances, the trust and dependence they all felt for the stage crew who supplied sound effects, lighting and in general just kept the show flowing. She found that there was nowhere else in the world where she would rather be.

Once at school for the final performance Beth found the atmosphere of the makeup room a mixture of excitement and sadness. The young cast members were excited about performing and sad that their time on stage soon would be over. Beth too was fighting mixed emotions but rather than worry about her time on stage being over she was more worried about her transportation home after wards. Mom had told Wade that the play got over at 9:30 but to pick her up at 11:00 at the restaurant where her teacher/director had reserved a room for the cast party.

Still experiencing the incredible adrenaline high from performing Beth walked out the backdoor of the stage and headed to the dressing room to change for the cast party. She heard him before she saw him. From behind her somewhere she heard the voice of her step brother calling to her. "Beth," he called. She wanted to pretend that she didn't hear him but her back had stiffened causing her to pause at the sound of his call. She knew that even with her best acting she wouldn't be able to pull off this act.

She waited as he approached her. When he got close he spoke. "Hurry up and change we've got to go."

"But, we have the cast party at the restaurant."

"Sorry, I can't wait that long. Lindy isn't feeling well and I have to get right home."

One of the other cast members who had been walking near by overheard and spoke up, "Beth, I bet my mom would be glad to give you a ride home after the party."

Excitedly Beth replied, "That would be great!" She turned toward her step brother. "Can I? You wouldn't even have to wait for me to change if I go with Val and her family."

"I'm really sorry Beth but Mom said for me to bring you home." He said seriously then turned to the nearby cast member. "Thanks for the offer though."

"Yeah, thanks Val." Beth said with her face falling.

"Hurry up Beth. I'll wait right here for you.

Beth barely spoke to anyone as she changed out of her costume and returned it to the costume closet. There was a flurry of excited activity going on around her but she felt invisible as she made her way through the excited cast and crew to the hallway beyond. Twenty minutes later she found herself naked from the waist down in the backseat of her brother's car with his crushing weight writhing on top of her. The bouquet of flowers that the director had given her and the other actresses was now torn and scattered between the seats after it had fallen from her lap as her brother dragged her over the seat to do his bidding.

When he finally dropped her off at home she looked at the wall clock in the kitchen and saw it was only 10:30. Once again she climbed into the shower and tried to wash away the feelings of shame and the smell of her brother.

Part of her had to laugh at the absurdity of her step brother and his lies. On the ride between the high school and his parking spot he had tried to engage her in conversation about the play claiming to have been in the audience but saying he had lost his ticket and program. She had set a trap for him by asking about a character who had died early in the show and he had no clue of what had happened and said something that was a total discrepancy. Beth had kept this knowledge to herself because she had learned long ago that calling him out on a lie would only result in more punishment.

Stepping out of the shower she once again noted the soiled panties. She wasn't sure what time her parents would get home so she added them to the collection in her bottom drawer thinking that she'd get a chance to rinse them all out and dry them one night when her mom went to visit her aunt in the upcoming week. Climbing in bed she tried to distract herself by reading but her mind kept going back to the cast party that she had missed and what she had been forced to endure instead. Tears ran down her cheeks and when she heard her mom and dad return she pretended to be fast asleep so they wouldn't see that she had been crying.

The next morning, she sat at the breakfast table with her parents. Her mom asked about the play and the cast party. She said the play went fine and blinking back tears she explained that she hadn't got to attend the cast party because Lindy hadn't been feeling well and Wade didn't want to leave her for that long. Both of her parents looked surprised when she told them that Wade had seen the play and told her that he had really enjoyed it.

Later that afternoon Lindy brought the baby for a visit. Beth was sitting at the dining room table doing her homework when she heard her mom greet the baby and her sister in law. Then she heard her mom say, "I'm surprised to see you out today."

Lindy's voice was questioning. "How come?"

"Well Wade told Beth that you weren't feeling well and that's why he picked her up early. She had to miss her party."

Lindy looked confused. "All I know is that he told me he had to pick Beth up at 10:00. He left around 9:00 in case she got out early."

Now it was Beth's mom who sounded confused. "Huh? Beth thought he'd told her that he had watched her play."

Beth went back to her homework smiling yet hoping that this didn't somehow get her in trouble with her step brother. She tried to finish her homework but found that she couldn't concentrate on the novel she was reading for her English class. She put it away thinking that she'd get some time for reading later. As she returned her school books to her room she found herself restless and in need of something to take her mind off of the dark thoughts that kept intruding into her day no matter how hard she fought to keep them back. She spied her tennis shoes in the corner of her room and decided to go for a run.

On her way out she greeted her sister in-law and nephew then explained to her parents where she was going. From the point that she stepped out of the garage and worked into a steady jog her mind went back over all of the unfair and unpleasant parts of her life. Her speed increased, her steps became more and more determined. On and on she traveled as she thought back over the last few weeks.

Finally she thought about the cast party that she had been dreaming of going to since opening night when she first started to realize that one of the male cast members was paying special attention to her. His name was Roger and once she thought about it he was really nice looking. She knew she'd never be able to have a real boyfriend but it would have been nice to hang out and talk to him for a while. She tried to console herself by remembering her parents rule about not dating until she was sixteen.

On and on went her thoughts and on and on she ran. When she got to the point of remembering just how she had spent the time after the play the previous evening she pushed every ounce of strength into her run. Up and down her knees went with her arms pumping in rhythm. Harder she pushed herself. Faster she ran. She was unaware of her fiery muscles or the raw burning in her lungs until a tight knot formed in her left calf.

"Uhhhhhh," she moaned as she slowed to a hopping stop. Bending down she rubbed out the muscle cramp and flexed her calf gingerly. Once she was satisfied she turned and continued her run. This time she tried to keep her pace more reasonable but when she remembered that today was Sunday and tomorrow would be tutoring day at Wade's she once again poured on the speed. This time it was her churning stomach that brought her to a stop.

Gasping for breath she found that her stomach was tightening and releasing regularly. She managed to bring herself to the roadside ditch where she rid herself of the contents of her stomach. Once her stomach settled and her pounding heartbeat slowed she turned and headed back towards home. Managing something like a slow jog she was amazed at how far she had run. She'd have to ask her dad to measure the distance with the odometer in the car but she was sure she had run at least three miles without even remembering traveling some of the roads it took to get here. The taste in her mouth made her wish for a drink of water and a toothbrush or at least a piece of gum. This thought kept her inspired the rest of the way home and the dark memories seemed to stay away.

After quickly downing a full glass of water, brushing her teeth then a quick shower Beth found that she could now concentrate on her reading assignment. At least she now had her homework done she thought as she went to the kitchen to help her mom with dinner.

## CHAPTER FOURTEEN

### Punishments

Beth stood gaping in amazement at the doorway to her bedroom. She had no idea what had happened but knew she was in deep trouble for something. Staring at the floor in shock she noted that every piece of clothing that she owned had been torn from its hanger or dumped from its dresser drawer, her books and albums had been scattered around the room as if someone had just tossed them like Frisbees, and other random belongings were mixed in the chaos. When Robby had moved out they had traded her double bed for the bunk beds that had previously occupied the room her brothers had shared. The bedding was now torn off both of the bunks and tangled into the disarray of clothing on the floor.

"What the hell?" she wanted to shout but she knew better than speak that way in anyplace that her mom might hear. As she hung her book bag on the hook located on the outside of her closet door she caught a glimpse of her mom approaching from the hallway.

"What the hell kind of white trash scum are you?" her mom yelled and Beth had no idea if she was expected to reply so she stayed silent as the tirade of anger and name calling continued. "I have never seen such a filthy, low life, pig in my life!" she shouted. Then with a few more expletives she wound down with, "What the hell are you thinking?"

At a loss for words Beth just stood there wondering what had upset her mom so badly and could no way comprehend why her mom, the complete neat freak, would ever trash her room this way.

Eventually, she got the clue as her mom gestured toward the top of her dresser where four pairs of soiled panties were lying. "Why would you save that mess? She screamed. "I told you when you started your period to rinse your garments right away if you got blood on them."

Beth's stomach clenched with revulsion when she realized what this was all about. She once again didn't know if she should be angry or relieved. How dumb was her mom? None of those panties contained enough blood to look like menstrual blood and some didn't contain any blood at all.

"And, I just want you to know I didn't make any of this mess. Your father did and he wants it cleaned up and that underwear washed before he gets home. He also said to tell you if you want to live in squalor you can damn well find somewhere else to live." With this she turned and stomped away from Beth's room.

At first Beth was too shocked to move. Then as anger began to take over hot angry tears filled her eyes and spilled down her face. She shut her bedroom door picked up one of the uncased pillows off of the floor and buried her face in it. There she stood in front of her dresser sobbing. "I can't do this anymore" she cried. I just can't do this."

When her tears were spent she found the pillow case for the tear soaked pillow and systematically began sorting the bedding and clothes to put them back in order. It was well after dinner time when she finished the chore. When she remembered she had not had anything since breakfast that morning she was surprised to find that she didn't feel like eating anyway. She found her mom seated in the family room doing a word search puzzle. Dejectedly Beth explained that her room was back in order and the dirty laundry was done.

"You better make yourself a sandwich." Was her mom's reply.

"That's okay. I'm not hungry."

"Where do you keep your cigarettes?" her mom asked her.

"What?" Beth gasped in disbelief.

"You heard me. I said where do you keep your cigarettes?"

"I don't smoke so I don't have any cigarettes." Beth answered.

"Then who was smoking in Lindy and Wade's bathroom when you girls babysat last weekend?" her mom asked. "Does Haley smoke?"

"No," Beth said and finally fed up enough she blurted. "But Wade does. Lindy thought he quit when the baby was born but he still smokes when she's not home."

Her mom's eyes widened as she asked, "Is that true?"

"Yes, but now he's going to be mad at me for telling on him."

"Nonsense." Her mom replied. "He's a full grown man. He can smoke if he wants to." Beth's mom went to the phone and began dialing. She waited a minute then listened as she spoke. "Wade is Lindy there?" She paused for a beat then continued. "Do you by any chance keep an ashtray and lighter in your bathroom? Another pause. "Well Lindy stopped over this morning and told your dad and I that she thought the girls had been smoking in your bathroom the last time they babysat because she found an ashtray with cigarette butts in your bathroom." The pause was only half a beat this time. "Wade, it's not funny we searched Beth's room for cigarettes and were even considering calling her friend's parents. You better explain to your wife that it wasn't the girls." There must have been a funny reply because her mom laughed before she said, "Okay, she'll be there in a few minutes."

Upon hearing the final words Beth wanted to scream. Her mom turned toward her and said, "Wade's waiting to help you with your math." She stared at the girl for a moment then said. "I'm glad that you don't smoke but that doesn't excuse that disgusting mess I found."

Beth nodded which seemed to appease her mom. She retrieved her book bag, shoes and jacket then made her way slowly to her brother's house wondering just how much worse this day was going to get.

When she walked into her brother's house she got her answer. After grilling her about the cigarette search he made her satisfy him orally. Beth received a reprieve because just as he was near finishing they heard Lindy's car turn into the driveway. Wade scrambled to rectify his clothing and Beth sat down at the table in front of her book bag. As Lindy walked in with the baby she pretended she was putting her books away then hurried to help Lindy get the baby out of his car seat. Despite her feelings for her step brother and his wife she did like the baby, often felt sorry for him, and always made it a point to pay attention to him. After letting him grip her finger and coaxing a smile out of him she said goodbye to her sister in-law, choked out a thank you Wade for his homework help and left the house. As she stepped outside she thought cynically to herself that perhaps her drama class was paying off.

Once back at home she got ready for bed. As she lay in her bed she could hear her mom talking on the phone in the other room. She was talking loud and it wasn't hard to hear the words that she was saying or figure out that she was talking to her sister.

"I just don't know what to do with her Jeanne," she was saying. "She was saving pairs of her bloody nasty underwear in her drawers." Her mom paused and Beth felt a sense of total degradation as she heard the conversation continue. "It was just like cleaning out Rob's first wife's clothing when I married him. She too had saved her bloody underwear and Kotex in her drawers."

"What?" Beth wanted to storm into the room and demand of her mom. "That is not true! How could you be so mean?" as she heard her mom continue she felt sure that she was lying.

"Oh, yes she did. I just never told you before because I didn't want you to know what horrors I had moved into." With these last words Beth's thoughts were confirmed. Her real mom had never done anything so gross and her step mom was just being vengeful and mean. Beth tried to tune out the phone call. Embarrassment for herself and her real mom filled her. That her step mom could share those horrifying things with an aunt that Beth had come to like was mortifying. It took her a long time to fall asleep but finally she tuned out on the droning phone conversation and drifted off.

Later that night she was awakened instantly from her troubled sleep by the sound of her door flying open and slamming firmly against the wall. The lights were turned on and her father was roaring angrily. "Did you like the mess you came home to?"

Blinking painfully in the brightness Beth managed to stutter out a shocked "No sir."

"Well let's see how you like it again!" Her dad crossed the room, opened the top dresser drawer and dumped the contents on the floor. He continued on until every drawer was emptied and then moved on to the closet and started pulling out clothes and throwing them on the floor. Once the closet was emptied he moved on to the beds. The whole time he was telling her that if he ever saw or heard of a mess like that again she would have to find another place to live because he was not a pig farmer and refused to keep a pig in his house.

Beth couldn't control her tears. The horrible humiliation and shame that she was feeling was unbearable. Then her father stormed from her room telling her that this mess needed to be cleaned up before she went back to sleep. Once again she wished that she were dead. She wished that she had been brave enough with the razor blade to have completed the swipe across her wrist and then she would have never had to live through this day. She was mortified that her dad, her hero, the man that for which she endured atrocities, so that he could keep his wife could address her with such horrible scorn. Beth thought, "Just when you think your heart can't break any more it does."

A little voice inside her told her that she needed to put those thoughts away and clean up the mess. She glanced at the alarm clock setting on her nightstand and saw that it was 1:15 in the morning and realized that her father had just arrived home from work. She forced herself to get to work and when she was finally finished she noted the clock now said 3:30 in the morning and that it would only be an hour and a half before her alarm clock went off.

The next morning riding the bus to school she leaned her head back against the seat trying to doze but her hurt and anger kept intruding. When she gave up trying to sleep she focused seriously on a thought that had occurred to her just after the second time she had cleaned her room. It seemed that no matter how bad her life seemed to get it always went on. This thought only brought one question to mind. "Why?" She had asked herself this question many times before and still she never received an answer.

Her life-- it did go on. She kept going to school, coming home, visiting her brother and satisfying his warped sexual desires. Only now when he left her with soiled panties she took them with her into the shower rinsed them out then hid them at the back of her closet until they dried then she put them into the dirty clothes hamper. She only hoped that her mom never took it into her mind to search behind the clothes hanging in her closet.

The holidays came and there were the usual holiday gatherings. When she faced the Aunt who her mom had complained to about the soiled undergarments she experienced the omnipresent wave of humiliation and shame that seemed to travel with her wherever she went. When the aunt hugged her close and wished her a Merry Christmas Beth found that she couldn't look the woman in the face.

Her fifteenth birthday came and went without much fuss. Mom and Dad had given her a new outfit and a purse. Ellen had left them for her on the table, along with a note explaining she was visiting her aunt. Her birthday fell on the last day of the semester so her report card hadn't been sent home yet. She would get it the next week but being that it was a Monday night she was scheduled to go to her usual tutoring session.

To her surprise Lindy was at home and had a brightly wrapped gift for her. Inside the box were two novels by an author that both she and Lindy enjoyed. Beth said thanks and Lindy was quick to say, "After you read them can I be the first to borrow? I bought them a couple weeks ago and it has taken all my willpower to keep the covers closed."

"Of course," Beth replied. She didn't really dislike Lindy. In many ways she found her kind and nice to be around but unfortunately when Lindy was around Wade was too. Lindy was different. In some ways she was very naive and Beth felt sorry for her. She often spoke out without thinking which provoked Beth's mom to be harsh and judgmental toward her. Beth's mom often spoke out against Lindy's parenting, housecleaning, and anything else that came to mind. When this happened Beth wished that her mom would take a good look at the man who poor Lindy had married. "Do you want to read one now and I'll read the other then we'll trade?" she asked her sister in law.

"No, no. You read them first." Lindy said. "I've got plenty of reading material for now." Lindy laughed as she spoke also walking around the table toward Wade. When she was next to him she bent and kissed his lips. "Now I'll leave you two to the math homework and I'm off to play scrabble with Debbie. Michael is asleep and should be down for the night. See ya in a couple hours she said." Beth flinched as she heard the door close behind her sister in law.

She dove for her book bag but before she could get out her math book Wade had her by the wrist and dragged her away from the table toward the bedroom that he shared with his wife. Once there he proceeded to give her a very unwanted birthday gift.

When his desires had been satisfied and his threats issued in his usual serious flat tone he really did give Beth a gift that she felt was too good to be true. "I guess you haven't heard the news." Wade said.

"What news is that?" She only answered because she knew it would anger him if she didn't.

"Lindy and I have sold our house." He said. "We are moving to Saginaw."

The blood in her veins seemed to stop as her brother said this. Only if it were true she thought. No more tutoring sessions! She wouldn't have to be afraid when she was home alone. Please, she issued the prayer silently in her mind. If you are real, God, let him be telling me the truth. She brought her eyes up to meet his but as always the flat olive pits gave no clue to his thoughts. "Oh," she managed to stammer and he was quick to continue.

"We bought a beautiful house there," he said. "It has four bedrooms and a swimming pool. I'm sure you will want to come and stay with us often. Maybe Dad and Mom will let you spend the whole summer with us."

His last words made her flinch inside and she hoped her body language didn't reflect what she was thinking but as usual something had given her away. Her step brother put his hand on her shoulder where it quickly found purchase letting his thumb and forefinger grip tightly in the area where her shoulder and neck came together. The pain was intense and paralyzed her as he went on. "I know you enjoy our private visits together. I love you and will come to see you as much as I can. No matter what we will always be as close as we are now."

It was only about six weeks later that her stepbrother and his wife packed up and moved about an hour's drive away. The day they left Beth experienced a feeling of freedom that she had never felt before.

## CHAPTER FIFTEEN

### Shattered Peace

Up til now her life had never seemed so good. Time passed quickly. She loved school. Her math grades improved—which of course her step mom attributed to the tutoring sessions with her stepbrother. There was a spring musical that she landed a leading role in and none of her family attended. Her step mom begged off saying that she had no one to attend with and her father was working nights.

Easter came along with spring break. Wade and Lindy called wanting her to spend the week at their house but Beth managed to convince her parents that she had a sore throat. They were quick to believe her because one of her closest friends had mono and they decided it would be best that she didn't take the chance of exposing her pregnant again sister in law and her nephew to a possible illness.

Summer came and she landed a full time babysitting job making sure that she wouldn't have to visit her step brother. It was the best summer of her life. Her cousin Brad stayed with them. Her friend Lydia spent the summer at her cabin just down the street and the three along with the boy and girl that Beth babysat for became inseparable. On paydays Beth always felt as if she should share her paycheck with her friend and cousin because they often helped her by joining her and the kids at the beach or bike riding.

The only time she had saw her step brother was when he and his family came to visit along with many aunts, uncles and cousins to celebrate her aunt's birthday which fell on the Fourth of July. Beth made it a point to make sure that she was always surrounded by her cousins. At one point that summer after her friend Lydia said that Wade gave her the creeps because he always touched her hair Beth had alluded to Brad and Lydia that her step-brother was a pervert and had hurt her but, swore them to total secrecy.

By Fall Beth found a comfort zone that she'd never before experienced. She no longer felt reticent about going home after school or staying home alone in the evening. A sort of peace settled over her until it was shattered on one Saturday morning when she awoke to find Wade sitting at their kitchen table. He and Lindy were going away overnight and leaving their boys at their house for the weekend. As Beth poured herself a glass of juice her step brother explained that he'd forgotten the new baby's formula and that Beth should ride with him into town to get some.

"I can't." Beth said as her mind raced to think of an excuse.

Before she could find any words her step mom chimed in. "Sure you can. You don't have anything planned."

"I know." Beth replied. "But I'm not dressed and I need a shower."

"I can wait." Wade replied. "Our reservations aren't until this evening and I haven't seen you in ages. You'll have to fill me in on what's new and how you are doing in school"

Beth's fate was sealed as her step mom said' "Hurry up. Get your shower." An hour later she found herself naked and pinned beneath her stepbrother in the backseat of his car. He puffed and grunted shoving himself inside of her as he told her how much he had missed her and the repercussions that would happen if she told anyone about their love. "Love?" she couldn't help thinking. "I hate your guts!" She closed her eyes tightly and wished that this was all a bad dream.

When they arrived back home Wade sent her inside with the baby formula, that had actually been in the trunk of his car the whole time, and instructed her to tell their parents that he would see them on Monday when he and his wife picked up the kids.

## CHAPTER SIXTEEN

### Finding Freedom

Earlier in the year Wade had lost his job and now nearing October he still hadn't found one. One Monday when Bethie returned home from school she found her step mom crying uncontrollably. She explained that she was upset because Wade and Lindy were going to move because Wade had found work at a factory in another state. Beth did her best to comfort her step mom but inside couldn't help feeling total elation. Maybe now the nightmare life with her stepbrother would finally be over forever.

Despite the fact that her Mom seemed devastated by the news of the move she managed to babysit the two boys while Wade and Lindy packed and made a trip to Georgia to find a place for the family to live. When the twosome returned from their trip and came to pick up the two boys they were pleasantly surprised to find that a quick surprise party had been planned in their honor. The party guests included a variety of friends and relatives who were available on short notice.

Mid evening Beth's mom had sent her into the garage to put some food into the extra refrigerator there. When she had rearranged some things on a shelf to make room and deposited the bowl, she slammed the door, then turned to leave. To her dismay she found her path blocked by her step brother.

Thinking quickly she tried to duck around her father's car that was parked in the garage but she wasn't quite quick enough. Wade's arm seemed to snake out and quickly grab her shoulder. "I gotta go get some more stuff for mom," she tried to turn away from him as she spoke but his grip only tightened.

"That's okay. Lindy and Aunt Jean are helping her she won't even miss you." As he spoke he used his tightening grip on her shoulder to steer her toward the door to her father's workroom that was located at the rear of the garage. Once he had her inside he closed the door tightly, locked it and pulled her to him. "I'm going to miss you." he spoke huskily.

Beth's stomach rolled. His breath smelled of stale cigarettes and soured food. She wanted to scream out that she wasn't going to miss him but when she saw him reach out and grab a large screw driver off her father's workbench she found she couldn't form a single word. "I'm not sure when we are going to be able to come back for a visit." he said.

"I know," trembling she managed to stammer, "But mom's going to be looking for me."

"She's too busy crying in her beer" he sneered. "We've got time." As he spoke he pushed his midsection against her backing her up against her dad's workbench.

Once again her mind raced for something to dissuade him with. "Wade, we can't do anything." She gasped, "I've got my period."

His pause was only momentary then he flipped the screwdriver between his fingers like a majorette twirling a baton. "That's okay," he said, "Guarantees you won't get pregnant." He dropped the screwdriver back on to the bench then grabbed her wrist roughly pulling her hand toward the fly of his jeans. "Undo my pants and get my dick out." he ordered. "Stay quiet and be fast." He leaned away and watched her fumble with the closure of his pants. Growing very impatient he roughly shoved her hand away and quickly opened his fly himself.

He was tugging at her clothes when they heard someone outside the workroom in the main part of the garage. He froze and waited. Once the voices drifted off and the clunk of the door closing verified that the garage was once again empty he continued his efforts. Each motion was precise and efficient. Once she was naked from the waist down he pushed her up onto the workbench and positioned himself strategically between her legs.

She squeezed her eyes shut tightly as he used his fingers to guide himself inside her. He didn't even wait for her skin to stretch and accommodate him. He immediately began roughly pumping back and forth at a frenzied pace. Biting the inside of her cheeks to keep from crying out Beth was thankful when he stiffened and spasmed signifying that the encounter would soon end. The whole time she kept telling herself that he was moving away and this nightmare would finally be completely over. As he finally pulled away and began adjusting his clothing back into place he was issuing his usual warnings.

Beth restored her own clothing and pushed past Wade to exit her father's work room. When she saw the garage door opening she pretended to be turning away from the refrigerator and headed back toward the house entrance. "Beth," she heard her sister in law's voice, "Have you seen Wade?"

"Nope," she managed to croak quietly and stepped quickly into the house. Keeping her head down she managed to avoid eye contact with anyone as she made her way to the bathroom. All the way there she was hoping that Lindy found Wade in the workroom and he would have to explain.

The next morning amongst many tears from her mom Beth stood with her parents and watched as Wade pulled away in the big U-Haul truck followed closely by his wife and two sons in the family car. With a huge sigh of relief Beth thought she had finally been set free.

The fall continued toward winter. Robby and Joy married and Beth continued on with school, cheerleading and the drama club. She enjoyed her first official school dance having been given special permission to waive the 16-year-old dating rule in order to attend the Christmas formal at school. Her date was nearly as shy as she was and at the end of the night Beth found she was happy that the date was over.

That January she celebrated her 16th birthday and having completed Driver's Ed the summer before she obtained a driver's license. Life was finally looking her way. Her brother Rob and his new wife had moved into a home within walking distance and Beth visited them frequently. During one of these visits Beth found out that once again she would be an aunt and a Godmother. Rob and Joy were going to have a baby that fall.

Winter turned to spring then moved on to summer. Brad, Lydia and Beth were nearly inseparable. They fished, swam, sunbathed and laughed nearly constantly. Beth's mom and dad purchased a motor-home and took up camping on weekends. Brad's family and Beth's camped together several times throughout the summer and Beth was allowed to bring Lydia along. She couldn't believe it was real. Beth was living without a shadow hanging over her and she had never felt so relaxed and happy. She was getting along well with her mom and the two often enjoyed seeing movies and shopping while her dad was working.

As summer came to an end Beth's reprieve seemed to also be coming to an end. Part of her wanted desperately to think that it would continue but Wade and Lindy were coming for a weeklong visit and a dark cloud of dread was preceding them. They along with their two children were going to stay in the motorhome parked at the end of the house. The same week that Brad returned to his family in Midland Beth's stepbrother and his family nestled snugly into the motorhome for their visit.

It was the second evening of their visit when the family was sitting around a small campfire at the end of the house. They were all relaxed and talking about the past year when all of a sudden Wade spoke up, "I have to go get some cigarettes," he announced "Bethie why don't you show off your new driving skills and drive me to the store."

To the rest of the family it sounded like a carefree suggestion but to Beth it sounded like the proclamation of a prison sentence. "Nah," she tried her best to turn him down but he proceeded to cajole her. "You can drive my car-or are you too chicken?"

Though everyone else heard his taunt as teasing she knew that there was a dual intent and totally understood the undertone of his invitation. He kept up until her sister in law spoke up. "Will you guys get some milk while you are at the store? That way we'll be sure to have enough for breakfast."

Beth stayed seated in the lawn chair but when her brother came over and grabbed her arm she didn't see how she could get out of going with him. She found herself on her feet quietly following him toward the driveway where his car was parked. He tried to hand her the keys but she refused to take them so he went to the passenger side of the car and opened the door for her. Seeing no way out she climbed inside and Wade took his spot behind the steering wheel.

There was a store only a short distance away but to Beth's dismay Wade failed to turn on the road that would take them there. Heart pounding Beth said, "You missed the turn."

"Nah, we are just going to take a little detour." Wade said. "I think you should welcome me home properly."

"They are waiting for us at the fire." Beth spoke with a brevity that she really wasn't feeling.

"It'll be a quick welcome." He replied as he negotiated a turn into the next bayside subdivision.

Beth wondered hopefully if she could jump out of the car and make a run for it, but she realized that the opportunity for that had passed. She held her breath as he drove to the end of the road far beyond the last house. He pulled the car into a turn out with the headlights pointing out over the bay. Everything seemed to be happening in slow motion. Beth watched on edge as he doused the headlights and adjusted the radio volume before reaching across the seat toward her. "Come over here, you." He growled huskily.

Something brave took hold inside her as she replied. "Don't you touch me."

"Aw, come on. I know you missed me." Wade slid toward her.

"No I didn't. I wish you had never come back! Just stay away from me and drive to the store." Her tone was flat and unquavering despite how hard her heart was hammering inside her.

Wade's eyes flashed in the dimness from the dashboard lights and Beth could see his anger growing but still she didn't back down. "What did you say?" came his astonished question as he shoved himself farther across the seat toward her.

"You heard me." she kept her tone low and serious.

Wade used his body weight to pin her against the door on her side of the car. "I think you have forgotten just what I can do to you." he growled. "Do you want mom and dad to know what a little slut you really are?"

"I don't care!" came her quick reply. "Keep your hands to yourself." She ordered as she struggled to keep her hands away from his grasp.

"That's no way to treat me on my first visit home." His tone changed to one of pleading innocence but Beth was having none of it. She grabbed his hand that was trying to reach between her legs. Using all of her strength she bent one of his fingers backwards.

"Ahhh," he groaned, "So you like it rough now."

"I don't like it at all! Get away!" she yelled as all semblance of control rushed out of her.

"I've got everything you want!" Wade growled and grabbed her shoulders shoving her down on the seat below him. He pinned her to the seat by straddling her. He was trying to pin her with his knees to her biceps but she crossed her arms across her body so he had to settle to holding her arms in place with one hand.

He was much stronger than she and something inside her told her to wait and bide her time. She quit struggling as he leaned back and fumbled with one hand at his waistband. He freed himself from the restraints of his shorts and was reaching toward hers when she saw her opportunity. She wriggled one hand free and he was so intent on what he was doing that he didn't appear to notice. His erection was bouncing in between them and Beth's stomach heaved as she caught the familiar scent of his body. Gritting her teeth tightly she used her free hand to reach out, grab the bouncing penis and gave it a hard yank.

"Yeeeeiiiiiii," he roared and shifted his weight back away from her with both of his hands going immediately to his groin.

She didn't waste any time in taking advantage of the moment his weight shifted. She used her legs to propel herself out from under him. Kicking her way to a sitting position she reached behind her and pulled roughly on the door handle. Her effort opened the passenger door. Scrambling backward she tumbled to the graveled ground outside of the car.

Springing quickly to her feet she turned her head from side to side looking for a place to go. Wade's car was blocking the path back toward the road and he seemed to be getting himself together enough to climb out of the car to give chase. She took the only opening she saw and ran quickly toward the stretch of ground that met the water's edge. Dodging cattails she left behind her shoes and made her way out into the water. Behind her, even with the sound of her splashing steps, she could hear Wade's progress. The car door opened and closed. Then the rustle of gravel and stomping thuds on the shoreline told her that he was making his way toward the water. She kept moving with no real idea of where she was going. All she knew was that she had to get away from him no matter what the consequences.

Once the water grew waist deep she lowered herself until only her head protruded above the water. She pushed on using a combination foot push and breast stroke to move forward much more silently. She turned back and stole a glimpse back toward where she had been. It took a minute to find him in the darkness but there he was about knee deep in the water apparently pausing to catch a glimpse of her.

"Bethie," across the water came a stage whispered shout. "Get back here! What do you think you are doing?"

She could think of all kinds of retorts but instead she kept silent as she turned away and propelled herself farther away along the shoreline. She knew better than head out into too deep of water. It was dark and she had no clue what she might encounter out there but she had boated and played along this shoreline enough to know that she was pretty safe just following its contours.

Behind her she heard more calling and splashing as her step brother waded out deeper. "Get back here. Mom and Dad are going to be pissed. You are in so much trouble. Beth where are you?" Even though his tone had changed she knew better than to turn back. Her resolve strengthened with each stroke. Finally, he quit calling to her and it was only a short time later that she heard the sound of a car door opening. When the headlights came on lighting a large area of shoreline to the side of her she sunk lower took a breath and swam under water as far as she could making sure to break the surface as silently as possible when she needed air. She continued the process of gulping air, diving and swimming until she heard the car engine start.

Sinking below the surface she kept her eyes opened and watched as the car's headlights traced a path across the surface of the water. Once the lights passed over her she surfaced and continued her journey along the shoreline. Making sure to stay in the same depth of water she used the combination walk and breast stroke to keep moving. She was coming up on the area where several cabins dotted the shoreline. A few had lights on while others sat in deserted darkness. She thought about going ashore but she could see her brother's headlights clearly as he drove up and down the road.

As she watched the reality of her situation was beginning to set in. What was going to happen she wondered. Wade could hardly go back to the house without her and if he did what explanation would he give? What about her? How could she go back home without Wade. Plus how could she explain the fact that she was soaking wet? What was I thinking? she wondered as she continued along the shoreline. She noted that her brother's car had made several trips back and forth along the road where they had parked then turning back she saw that the headlights finally turned and pointed perpendicular to the road meaning that he was leaving that subdivision.

Not wanting to head to shore too soon in case he came back she continued until she knew the stretch of shoreline she now followed had switched to that of the next subdivision. This was the subdivision that contained the store where they had been expected to go. Once again she knew not to head to shore too soon but she also knew that between her and the store was a boat launch channel that was quite deep. She would either have to go to shore before then or swim the width of the channel. Even though her teeth were now chattering she decided to wait until she got to the boat launch channel to decide what she was going to do. Until then she told herself not to think and just keep going.

Much sooner than she expected she found herself at the edge of the boat launch channel. On shore bordering the boat launch she saw the combination grocery store and tavern that was supposed to be their original destination. Just as she had decided to head for shore and not risk swimming the channel she caught a glimpse of something that made her change her mind. Parked in front of the business was her step brother's car and just entering the business she spied her step brother.

This view made the decision for her. She crept forward in the water and swam silently across the channel. Once across she climbed ashore. Ducking low and hoping not to be seen by anyone she quickly crossed a small point of land then headed back into the water of the beach beyond. This area of shoreline was bordered not only by the small business but a strip of cabins and then a public beach. From her position in the water she watched as her step brother's car pulled out from the parking spot and headed away from the store.

She knew she would have to get out of the water at the public beach. The shoreline between there and her parent's house was rock strewn, rugged, and she would have to traverse areas of much deeper water. There would also be another boat launch channel to cross and knowing that a few years previously a young boy had drowned there she had no desire to swim across it in the dark.

She continued in the water until she was just a few cabins before the public beach. On shore she could see a small bonfire with a few figures silhouetted in front of the dancing flames. She moved as silently as she could which allowed her to hear the fire goer's voices drifting across the water toward her. Angling her path toward the public beach she recognized one of the voices and quickly figured out who probably belonged to the other voices.

Pausing to be sure, she listened closely, and then knew definitely that the voice carrying clearly over the water toward her was her brother Robby. Glancing toward shore she realized that the bonfire was located on the beach in front of one of Rob's friend's houses. Without thinking twice she turned and headed straight for that fire.

"What the hell," came the comment across the water toward her, "Is that someone in the water?"

Her teeth were chattering too hard or she may have answered but instead she kept wading toward shore. As she made her way out of the water she heard her brother swear in disbelief as he jumped to his feet. His friends John and Joe quick to follow.

"Bethie?" he came toward her. "What the heck?"

Once she saw him all of the emotions that she had so stalwartly been holding back bubbled to the surface. She opened her mouth to form a reply and instead let out a strangled teeth chattering sob. At this her brother pulled her close and his friend John grabbed a large beach towel off of the nearby clothesline and quickly wrapped it around her.

"Hey, you're alright," her brother crooned softly over and over until the worst of her sobs subsided.

"Let's get her inside." John suggested and with Robby on one side of her and Joe on the other they guided her into the cabin.

Once inside John handed her a thick sweatshirt and instructed her to put it on. She pulled it on over her wet shirt and felt somewhat warmer. She was grateful for the chair he pulled out for her and as she sat down Robby could wait no longer. "What happened? Why were you in the water?" came his questions.

Unable to think of anything else she let the whole sordid story pour out of her. As her words answered his questions she could see his anger grow. "That Fucking Son of a Bitch!" he roared. "I'll kill that fucker." he added making his sister's tears start anew.

"You can't!" she cried. "Please Robby, you can't do anything."

"What are you talking about? He can't keep hurting you!"

"But you'll get in trouble! You have Joy and the baby coming!" Beth retorted with her words tumbling on top of each other. "If he finds out I told he'll hurt you and mom and dad. If you do anything to him, you'll go to jail."

Robby was pacing back and forth angrily. His fists were clenching and unclenching with each step. He only paused with a look of disbelief when his friend spoke up. "Your sister's right Rob." he said. "If you do anything to Wade you may hurt your wife and child."

"Robby, please don't do anything!" She pleaded.

"John where's your gun?" came his reply.

"Whoa buddy! Don't even think like that." John's tone was serious. "We need to come up with a plan where no one gets hurt and that ass hole gets what's coming to him."

"My mom and dad got to be looking for me. What time is it?" Beth asked. "I don't know if Wade went home without me or not."

"Nearly 10:45." John supplied as he glanced out his window. "What time did you leave home?"

"I'm not sure but I think it was a little after nine. It was still pretty light out."

"We need to get you home." Came John's reply. "Why don't I give your sister a ride home. You and Joe stay here Rob. I'll see if I can catch up with Wade and invite him over for a little party."

"No, don't you guys get in trouble!" Beth's tone was pleading.

"Wait a minute," John interjected. "Look outside Bethie. Is that his car?"

With what felt like a brick in her throat she got to her feet and stole a glance out the window where she could see the white car that was slowly creeping down the road. With a sick feeling in the pit of her stomach she croaked, "Yes."

With her one word Robby dove for the door but his friend Joe grabbed him before he could dash outside. "Wait." he ordered. "Let me go get him."

"Please, don't." Beth was crying again and this time it was John who hugged her.

"Don't worry. We are just going to make sure he doesn't hurt you again." his tone was reassuring. "Here are my keys Rob. Use my car and take your sister home then come back." Rob looked like he was going to protest. "We'll just invite him in for a beer. We won't start the real party without you." He gestured for Joe to continue outside then toward a door leading to the garage. "Go this way Rob, so he doesn't see you two."

John squeezed the girl's arm reassuringly as she followed her brother through the door and into the garage. Beth ducked down as they pulled out of the driveway and away from the house. Peeking out she saw that Wade had parked his car and was walking with Joe toward the bonfire at the front of John's house. Through the open car windows Beth overheard Joe talking to her stepbrother. "Yeah, your brother will be right back he just took Beth home. I guess she was at a party that got a little wild and we saw her walking home so Rob gave her a ride."

As they drove toward her house she once again begged her brother not to do anything that would create problems for him.

"Don't worry about it." he reassured her. "When you get home just tell everyone that Wade saw us and stopped for a beer. You can say we were goofing around and I threw you in the water. From here on out if Wade even looks wrong at you--you just let us know. He'll never touch you again Beth."

When Rob pulled the car into their driveway they could see everyone was still sitting around the fire. Rob got out of the car with her and Beth was glad for the darkness and his quick thinking as they approached the fire. Rob spoke before anyone else could. "Hi," he started. "We ran into Wade and Beth outside John's house and Wade decided to have a couple beers with some of his old friends. Bethie brat," he used his nickname for her, "Managed to get herself thrown in the water so seeing I was the one who did it I thought I should bring her home so she could get dry."

There were a few chuckles at his explanation and Lindy spoke up in a joking tone. "Well that's just like my husband to get out of putting the boys to bed."

"I don't think he planned to stop." Rob explained. "We stopped him and one thing led to another but now I'd better get John's car back. See you all later." He turned from the fire as Beth pulled off the sweatshirt and handed him it and the towel that she had held wrapped around her.

"Tell John thank you." she said meaningfully to her brother then added to her parents. "I'm going to get out of these wet clothes." As Rob started the car and backed out of the driveway she made her way into the house and headed for her bedroom where with still shaking hands she peeled off her wet clothes and exchanged them for the baggy shorts and tee shirt that she liked to sleep in.

Returning from depositing the wet clothes in the laundry room she could hear her family still sitting around the fire just outside her bedroom window. Knowing there was no way that she could sit there with them and keep up the facade of normalcy she pulled back the curtain on her window and said, "I'm going to bed. Good night everyone."

She heard their replies as she doused the overhead light and crawled into bed. Knowing that she'd never be able to sleep she turned on the reading light and picked up the Stephen King novel that was on the nightstand. Still shivering she tried to read but even her favorite author couldn't keep her from wondering what was going on elsewhere at that moment. Her imagination both fulfilled her dreams and scared the daylights out of her.

All of her stepbrother's dire warnings kept coming back to her. She had told and now he would know it. She was terrified at what might be happening at that moment and what the future repercussions of her actions would be. She heard her family retreat from the bonfire, the squeak of the motorhome door as Lydia headed off to bed then shortly after the screen door of the house as her parents made their way in for the night.

Her imagination ran rampant. Would Wade come home and kill everyone or would he just torture and kill her? What was going to happen? It seemed like hours later when she heard a car approach then pull into the driveway.

She sprang out of bed and went to the window where she peeked through the crack in the curtains. It was very dark but the streetlamp down the road threw enough light that she could see the form of her step brother as he got out of his car and headed toward the motorhome where his family slept. She wasn't sure but she thought that he was moving slower than normal and even seemed to limp a bit as he climbed the steps into the camper. "Oh no," she thought. "He's really going to kill me for this."

At that thought she stepped away from the window and looked around her room frantically. Her racing thoughts spurred her into action. As quietly as she could she inched her dresser along the wall until it completely blocked the closet door guaranteeing that Wade would not be able to enter her room from the attached closet in the living room. Next she looked toward the door that led to the hallway beyond. Using all the strength she could muster she lifted one end and dragged the entire bunk bed set until the end of the bed was covering the first few inches of the door. Now there was no way that Wade could get into her room without making enough noise to wake her parents.

She felt exhilarated yet scared to death. What if Wade hurt her family, she thought, being barricaded in her room would do her no good then. Heart sinking, she crawled back into bed where she lay wide awake and listening for the motorhome door to open. Hours later, when she finally heard it, she was still awake and there was bright sunshine filling the day and it was one of her two nephews who scrambled down the steps with his mother following close behind.

Looking around her room she decided that imminent danger was not a problem so she should put her furniture back where it belonged before someone discovered her rearrangement and questioned her. When that chore was done she pulled on a bathing suit, which was her usual summer attire, and added an oversized tee shirt over the top. A plan was forming in her mind and she hoped to pull it off.

Once in the kitchen she retrieved a cereal bowl and spoon and put them in the sink as if she had already eaten. This would satisfy her mother's rule that she was not to leave the house without eating breakfast. Next she went into the bathroom where she quickly scoured the sink, tub and toilet which was her daily assigned chore. With this done she scrawled a quick note telling her parents that she was going for a bike ride, left it on the table and headed for the door.

Just as she was wheeling her bike out of the garage she heard her sister in law call to her. "Where you off to so early?" the distinctive whiny tone drifted across the yard toward her. As much as she wanted to ignore the voice, climb on the seat of the bike and pedal away she just couldn't bring herself to do it.

She turned back and answered in what she hoped was a bright tone. "Just for a bike ride."

"Oh," Came the reply, "Could you do me a really big favor first?"

Beth's hopes fell as she formed her reply, "Sure, what do you need?"

"I just need to take a quick shower. Could you please watch Mike? Mitchell and Wade are both still sleeping." She gestured toward the camper as she spoke. "I wanted to take a shower last night but Wade stayed out so late I just went to bed." Beth's look must have given away her reticence because Lindy went on. "I'll be really quick. I promise."

Feeling trapped she could find no other reply. "Okay." She returned her bike to the garage then took her nephew by the hand wanting to get as far away from the motorhome and a possible encounter with her stepbrother as possible. "Let's go for a walk."

She led the toddler along the edge of the road where she allowed him to meander along and stop occasionally to pick up a stone or inspect a roadside dandelion. They moved slowly and she made it a point not to turn back until she was sure Lindy had enough time to have showered. When they were nearly back to their yard Lindy and her mom both came out of the house and strode forward to greet them.

As Beth watched her mom stooped and gathered the little boy into her arms. "Hey you," she cajoled her grandson. "Give me some kisses."

Lindy turned toward Beth as she next spoke. "You weren't the only one who got thrown in the water last night but you were the lucky one."

"What?" was all she could manage as a reply.

"Yeah," she nodded affirmation as she spoke. "The guys were horsing around and threw Wade in too. However, he was either too heavy or they missed--he got all banged and bruised up on some rocks when they threw him."

Beth was glad that she didn't have to respond because her mom jumped in gasping as she spoke. "Oh no! Is he okay?"

"Yeah, he'll be fine." Lindy assured her. "He just looks a little worse for wear."

Not knowing what to say or do Beth turned away and said, "Mom if it's okay I'm going for that bike ride now."

Lindy chimed in as her mom nodded. "Thanks for keeping an eye on my little monster for me."

"Mike's a good little guy." she replied and turned away.

Quickly Beth retrieved her bike from the garage and pedaled away while scary confused thoughts filled her mind. She wasn't even quite sure where she was going but pedaled on anyway. It was still quite early and she noted as she pedaled past Robby and Joy's house that no one appeared to be awake so she kept right on going. Thoughts of the previous night filled her mind and even though she hadn't slept a wink she felt like she could keep pedaling forever.

Thinking of the day ahead she wondered how she was going to get through it then even more concern filled her as she thought that the visit of her stepbrother and his family was scheduled to last until the following weekend. How she wished that she could just stay away from home for the entirety of their visit but she knew that would not be possible.

Sadly she turned back and rode toward home knowing that she'd have to find a way to get through the next week. Her hopes picked up when she remembered that her mom had planned a cookout and invited her aunts and uncles for dinner. This meant that Brad too would be returning and was planning on spending one final week with them before they went back to school.

Once she got home she made it a point to offer to help her mom in the kitchen as she prepared for the company. It was well after noon and the company was already arriving before she even got a glimpse of her step brother. When she saw him she nearly guffawed aloud.

Turning away quickly she wasn't sure whether her reaction was shock or jubilation. Wade had a huge bruise on the side of his face that extended from his eye nearly to his chin. She later heard him explaining that some friends had been trying to throw him into the water but he had fought so hard that they had dropped him as they tried to swing him out over the seawall and into the water. He lifted the side of his shirt to reveal even more ugly purple patches along his sides and rib cage.

It wasn't until the end of the day, after all of the company had left and the only ones left at the bonfire with her were her friend Lydia and cousin Brad, that she realized her stepbrother had never even attempted to speak to her. It seemed nearly too good to be true. That night she and Lydia slept in her bedroom and let Brad sleep on the couch in the living room where he could watch tv. As she dragged the dresser in front of the closet and slid the bunk beds across the door she explained to her friend that this was insurance that Brad would not come in and pull pranks on them during the night.

Beth managed to stay very busy with her cousin and friend and avoided her stepbrother and his family as much as possible. During the middle of the week an argument broke out between her mom and step brother. Beth and Brad had been getting ready to go fishing and were standing in the driveway making sure that they had all of their equipment when raised voices in the front yard attracted their attention.

She heard Wade's deep voice raised saying "Just shut your fucking mouth."

At this Beth saw her father cross the yard quickly, lift Wade off of his feet and slam him into the side of the motorhome. "You don't ever talk to your mother that way!" her father roared. "Pack up and get the hell off of my property right now!"

Beth and Brad stood in the driveway both gaping in disbelief. It seemed like everyone stood frozen in shock then Wade spoke. "Lindy pack up. We're going home."

Hearing his words Beth felt like cheering aloud but instead she turned to Brad. "Let's go get Lydia." It was only a short while later when the three teens who sat fishing along one of the boat channels saw Wade's car tear off down the road leaving a plume of dust behind it.

Filled with elation at this departure Beth finally found the words to tell her two dearest friends some of the horror story that she had endured by living with her step brother. She swore them both to complete secrecy and she never doubted that her secrets would not stay safe. Brad spoke up saying he wished he could have witnessed what Rob and his friends had done to Wade and Lydia also spoke saying that Wade had always given her the creeps especially when he made it a point to touch her long hair.

As the adult Beth walked back to her car her mind sped through other memories. None of which instilled as much pain and turmoil as those she had already visited. She encountered a boyfriend or two, some with smiles and some who just made her shake her head.

Eventually Wade and her parents had put whatever had angered them aside and once again established a close relationship. When Wade, his once again pregnant wife, and their two children moved back to Michigan into the motorhome until they could afford a home of their own Beth found an opportunity to move out. Despite her parent's disapproval, just shy of her 18th birthday and over a semester away from graduation, she moved away from home. Working two jobs and going to school kept her very busy.

Despite her step mother continuously calling the police and reporting her as doing and selling drugs. The principal calling her to the office daily and questioning her about her living situation. Beth managed to graduate ninth in her class. However, when she went to the counselor's office she found out that her dreams of college would have to be put on hold. It seemed that no matter where she lived she had to claim her father's income and that made it so she did not qualify for any financial aid. When she was finally brave enough to approach her parents via telephone she was told by her step mother that the only way they would even fill out the paper work was if she moved back home and went to college to be a beautician or a "secetary". Her step mother's mispronunciation of the word secretary nearly made her burst out laughing as she hung up the phone.

## CHAPTER SEVENTEEN

### Manipulations

As she settled back into her car Beth headed away from those memories and on to others. Though she had never again physically suffered through Wade's forced attentions her life still was not free of him. Once her parents had put away some of their anger about Beth moving out they were adamant about including her and her new boyfriend in family affairs. As she and Rob agreed years before they would keep the family peace. They had agreed that for their parent's sake they would manage to put up with Wade. Beth was able to endure Wade's presence at family functions but she was always leery and would never put herself in a position to be alone in a room with him. Rob too would just keep his distance.

Eventually she met someone, they moved in together, married and moved to a small town about 20 miles away. She and her husband, Ben, opened a small business and were expecting their first child when Wade once again made a direct intrusion into her life.

Rod and Joy had also moved to the same town. The two couples along with Rod and Joy's three children were together frequently. When Beth found out she was pregnant they were quick to ask Rob to be her baby's Godfather. The announcement was made at Christmas and only a few days later Beth's dad took her aside and angrily asked, "Why do you constantly try to divide this family?"

Beth was completely taken aback. "What?" was all she could stammer.

"Wade and Ellen are both very hurt." he replied.

Still feeling left in the dark, "About what?" she asked ignoring the feeling of dread in her stomach and thinking there must be some misunderstanding.

"You know damn well what! After promising Wade that he would be the Godfather to your child you asked Rob." Her dad thundered.

She had found herself so taken aback it was a few beats before she could even find her voice. "I" she was incredulous, "I never asked Wade to be the baby's Godfather." Just the thought made her stomach churn and both hands moved protectively to her swollen abdomen. "Who told you that?"

"Wade," her father added, "He's so hurt by this that your mother said he cried when he told her."

"Dad, I never asked him and I don't know why he would ever say I did." The first part of her protest was totally true but suspicions about the second part were multiplying in her mind by the second. Anger overcame her and at that point she told her father that she just had to go and they could talk later.

The present day Beth found herself still nearly as angry as she had been back then. She was once again leaving the location of her parents' home and driving toward her own via the same route. This time however, she was not overcome with tears, she was remembering. These memories were fueled with anger.

Back then she had returned home to her husband who held her until she had calmed down enough to tell the story. He had known, since before their wedding, what she had endured at the hands of her step brother. Despite his better judgment he too had kept the secret in order to spare her parents. Now however, he was agreeing with Beth that her parents needed to know the whole truth. That evening he went with her and sat holding her hand as she spilled the story. She held back as much of the horrific details as she felt she could in order to still protect them but she did tell them that Wade had groomed and abused her from the time she was four years old until she was sixteen.

Her father sat in shock and finally spoke. "What do you want to do with this? Do you want him to go to jail?"

Instead of answering what was truly in her heart she spoke. "I only want you guys to understand why I don't want to be around him and would have never asked him to be the Godfather to my baby."

At this her stepmother erupted. "Why should we believe this? You are lying! Robby did those things to you. Wade would never!"

With Ellen's words Ben spoke out with calm reasoning. "Ellen he did all of those things and much worse. He raped her repeatedly. There is no reason she would make up something that horrible."

Angry fire flashed from her stepmother's eyes as she retorted. "She and Robby have hated Wade and I from day one. This is just another way that they will try and break up this family and now she has you doing it too."

At that Beth rose and said. "Well, I've said what I came to say. I think it's time for us to go. I never wanted to hurt either of you. I just want you to understand." With her heart in her throat, tears in her eyes, she and her husband had left.

After a very sleepless night it took all of her courage to pick up the phone and dial her parent's number. When the connection was made and the cursory greeting was over with the words her mother told her left her in shock. "Wade told us everything."

she said. "He has even gone to counseling. He said he tried to apologize to you but you would never talk to him." Feeling relieved and off the hook Beth thought this chapter of her life was finally closed. She doubted that Wade had ever admitted his actions or went to counseling but at least her parents would finally understand.

A few years passed. Life went on much as it had before. Beth now had three sons. She made it a point to never allow her children to be in a situation where they would be alone around her stepbrother but for her parent's sake she still participated in family gatherings and holidays. She even invited Wade and his family to their home on Christmas eve in order to make it more comfortable for her parents.

On one such occasion Wade's middle son confided to Beth and Ben that he had caught his father having sex with the fifteen-year-old exchange student who was staying with the family. Wade had taken the boy by the throat and threatened to kill him if he ever told. The boy had gone to his grandma (Wade's mother) with the story and she advised him not to tell. When the boy looked to his Aunt and Uncle for guidance they both advised him to tell his mother.

Beth's parents, who babysat frequently, were given strong orders that under no circumstances were her children ever to be left alone with Wade and as soon as her boys were old enough to understand they too were told never to be alone with Wade.

Meanwhile, Wade and Lindy divorced. Lindy was devastated and would spend hours on the phone pouring her heart out to Beth. She even asked Beth about her allegations of Wade being a sexual predator. Beth would wince and bite her tongue as Lindy poured out stories of Wade's weird sexual appetites and the fact that he had sex with another woman while Lindy watched. Beth strived hard to convince her ex sister in law that she was now much better off.

Wade quickly met and had planned to marry someone new. Beth was horrified to find out that the fiancé had two young children, a boy and a girl. After much soul searching she decided to warn the woman. She had tried on several occasions, at family functions, to get the girl alone for a chat. She had even gone so far as to set up a luncheon date but the woman canceled. To Beth's horror and later to that of Wade's new family the wedding took place.

The marriage was short lived. Beth had received a phone call from a blocked number. The caller had been Wade's new wife saying that she was in fear for her life and was leaving the state. She asked one question of Beth, "Why did you want to have lunch with me before I married Wade?"

Beth didn't hesitate to answer her, "Because I wanted to warn you that my stepbrother is a child molester and I was afraid for your kids."

"He made me cancel that day." she explained. "He said you'd try and tell me a bunch of lies because you were friends with Lindy. I was stupid and believed him. He even manipulated me into marrying him. He proposed in front of my church congregation and asked my father's permission first. How could I say no? I'm sorry." With those last two words Beth was left holding a phone that was issuing forth a dial tone. Wondering what could have possibly happened Beth hung up the phone.

More time passed. Beth's family and Rob's were still very close. They enjoyed cook outs, boating and fishing together, camping trips and frequent sleepovers between the kids. On one morning, just after the two families had ushered in the new year together Rob was having coffee with she and Ben, Beth shared the news that her father had told her the previous day. Wade's new wife had left him via a women's shelter. The reason for this--Wade's eldest son was going to a juvenile facility for sexually molesting her little boy.

Beth was very upset by this and shared her thoughts. "The chain of sexual predators is continuing." She ranted. "I think this is learned behavior. I will lay money that Wade has abused him or somehow taught him this." She also went on to explain that she had talked to the county prosecutor and told him about her stepbrother. The prosecutor had explained that the statute of limitation for the crime committed against her had long since ran out but perhaps she should tell her story to her nephew's counsellors.

Later that day, after returning from ice fishing with his brother in law, Ben told Beth that she needed to talk to Rob. When she asked why Ben's reply chilled her to the bone. "Because he told me that you weren't the only one that Wade abused."

Leaving her sons in the living room with her husband, Beth went to the phone in their bedroom where she could speak in private. When she heard her brother's voice on the phone she grimaced and plunged forward. "Robby, Ben told me that I should call you."

"Yeah, I knew he would." Came the solemn reply.

"Wade did those terrible things to you too?" As much as she didn't want to hear the answer she knew she had to.

"Yeah," Beth heard the catch in his voice and her heart broke for him as he continued. "It was different for me. Beth, I should have fought back. I should have been stronger."

"Robby, it wasn't your fault. He is a predator and I know how he operated. There wasn't anything you could do. He is an evil manipulator. We were kids." Beth was scrambling to recall all the things that the counselor had said to her.

"I know. I just wanted to tell you that I would talk to Mike's counselor too if you think it would help."

Speechless Beth listened as her brother went on. "But right now, I just can't think about this anymore. I'm going to watch a movie with Joy."

"Okay." She reached for a lighter tone, "Love you brat."

"You're the brat." Came his reply. "Love you too." Then she heard the clunk of the phone.

Back to the present Beth let out a huge sigh. If I had only known, she was thinking. That had been the last conversation she had ever had with her brother. Two short days later, just a couple months short of his 38th birthday, the brother that she had idolized had dropped dead from a heart attack. Calling her nephew's counsellor was now the farthest thing from her mind.

Getting through the funeral, struggling to keep her emotions in check and trying to do her best to be there for her sister in law and her two nieces and nephew was her first priority. As time went by she marveled at her sister in law's strength. Beth witnessed firsthand how despite grief and loneliness Joy gathered herself around her children, working to make sure they had a good life and to fill the horrendous void left by the loss of their father. Beth had never felt anything like the grief she felt from losing her brother but watching the strength of her sister in law she managed to tuck away her pain and keep going.

When it was time for Rob's oldest daughter to graduate Joy planned a special celebration. Announcements and invitations were sent out and party plans were in full swing. Wade, now divorced from his second wife, was now back together with Lindy. A week or so before the party Beth received a phone call from her father. He was very upset because it had been brought to his attention that Wade had not been invited to that graduation party.

"If Wade's not invited to this party I will not go either." came his angry words.

"Dad, how could you do that to Robby's daughter?" Beth was shocked.

"They've done that to themselves. There is no reason for them to deliberately exclude Wade and his family."

At that Beth felt ice water run through her. "Dad, there is plenty of reason." she tried to explain. "Before Robby died he told us that Wade had molested him too."

"You are making that shit up! Wade never did anything to Robby" came the angry retort. "Why do you keep doing this?"

"Dad," She countered, "Mom even told me that Wade admitted everything back when I told you guys what he'd done to me."

"That's right he did." Her father agreed. "Wade told us in detail about the affair you and he had when you were sixteen and how you nearly destroyed his marriage. He even told us that he went to Lindy and their priest and confessed."

"What?" Beth was incredulous, "Dad do you really believe that?"

"What more do you want?"

"I want you to believe your children and not the lying pervert who molested not only one but two of your children." Her heart was breaking but at the moment her disbelief and anger was guiding her. "How could the man who had always taught her that the truth was the most important thing have bought into Wade's lies? How could the father who she had always loved and respected no matter what be deserting his own children this way? How could he choose an evil child molester over his own flesh and blood?"

Her father's next words interrupted her thoughts "Beth he's done everything he could to make amends and still you have this vendetta against him."

"I have no vendetta Dad. I have nothing but truth. Look at the evidence--his own son repeated his actions and Mitch even told Mom about catching Wade in their barn with one of their exchange students. I don't want to be near him and I don't want my kids or anyone else's anywhere near him!"

"If that's how you feel you are no daughter of mine and I'm done with you!" Using every last bit of self-control that she could summon Beth answered, "That's too bad because I love you Dad." she put down the phone and sank to the floor. Her chest hurt so bad that she couldn't even pull in a breath. Five years later her father passed away with those being the last words ever spoken between them. All Wade's threats had come true.

## EPILOGUE

There had been no contact between Beth and her parents for nearly five years but it had been Beth who her step mother called at 4:30 in the morning when she found her father lying dead in the hallway of their home. From 20 miles away Beth called an ambulance and one of her parents neighbors to go and stay with Ellen until the ambulance arrived.

Beth stayed by her step mom's side during the funeral and maintained occasional contact but due to Ellen's push to involve Wade she found it best to keep her distance.

From a cousin, only months later, Beth heard that Ellen had married her widowed father. Not only had the man been Beth's father's brother in law--the man had been one of Beth's father's best friends. From a distance Beth heard stories of Ellen's manipulations. The family home had been sold and a brand new one built. There were rumors of the manipulated destruction of a close knit family that had never before had secrets. Wade and Lindy frequented the picture. The man's health failed. His formerly controlled Parkinson's Disease had worsened. By some saving grace a divorce ensued.

Once allowed back into the picture, Beth's cousins helped their father reclaim his health by maintaining his medications but were unable to recoup the thousands of dollars that had been given to Wade and Lindy in the form of checks.

Beth had suspicions regarding this matter. Wade and Lindy had both obtained some education in the medical fields. He as a EMT she as a RN. Beth wondered if the two of them had been helping to medicate Ellen's new husband.

There was more suspicion regarding Wade and his mother. After the divorce from Beth's uncle Ellen had found another interest. She had met an elderly neighbor man and the twosome was often seen out together. Wade was often present doing odd jobs and chores for the man. The man took ill and it was Ellen who was made his official caregiver despite the objections of his family. After the gentlemen's death a lawsuit incurred and Ellen was ordered to pay a large sum of money back to the man's estate.

Ten years after her father's death Beth received a phone call from a state police officer. The officer was asking for information regarding her step brother. It appeared that there were criminal sexual conduct allegations against him. Beth gave the officer as much information as she could but it could only serve as background info and not true evidence. Beth still frequently checks the sex offender's list to see if those allegations were ever proven.

Made in the USA
Monee, IL
24 February 2021